BETH BOLDEN

Chapter One

CARLOS WAS DRUNK.

Luca stared in disbelief at the man who was the head chef at his family's flagship restaurant, Nonna's Fine Italian, as he upended a bottle of Marsala wine and let the remainder trickle down his throat.

"What are you doing?" he demanded.

Carlos, who'd worked for his family for nearly twenty years and was *practically* family, shrugged.

"He and Lydia broke up," Marcella, Luca's younger sister, supplied. "He's heartbroken."

"You mean he probably worked too hard and she got tired of waiting at home, alone," Dario, Luca's younger brother, muttered under his breath. Not helpful, but probably accurate.

Carlos began singing Puccini's "Nessun Dorma" very loudly and very poorly, and Marcella shot Luca a look.

"Do something," she hissed. "I called you here so you would *do* something."

The problem with being the oldest of seven siblings and in charge of his family's business was that any hiccup, any issue, any problem, automatically came to him. Were the others capable? *Supposedly.* But it wasn't like Luca ever saw them handle anything on their own. He was always their first line of defense. And the second. And often the third.

For better or for worse.

Tonight, it was definitely for worse.

"Get him out of here," Luca said succinctly.

"Where should I put him?" Marcella asked.

She was smart. Capable. Raising two children while managing the front of their three sit-down restaurants with confidence and certainty. Yet when faced with the crisis of Carlos, drunk off his ass and unable to manage the kitchen for dinner service tonight, she looked lost. Helpless.

You know why they're helpless. You made them that way.

He had. He hadn't wanted to. Or *intended* to. But when he'd first taken over the family business—okay, for the last five years, after he'd officially been handed the reins to Nonna's—he'd become a little bit of a control freak. Nonna had instilled in him not just the belief that the Moretti family always came first, but the absolute certainty he either knew or would figure out the right thing to do in every situation.

Only in the last year, after the falling-out with his brother Gabriel, had Luca begun to question what he was doing to run the business—and *how* he was doing it.

"I don't know. Put him in an Uber and send him home," Luca barked. "Marcella. Dario. Figure it out."

But Marcella, normally so *fucking capable*, still looked lost. Dario, one of the fundamental and key pieces of the Moretti business, didn't move.

"Marcella. Dario. *Figure it out*," Luca snapped, barely hanging on to his temper. It took a level of patience he wasn't quite sure he possessed.

"Fine, fine, Dario, *do* something," Marcella said, directing another look at their younger brother.

Dario finally nodded. "I'll take care of him," he said. "But what about service? What will we do without Carlos?"

"You need someone to run service tonight?" Luca questioned, and they both nodded. He'd known it from the moment he'd gotten her first text and also what he'd be doing about it, though deep down, he'd sort of hoped things might shake out differently. But that ship had sailed a long fucking time ago.

"You know we do," Dario said, looking frantic. He was not at his best behind the stove. The whole family knew it. His genius was in numbers. Put him in front of a computer with a budget and a spreadsheet, and he was in heaven, but he couldn't sauté to save his life.

Marcella was not much better. Plus, she usually did her rounds early, among the three restaurants, and then went home, to tuck her kids into bed.

Luca already knew he'd be spending the evening tonight behind the swinging doors, not in front of them. So much for the date he hadn't really wanted to go on. Maybe it was better this way.

No maybes about it; it's definitely better this way.

"I'll do it," Luca said. He'd learned to cook from Nonna herself. She'd taken especial care with him, not only instilling in him the responsibility for the Moretti family, but making sure he knew the recipes, too. He could prepare all of them with his eyes closed.

He set his phone down on the stainless steel counter that ran the length of the big kitchen, and with deliberate movements, shrugged off his suit jacket, carefully hung it up on a nearby hook so it wouldn't wrinkle, then began to unbutton his cuffs and roll up his sleeves on the crisp white button-up he was wearing underneath.

"Apron," he demanded crisply, and Marcella handed him one. He tied it on and went to inspect the main kitchen. It was spotless—at least he could say that for Carlos. The staff was in the back, prepping, but with questions in their eyes.

When he came back, Dario and Marcella were dragging Carlos off, and he was still singing, off-key, and *horribly*, about losing his lady love to. . .well, something. He'd mangled about half the lyrics of the aria and Luca didn't remember the real ones.

Maybe, Luca thought, *he lost her to his own fucking stupidity.*

Who got drunk on Marsala? It wasn't even *real* wine. It was . . .well, it wasn't good for drinking, Luca knew that much, because when he'd been eleven and still a little bit wild, he'd snuck some once, and Nonna had caught him red-handed. The wine had made him lightheaded, but it hadn't been worth it because it had tasted like crap. "Because," she'd said firmly, scolding him, "it's not meant for that, Luca. It's meant for garlic and mushrooms and thyme and chicken. You will try it that way and you will see."

She'd cooked him her own recipe of chicken marsala that afternoon and he'd seen exactly what she'd meant. *Tasted* exactly what she'd meant and never forgotten it.

He'd also never forgotten the steely look in her dark eyes.

The inevitable disappointment.

That day he'd vowed never to disappoint her, or any of his family again.

So at twelve, when his friends at church had plotted to sneak into church and steal the communion wine, he'd said he was busy.

When they'd snuck out at sixteen for beers and to raise hell on the quiet streets of their town of St. Helena, he'd stayed home.

Even in college he'd kept his head down, studying hard, trying to be worthy and ready when his parents decided to retire.

Then Nonna had died, and grief hadn't changed him. Instead, the knot of sadness had coalesced into a desire to be everything she was. Steadfast. Responsible. Never shirking a single duty to her family.

From the moment he'd graduated, early, with his MBA, and come back to St. Helena, to the family fold, he'd been the real power behind the Morettis.

His father, Matteo, and his mother, Nicoletta, were sweet, but they weren't tough. Not tough enough, anyway.

The Morettis required someone strong and capable, someone to protect them and to watch their interests, and Luca had become that.

Exactly, he'd believed, what his family needed.

Then Gabriel had left, with Ren, their cousin, and at first Luca had told himself a pretty lie, that they were leaving to expand the Moretti empire, branching into the food truck business.

But in time, it became clear, they'd left to get away from him.

He and Gabriel had never been close. But the truth still stung.

Then Ilaria, his youngest sister, had announced she had no interest in joining the family business. She'd gone to school in San Francisco and decided to stay. And then six months ago, to his shock, Chiara, the second youngest, had joined her.

Luca had been furious, at first.

Now he was just resigned. Resigned and worried, deep down, that he'd fucked all of this up.

But there was no time to think of that now—no time to think of that normally, which, Luca believed, was better all around.

He turned to the stove.

Carlos had barely started the marinara sauce for the night's service. The huge pot was sitting on the stove, cold now, but it had clearly gotten hot and then *too* hot, because when he glanced in, he saw the garlic had burned black in the olive oil.

"Goddamn it," Luca muttered under his breath.

He lifted the big pot and took it to the back, to the dishwashing room, himself.

Putting it in the big sink, he ran the water as hot as he could stand, and scoured the pot as well as he could.

The last thing he wanted was for the taste of burned garlic to get into the new batch of sauce, and to do that, he had to make sure that every single inch of the pot was clean.

Once he was as sure as he could be, he gave it one more rinse, because nobody could ever accuse Luca Moretti of not being a perfectionism stacked on perfectionism, then dried it off and took it back to the prep kitchen.

The rest of the staff gave him a wide berth, but, Luca was pleased to see, continued to work hard at their jobs, getting ready for the night's service.

He set the pot back on the stove, poured in the olive oil and pulled out the garlic, chopping it and then grinding it with salt into a fine paste on the cutting board, just as Nonna had shown him how to do so many years ago.

"Nobody wants a huge bite of garlic, even if it's perfectly cooked," she'd lectured him.

Once the garlic paste was cooking in the olive oil, he added red pepper flakes and oregano, and then turned to the gigantic cans of whole San Marzano tomatoes that Nonna's imported from Italy by the pallet.

Finally, the sauce was simmering away, and he added the huge bunch of basil in, tied with a string, to impart flavor as the sauce cooked.

He kept a close enough eye on all their restaurants that he had a good idea of how Carlos ran things here at Nonna's flagship, and as he started the nightly meeting of the staff, he noted with pleasure nobody batted an eye at anything he suggested.

Just before five, Marcella came into the kitchen. "Dario and I got Carlos home," she said. "You good in here?"

Luca glanced up. "Yes," he said. "Everything's under control."

But she looked skeptical still. "How many years has it been since you worked on the line? Ten at least."

He shrugged. "Nothing changes. The recipes don't change. And the staff is capable. They can pick up my slack. I'm just here as . . .well, like Carlos is. As a figurehead."

"You sure that's all Carlos is?" Marcella questioned.

"Marcella," Luca said, losing his patience finally, "the man was guzzling Marsala wine. He's a fucking figurehead. Check on the other restaurants and then go home to your kids, okay?"

"Fine." Marcella turned and stomped out of the kitchen and Luca had only a minute to regret losing his temper before orders started piling in, and then he couldn't think of anything at all.

All Luca knew when Elia, one of the line cooks, tossed the last receipt in the trash, officially ending service for the night, was that Carlos had, in fact, *not* been a figurehead.

In a hard-won battle, Luca stayed on his feet and didn't immediately slump to the floor in exhaustion. He'd done this, at one point, working the line for six months straight because his father and Nonna had believed the experience would be a good one. Of course, as Marcella had reminded him earlier tonight, that had been ten years ago.

Though, probably more like twelve.

Still, he was in shape. The best shape, he'd believed, of his life.

But he was worn down, short-tempered, annoyance spiking at anyone who even glanced in his direction.

No wonder Carlos had resorted to the Marsala.

"Tough night, sir?" Elia asked. He was one of their youngest line cooks, a friend of a cousin, or something or other. Luca remembered hazily he'd argued with Carlos about hiring him, but Carlos had said if he couldn't hack it, he'd know.

Ironically, it seemed it was Luca who couldn't hack it.

"I'm just unused to working in the kitchen, behind the line." Luca managed to put a handful of words together and was proud they were all coherent.

"Too much time behind the desk? I couldn't do it." Elia sighed. "I'd go mad in a minute."

"You'd be surprised how comfortable you can get," Luca warned. He scrubbed a hand across his face. "Will you handle the cleanup?"

"Of course, sir," Elia said firmly. "We've got it."

Luca rarely let someone attempt anything without immediate supervision—because what if they failed?—but tonight he cut a piece of eggplant parm from the leftovers in the pan and headed through the dark, empty dining room to where the big polished walnut bar lay across the back of the room. Sat down on one of the barstools and Donna, one of the Morettis' longtime bartenders, took time from her nightly cleanup to pour him a glass of Chianti without him asking, sliding it over to where he sat with a single sympathetic look that spoke volumes.

His shirt was stuck to his back with sweat, dotted with sauce, and absolutely gross. He tugged it off and tossed it to the floor to dispose of later, leaving him in only his white tank.

Maybe burning would take the stench away.

He'd just picked up his fork when he heard a commotion, coming from where the wait staff were closing up the front of the house for the night.

Luca sighed heavily and traded his fork for the glass of wine, taking a long sip, ignoring the irony that earlier he hadn't understood how or why Carlos could be driven to drink Marsala.

Because only one person—or one couple—could cause that kind of excitement.

Everyone was always full of dread when *he* showed up. He saw it in their faces, even though they tried hard to hide it. But when his father and mother showed up?

Adulation and excitement like they were the middle-aged versions of Italian rock stars.

He turned, just as Nicoletta walked into the bar.

"Oh, Luca, you looked absolutely terrible," she said, wrapping an arm around him and smacking a kiss onto his cheek. "Did you work for Carlos tonight?"

"No, I just felt like working myself to the bone on the line cause it had been too long," Luca said dryly.

"Dario came by the house for dinner and said Carlos was 'incapacitated,'" Matteo said, appearing next to his wife.

"Are you really feeding him still?" Luca muttered. "He's a grown ass man—he should be able to feed himself."

"Or maybe just wants to see his parents," Nicoletta said firmly. "What happened?"

"Carlos got dumped. Carlos got drunk. I subbed. End of story."

Nicoletta's expression immediately morphed into sympathy.

But it wasn't for him.

Of course not.

"Poor Carlos," Nicoletta said.

"Must be grave for him to turn to drink," Matteo echoed.

"Or it was just handy," Luca observed. "The wine was *right there*."

"As always, great work, son," Matteo said, patting him on the shoulder. "You do the most for our family."

He did. He knew he did.

It had always been his goal, but did that mean it was right?

He wasn't sure he knew anymore.

Certainty was no longer his constant companion and that was worrisome.

"So true," Nicoletta agreed. "And that is what we came here for, actually, because I have had a really . . .panicked email from Giana."

Luca had picked up his fork again and had a mouthful of eggplant and cheese halfway to his mouth. "Your sister Giana?"

"Yes, you know we invested in the deli she and her son started?"

"You mean the deli the Morettis invested in?" Luca asked archly.

It had been five years ago, right when he'd first been getting his feet under him as the de facto leader and Nicoletta had, Luca was not ashamed to admit, bulldozed right over the half a dozen serious concerns he'd had.

Starting with the fact that Giana was flighty as hell, and her son was a waste of space. He'd never believed they could make a go of the family business, but they were starting it across the country, and maybe good Italian food was so scarce in the wilds of South Carolina it wouldn't matter how poorly the business was run.

Their loan payments had always come in. Sometimes late, but always eventually showing up, and he'd put them out of his mind.

But now that worry cropped up again.

"Yes, yes, that deli, of course," Nicoletta said, waving her hand. She took a long pause, for dramatic effect, but it was completely lost on

Luca because he already was ninety-nine point nine percent sure what she was going to say. "Giana says the deli is in trouble. They need help, Luca, darling. Can you help them?"

Luca barely refrained from rolling his eyes. "Sure, I'd be happy to look over their accounting, if they'd like to send it over. Make sure they copy Dario, too."

"Luca," Nicoletta chastised. "If it was a matter of numbers, you know I would ask Dario, but this is bigger than that. It needs . . ." She paused and again he knew exactly what was coming, but that didn't mean it felt any better to hear it. "It needs your touch, Luca. Your personal attention. Please. For Giana. For Enzo."

"Mama, I can't go to South Carolina. There's way too many things that need my attention." It was a last-ditch effort. He knew it would be in vain but he tried it anyway.

The pull of helping Morettis was too strong. The ingrained need in him to do everything he could. Even if Giana was an idiot and her son even worse.

"I know you do, Luca, darling, but you can take a few weeks, maybe even make a little vacation of it. The town is very sweet, very relaxing, right on the water, or so Giana says. Maybe we will go there this summer for a vacation of our own."

Luca didn't hold back his eye roll this time. "If it's so fucking picturesque, why can't they run a successful business there?"

Nicoletta slapped him on the side of the head. "Language, Luca."

He stared at his plate. He did not want to go to wherever it was that Giana and her stupid son were running a Moretti business into the ground.

But this was family.

He'd done so much worse for family.

"Maybe this will even give you a new perspective," Matteo added, probably trying to be helpful, but not realizing he was sinking further into the black hole his wife had already vigorously dug.

"A new perspective on *what*?" Luca asked. Even though he already knew what that was.

Italian goal number one: to support the family, and more importantly the family's *business*, and help it become as successful as possible.

Italian goal number two: to make even *more* family to benefit from number one.

Luca was always going to be fucking fantastic at number one, and terrible at number two.

It wasn't like there weren't possibilities for children for gay men, but Luca had never been interested in having kids of his own. He'd never even had a real relationship. Not ever dated a guy for long enough who he felt like introducing to the insanity that was the Moretti family.

In this particular vein, he was an absolute disappointment. He knew it. Nicoletta knew it. Matteo knew it. And his parents were too relentless to ever stop alluding to his one failure: meet a nice Italian boy and make a nice Italian family together.

"You know what he means," Nicoletta chided. "You are so *lonely*."

"No, I am so *busy*," Luca argued. "So busy trying to keep Nonna's in one piece."

"Nonna's is fine. You work hard. Dario works hard. Marco and Marcella work hard. Gabe and Lorenzo work all the time. Even Chiara and Ilaria are trying to do something. But they all have *lives*, Luca. You do not."

Luca finished eating his eggplant. Took a long sip of wine. He didn't really want to bring this up because he rarely talked about his personal life. Not that his parents weren't accepting. They *were*. But they always wanted the next date to be the man he was going to marry. And Luca didn't even know if he wanted to marry anyone at all.

So it was just easier to keep quiet about it.

But this was too much.

He couldn't swallow it down any longer.

He stood, his exhausted legs screaming. But he stayed steady, because that was Luca. He always stayed steady. He looked his mother right in the eye. "Fine. I will go to Indigo Cove or Geranium Bay or whatever it's called. I will go there and tell Giana and her idiot son exactly what they are doing wrong. Because I'm sure the list is long. But I want you to know, before I was called in tonight, I *did* have a date. A *life*, as you so pleasantly put it. But I had to put it aside for Nonna's. I don't mind doing that, but what I do mind," Luca said, lowering his voice, "are the lectures."

Nicoletta stared at him.

He rarely worried he was too harsh. His exacting standards often lent themselves to a kind of ruthlessness. It was just something that came with the territory, and something he'd come to terms with ages ago. It was how Nonna's continued to flourish and prosper. Every time he thought of how Gabe's face shut down, how he'd rejected both Luca and his assistance, he reminded himself of all the good he'd done. How he'd shepherded the Moretti business through every tough situation they had encountered.

But today, he worried.

"Mama," he said, knowing he should apologize, but instead she held up a hand.

"No," she said firmly. "No. I know we expect much of you, Luca. You are the eldest. You run everything, and you do it brilliantly. Nobody could argue with that. But I wish you had gone on the date tonight. We could've handled it. I could have worked the line—Elia is coming along so much better. We could have done *something*. We could've gotten Marco to come over from the other restaurant. You deserve to have good things too." She paused. "Do you like this boy a lot? Have you been on many dates?"

No, and *no.*

Luca was regretting ever bringing the date up, because now her eyes were gleaming with all the possibilities. "Mama, no, *no.* He's just a guy from the gym. I didn't even want to . . ."

"But." Nicoletta grasped his arm. "How will you ever find anyone if you don't *try,* Luca?"

She was so heartfelt, so *earnest,* he couldn't even roll his eyes. It felt wrong to do it.

"I don't know," he admitted. And he didn't know. That *was* the truth.

Wasn't he happy the way things were, with his work and his family? Well, maybe he wasn't happy, but at least he was satisfied with how things were, and wasn't that really the most you could hope for?

Why couldn't other people see that?

"Promise me," Matteo chimed in, holding his shoulder again. "Promise me you will take a few weeks to sort out this problem of Giana's and then take another week, just for you. Relax. Go to the beach. Don't worry about us. We will be fine."

Luca thought his father's confidence in their fineness without him was misplaced, but he knew he couldn't keep arguing about it.

Some disaster would happen and he would have to come home to deal with it, and that was fine. He wouldn't even be disappointed.

The last thing he wanted was to go to South Carolina at all. The last thing he was going to want to do was stay.

Chapter Two

Oliver Billings loved the rhythm of the morning.

He knew some bakers hated the hours—getting up so early that most people wouldn't even consider it morning, but a very, *very* late night—but getting up before dawn crept over the rise of the ocean had never bothered Oliver. He'd always been a morning person, anyway.

Then there was the little burst of joy he felt every single time he unlocked the door to his own bakery and cafe.

He'd started out baking cookies, cupcakes, and big special occasion cakes in his kitchen at home. But even though Indigo Bay was a small town, the residents had a sweet tooth, and soon he'd needed to expand out of his space and add some help.

He'd had his eye on this tiny, tucked-away empty corner property at the end of Main Street for ages, and he'd felt such a rush of achievement when he'd unlocked it with his own set of keys for the first time, almost five years ago.

At first he'd only sold pastries in the mornings, along with coffee, courtesy of Taylor, his bright red Italian espresso machine. But when he'd started selling out of the muffins and doughnuts and hand pies—both sweet and savory—he'd expanded, adding in breakfast and lunch sandwiches, built on bread he baked fresh daily.

Long-term, Oliver had a dream of staying open for dinner. He'd need more staff—and some professional help with the menu—but that was far enough off that it was still just a fun idea he liked playing with in his evenings.

After turning the key in the lock of the back door, Oliver let it close behind him and hung the ring of jangling keys up next to the door, grabbing the apron from the hook next to them.

He tied it on and flicked on the lights, all the shiny stainless steel momentarily blinding in the sudden brightness.

Aaron, his assistant and intern, would be in soon to help Oliver with the morning's bake, but for now, it was just him.

He flicked on his Bluetooth speaker, picked one of his favorite playlists and let the strains of the music get him moving.

First, dough, because it would need time to rise.

He made bread dough, pastry dough, and lastly, the pie dough for the many different variations of hand pies that were the bakery's specialty.

There was a beautiful rhythm to this too, the mixing, followed by the kneading, followed by the rise in the warmest part of the bakery, already chasing away the chill of a spring morning. By noon it would be warm here, even though it was only early March in South Carolina, but it was so early there was still a definite chill to the air.

Then, while the bread rose, Oliver moved onto muffins, which they baked fresh every morning. It was an unusual day where they didn't sell out completely.

As the huge vat of dough swirled in the biggest mixer, Oliver prepped the ingredients. They had the standards, of course: blueberry, chocolate, banana walnut. They had others, too, that he really enjoyed experimenting with. Chai spice pumpkin with a cream cheese drizzle that was to die for. Apple cinnamon pecan. Coconut pineapple with an unexpected swirl of mango purée in the crusty top.

He also sold baked goods to the many bed-and-breakfasts in town, and they loved his muffins, so he made sure to make enough to fulfill his standing orders.

Once the dough was scooped out into the army of trays and he'd started rotating them through the big oven, Oliver wiped his floury hands on his apron and glanced at his watch. Aaron should be here, to help prep the sweet dough and the various pastries they crafted out of it. Cinnamon rolls full of butter and pecans, chai spice twists bursting with flavor and an unexpected hint of cayenne pepper, and finally the *pain au chocolat* that had gotten Aaron hired in the first place.

He was young, much younger than Oliver had wanted, but when Aaron had brought in some of the chocolate croissants he'd baked, Oliver had realized that age was just a number. The pastries were *that* good, bursting with butter and chocolate that wasn't really all that sweet, but addicting, all the same.

Aaron might be young, but he was unfailingly reliable. He'd been here at three thirty for the last three years. Oliver couldn't remember one time he'd ever been late.

But he was late this morning.

Wiping his hands much more thoroughly, Oliver pulled his phone out of his back pocket and pulled up their last text convo, from a few nights ago, when Aaron had sent him a shrimp toast recipe that he thought they could adapt for the lunch crowd. He sent a new message, asking Aaron where he was and adding that he better not have overslept. It was Thursday, and they were always busier toward the weekend, when people felt like they needed an extra boost to get through the rest of the work week.

In a few hours, Marjorie would be in, to help make espresso and coffee and serve the handful of tables that Oliver had managed to squeeze into the tiny space.

If they ever did stay open for dinner, he'd have to figure out a way to expand. Mrs. Casey, who owned the antiques and knickknacks store next door, was always making noise about retiring. *One more year, with this kind of success,* Oliver told himself as he slipped his phone back into his pocket, *and you can devote yourself to convincing her it's time to retire and then you can rent her space and knock down that wall.*

Five minutes went by and then ten, but Oliver's phone didn't vibrate. He sighed and pulled the ingredients out for the cinnamon rolls, brick after brick of butter, and then began to mix the dough together, letting the wiggle of annoyance sift through him as he mentally rearranged his schedule for the morning. He could always call in his mom. Joy was an incredible baker, and he'd learned so much from her, but he didn't like to involve her, because this was his domain—and because she was already so busy, running the biggest bed-and-breakfast in town.

Plus, if she came, she'd harass him again about having a big party for the birthday he didn't want to acknowledge.

It was bad enough that she'd enlisted Marjorie—whom he'd forbidden from mentioning it within his hearing.

No, he couldn't call Joy. He'd just figure out how to manage on his own.

Oliver was done with the cinnamon rolls and had just moved onto the Chai Spice twists when the back door opened hard, nearly slamming open and then closed again. Oliver's fingers moved quickly, dropping butter into the big vat as it mixed the dough.

"God, I'm so sorry," Aaron said in a rush, and Oliver lifted his head.

Oliver didn't have to look at his watch to know that Aaron was almost two hours late. Today was seriously going to suck as a result. He was way behind on prepping the rest of the morning's bake, and he was afraid the bread might have been overproofed, because he didn't have as deft or quick a hand as Aaron did with the pastries. He used to, but Aaron had been solely in charge of them for nearly the last two years, and Oliver was out of practice.

"Where were you?" Oliver asked. His voice remained steady, because Aaron sounded *so* frantic. There wasn't a reason for both of them to freak out. And he'd learned from watching his mother at the bed-and-breakfast his family had owned for the last two generations that you always caught more flies with honey than with vinegar.

Aaron was an exemplary employee. There was no need to come down on him like a ton of bricks. Not when he was clearly already stressed.

"Car wouldn't start, and phone was dead. Guess I forgot to plug it in last night," Aaron said, pulling on his own apron from the hook by the door.

"How'd you get here?"

"Caught a ride with a neighbor, once he was up for the day," Aaron said. "But I'm gonna need a ride back after the morning rush, to meet the tow truck. If it's not a problem." He looked worried, like it might be. Even though Aaron had worked for him for two years now, Oliver knew his management style still took the other guy by surprise.

But this way, he was guaranteed to always keep people. Nobody was ever going to leave because he was an asshole. No—they were going to *stay* because he was kind and gave them the kind of wiggle room they needed. The kind of wiggle room he'd wanted, *he'd* needed, when he'd worked at some of the big restaurants in Charleston, before coming back home to open the bakery.

"No, of course not, not a problem at all," Oliver said. It wasn't a big deal for him to drive Aaron home and back again. Maybe some bosses would've been mad at the extra task on an already busy morning, but shit happened, and he wasn't about to make Aaron's life even tougher than it already was.

See? Oliver thought. *Perfect, logical sense.*

Between the two of them, they got the pastries and the muffins done and then moved onto the hand pies.

They made a big selection of sweet and savory ones.

Bacon cheddar, with a hint of chives.

Sausage and brie, with a dollop of cranberry to give just the right amount of sweetness.

Apple, peach, and cherry, of course, because people liked the idea that they were eating fruit for breakfast, even if it was coated in sugar and the dough drizzled in vanilla honey glaze.

But then there was the butter pecan flavor, which was basically a total excuse to eat something decadent first thing in the morning and not feel even the tiniest bit guilty about it.

Marjorie arrived, bustling in with a huge bunch of wildflowers she would divide up among the tiny glass vases at the dozen tiny tables crammed into the cafe proper.

"Where's all my pastries?" Marjorie called out, and Oliver knew she was talking about the empty glass case that stretched almost the full length of the room.

"Up soon!" he called out. "Runnin' a bit behind today."

"That's not like you."

Oliver glanced up as he slid a hot pan full of pastries into the tower rack. "Yeah, I know."

Aaron was in the back, finishing up the bread, because it would be a fine line for them to get it baked and cooled enough to use for sandwiches this morning.

She took a few steps closer. Her lipstick was bright red today and matched her hair and the rims of her eyeglasses.

Valentine's Day might've passed a week ago, but that didn't mean Marjorie would ever give up her red and pink. She was like Indigo Bay that way.

"What happened?" she asked.

Oliver shrugged. "It's nothing. A problem with Aaron's car, easily fixed, hopefully. But after the morning rush, I've got to run him back home, to wait for a tow."

"Do you?" Her eyebrow rose, a slash of bright crimson against her pale skin.

"Margie," Oliver warned softly.

"You're too nice. You know that," she said.

"I *don't* know that, actually," Oliver said. He slid another pan of freshly baked pastry onto the rack.

The problem—or the blessing—with Marjorie was she'd known him for every year of his upcoming thirty years. She was his mother's best friend and had been his third-grade teacher. After retiring from the school system, she'd been at a loose end, and it had made perfect sense for him to hire her to staff the bakery in the mornings.

Take into account that she'd gone to Europe most every summer she'd had off and could make a better cappuccino than him? It had been a no-brainer move.

Except for the fact she'd never forgotten she'd been his teacher.

"He's young, he just needs structure," Marjorie said, referring to Aaron.

"He has plenty of structure, trust me," Oliver said dryly. Anyone who could consistently be here at three thirty every morning didn't need a lecture on routine.

"Alright, well you do know best," she said. "I'll go flip the *open* sign if you want to fill the case."

"Sure thing," Oliver said.

For the next four hours, he didn't have time to think about what she'd said at all, which was frankly better than him spending those four hours worrying that maybe he *was* being too nice.

He still told himself, as he dropped Aaron off to wait for the tow to the local mechanics shop, that he was being a good boss.

That was all.

But his mind wouldn't quiet, as he turned onto Main Street, and he debated with himself about stopping by Walter's greengrocery, seeing what he had that was fresh and new. Maybe some recipe testing would relax him—but then he was tired, too. It had been a long, hard morning. Harder than he'd had in a long time, and Oliver couldn't deny that Aaron was at least partially responsible for that. If he'd known how late Aaron was going to be, Oliver would've called his mother. Or asked her to run over and pick Aaron up, so he *wouldn't* be that late.

He was still going back and forth on if he wanted to swing by Walter's when a flash moving across the street, just past the heart of downtown, caught his eye and he slammed on his brakes without a single second to spare.

Oliver had the fleeting impression of a man, a *big* man, broad and tall and solid in a dark suit, which was unusual because not many in Indigo Bay bothered with suits.

His hands landed on Oliver's hood and then a pair of dark eyes turned on him and caught him right through the windshield.

Trapped him.

Even darker brows slammed down, and Oliver realized then, between the full lips, the wavy dark hair with its few silvering threads at the temples, and handsome face, that the man was full-on glaring.

Okay, yes, he'd almost hit him. But . . .there wasn't a crosswalk here. Then there was the phone in the man's hand. He'd been looking at it, Oliver thought, then rewound his brain, replaying what had happened again, and *yes*, he had been.

Crossing the street and not even looking where he was going, and now he was going to glare at Oliver for almost hitting him?

He should be *thanking* Oliver for not killing him.

His hand was shaking a little as he rolled down the window.

"The crosswalk is the next block down," he pointed, hating the way his voice trembled. *Adrenaline, it's just adrenaline.* But it was also the intensity in the man's gaze. The size of him. The ferocity of him.

He should've scared Oliver. But he didn't.

At all.

In fact, he was feeling rather the opposite of scared right now as the man curled his hands into fists and leaned around the side of the car.

"What?" he barked out. "The fucking *crosswalk?*"

"You know what a crosswalk is. A place to cross the street. Two lines. You try to stay between them? I find it's a great way not to get killed."

Oliver knew his overriding characteristic was that he was *nice*. Too nice, according to some people (*ahem*, Marjorie). But when faced with this man, it was hard—no, *impossible*—not to dish his snark right back.

The man stared at him in shock. He probably wasn't used to people returning his shit, but Oliver had.

Because Oliver was momentarily crazy? Or temporarily mesmerized by the intoxicating look of passion in the man's dark eyes?

Maybe it was the pissed off kind of passion, but it was passion nonetheless.

He straightened his back and prayed that his hands would stop trembling.

"Are you seriously trying to tell me what a crosswalk is?" the man said. His voice was deep and dark but also melodic, with a touch of something Oliver couldn't quite place. It wasn't French. It wasn't Middle Eastern. It was something else. Something beautiful.

Oliver had never been tempted to fantasize over a man he'd met in everyday life before. But he had a feeling he'd be hard-pressed to forget about this one.

"Well," he replied seriously, "I wasn't sure you knew, as you weren't crossing in it."

"You almost *hit me*," the man retorted.

"Exactly," Oliver chirped.

For a second, those eyes went harder. Hotter, too. And Oliver trembled, not just on the outside—but inside, too.

Then the man muttered something under his breath and was pushing off from the car, his long legs striding across the street, and all Oliver had left was a departing vision of a broad back, covered in flawlessly tailored dark fabric, and a sneaking suspicion he'd be looking everywhere for that face for weeks to come.

Because Oliver would have remembered him, if he'd ever seen him around Indigo Bay before, and he definitely had not.

Was he new to the town? Just passing through? Maybe he could call his mother and ask if she was currently housing a man best characterized as a tall, dark drink of grumpy water.

A honk interrupted his internal sleuthing. Then another.

Oliver glanced up into his rearview mirror. "Shit," he muttered. He recognized Chauncey Anderson's car and also his glowering expression, and hit the gas, wheels squealing as he finally departed the scene of the crime.

No, he hadn't killed the mysterious man.

But the mysterious man had definitely done something to him.

Chapter Three

Luca's heart was still beating a fraction too hard as he walked down the block to his cousin's sandwich shop.

Maybe it was because he'd nearly been hit while crossing the street.

Or maybe it was the way the man in the driver's seat had met his stare and hadn't flinched. Hadn't backed down, while he'd lectured him about what a crosswalk was, even after Luca had pinned him with his most effective glare. The one that silenced even the best of them, even his own family, most of the time.

It had been hard to get a full impression since Luca had only seen him through the windshield, heart racing at the near miss, and then through the side window, once he'd rolled it down, but the small snapshots he was left with showed him plenty to like.

Big hazel eyes hot with challenge. Soft pink lips. Hair covered by a bright purple beanie embroidered with a rainbow flag. A thin frame but surprisingly strong, if the toned arms peeking out from underneath his T-shirt sleeves were any indication.

Luca shouldn't have found him appealing at all. After all, he'd nearly killed him. *But,* an annoying voice in his head added, *he wasn't wrong, you weren't on the crosswalk and you were looking at your phone.*

He'd been absorbed in an email from one of Nonna's regular suppliers, something about veal going up in price per pound, and he'd been reading the email while mentally calculating what that was going to do their bottom line, when he'd felt rather than heard or saw the car come to a screeching halt in front of him.

Okay, yes, he shouldn't have been crossing there. He shouldn't have been on his phone.

But did he need to be lectured, too?

Luca didn't think so.

Especially not with such a smug, superior air.

Especially not by someone who looked like they played with toddlers for a living or knit sweaters for orphans or owned one of the ridiculously large number of bed-and-breakfasts dotting this town.

He'd tried to book a room at one of the larger hotel chains, but all of them were much further out of town. Finally, after worrying about Wi-Fi, electrical outlet availability, shitty mattresses, and terrible water pressure, he'd booked the best-rated one.

The Sweetheart Inn, it was called. Luca had barely gotten an impression of a huge Victorian with a pristine white wraparound porch and all the delicate woodwork picked out in various shades of pink and red last night when he'd come in near to midnight after driving in from Charleston.

But the bed had been surprisingly comfortable, the Wi-Fi faster than he'd anticipated, and the shower even better than the one Luca had at home.

And the muffins? He'd devoured three at breakfast and tried not to feel guilty when he'd asked the lady staffing the dining room if there was a gym nearby that offered a temporary pass.

If he was going to stay here for a few weeks, *and* the baked goods continued to be this irresistible, he was going to need one.

Giana had told him via text she and Enzo would meet him at the sandwich shop at ten thirty, right as they opened for the day's business.

He'd nearly texted back and said, *eight or nine is better*, but he hadn't, because part of diagnosing the problems was seeing them in their element. How did the business normally run, not just when big bad Luca came to visit?

On the plane ride over, he'd done some rudimentary research. The deli's Google reviews were not great, and there weren't many of them, almost none of them from locals, which was worrisome.

Also, Luca wished he'd been more aware, when they were in their development stages, just *where* Giana and Enzo were planning on opening, because the location was not ideal, off Main Street and tucked away down a side street, with far less foot traffic than they'd get if they were on the main thoroughfare through town.

Arriving at the shop, he perused the outside. He was struck by a certain lack of charm as he stood in front of the shop. The sign was not great, but not terrible either, and could use some improvement. Even the windows outside were dirty and looked like they hadn't been cleaned in months.

Nothing like the bakery he'd passed a few blocks back that took up one whole corner on one of the busiest parts of Main Street. He'd had a feeling the Sweetie Pie's Bakery and Cafe was Nonna's Deli stiffest competition, and from everything he could see, he understood exactly why Enzo and Giana weren't on top.

He pushed open the door and waited for the inevitable smell of delicious food to waft over him.

But there wasn't any.

Nothing at all. No aroma whatsoever.

Luca hesitated just inside the door, glancing around, at the basic but uninspired décor; they had the same traditional red-and-white checked tablecloths at their own Italian deli and also at the flagship Nonna's restaurant, but they were crisper there, and offset by modern lighting and sensibilities, combining the old with the new. But here, without those key updates, the inside just felt plain and old-fashioned. And *empty*. He looked, down to the smart watch on his wrist, where *yes*, it said it was indeed ten thirty in the morning on the dot.

As he waited for someone—*anyone*—to arrive, Luca continued to look around, taking in every detail and making a whole list of mental notes.

The menu was above the counter, and Luca was surprised to see how beautiful it was. This was *actually* the foundation of the restaurant and it should have been the focal point. Instead it was tucked away, hidden from the doorway behind a large refrigerated case holding bottled drinks.

Originally it must have been a large chalkboard, but the edges had been carefully sanded down, buffed to a satin shine, and a glossy finish added until the wood glowed. The menu itself, every item on it Luca recognized as well as his right hand, wasn't written, but *drawn* with quirky imagination and a real charm and flair, each letter with its own personality.

It was the only original piece in what felt like a poor, cheap copy of the Nonna's brand.

He cleared his throat, loudly, and just when he'd given up hope on anyone showing up, a small woman with dark hair liberally streaked with gray emerged from the swinging doors leading to the kitchen. She wore a spotless red apron, long on her short frame.

Following behind her was a man in his mid-twenties, a sullen expression on his face and an equally pristine red apron over his white T-shirt.

"Luca, darling," Giana said, kissing him on both cheeks after she'd reached him. "You remember Enzo, of course."

He gave Enzo a nod, and Enzo nodded back, the resentment clear in his gaze.

Okay, so someone else was actually unhappier about him being here than he was. Good to know.

"Are you not opening today?" Luca asked. Trying for casual. But the surprise in Giana's face probably meant he hadn't achieved it.

"Of course we are."

Luca frowned. "Are you . . ." He hesitated. He didn't usually step so carefully around his immediate family, but he didn't know his mother's sister all that well. She'd moved to the east coast thirty years ago, met a fellow Italian in New Jersey, and to the family's dismay, he'd left her eight months pregnant and disappeared. Luca was half-convinced he'd be found someday in the river, wearing cement shoes.

He was no good, his mother sniffed, whenever Giana's situation came up. *No good at all.*

The family had come together in support of her, and that was why, Luca was sure, when she'd asked for seed money for the business with her son, Nicoletta and Matteo had made sure she got it.

But, Luca was beginning to see as he looked around the deli, maybe they should've been given not just the money, but additional assistance, too.

"We're open," Giana said firmly. "Of course we are open."

"But you're not . . ." Luca took a deep breath. He hadn't expected this to be so awkward. He *liked* his aunt, at least the half a dozen times he'd met her. He didn't know Enzo well, but from what he'd heard of him, he wasn't sure he'd feel the same way about him—but still it wasn't easy to come in here and demand to know why they hadn't started cooking yet. "Where is the food?"

"In the back of course," Giana said, shooting him a confused expression. "We have a full commercial kitchen."

A tense moment followed. He finally decided if he wasn't going to be honest, there was no point in him flying all the way out here. Plus, this had his *Nonna's* name on the front of the building, and he wasn't going to tolerate anything less than perfection. Same as he did at home.

"But I can't smell it," Luca finally said.

"Oh, *oh*," Giana said, with a chuckle. "We cook every few weeks. And then freeze everything. Just heat things up to order. Come in the back, and you will see."

Luca followed, silent, but ninety-nine percent sure that he hated this plan.

Giana showed him the walk-in fridge.

Then the freezer. Loaded with bins and bins of red sauce and meatballs. Chicken and eggplant parm. Lasagna in pans stacked high.

He took in the bags of bought sourdough and focaccia.

Tried not to let the shock show on his face, but it was there, rippling inside him.

Surely his mother had imparted the basic expectations of using the family name. Fresh ingredients, *freshly* prepared, always. Bread baked in their own kitchens. Sauce made from scratch every morning.

Even Gabriel and Lorenzo, with the limited resources they had in their food truck, did it right.

"So," Luca said heavily after Giana finished the tour, "what is the biggest problem?"

She wrung her hands, looking devastated. "Business is . . .not good. We've had to reduce staff, change suppliers several times to find better deals, and still . . .not good."

"And getting worse," Enzo supplied dryly, speaking up for the first time since Luca had appeared.

Giana shot her son a look. "Enzo manages things here, day to day."

"I see," Luca said. Thought that maybe he did.

He'd definitely noticed every single shortcut they'd taken.

Shortcuts he'd never permit in any of the other family restaurants.

"We're doing just fine here. Winter's just a hard time, and that's—"

"That's not why," Luca said, cutting Enzo off, ruthlessly. At first he'd been strangely hesitant to involve himself, but now that he saw the breadth of what had been done—or *not* done—he couldn't help himself. "The bakery down the street is thriving. I saw a line out of the door."

"Oh, *Oliver*," Enzo said bitterly.

"Who's Oliver?"

"Oliver owns the bakery," Giana explained.

"Ah," Luca said. Unclear as to why Enzo was so bitter about the man, except that maybe it was because his business was so much more successful. "The point remains. He's busy. You're not."

"How do we fix it?" Giana asked, wringing her hands together.

Luca, who was equally annoyed at her and at himself, and for the exact same reason—for letting things get this bad—cleared his throat. "I need to do some more research. Can I sit at one of the tables? Observe a regular service?"

Enzo and Giana exchanged glances, pinging Luca's bullshit meter even more.

"Of course," Giana finally said.

An hour and a half later, he realized why she'd been so uneasy.

In ninety minutes since Enzo had flipped the *open* sign, they'd had exactly one customer, a gruff older man in a worn-out Durham Bulls ball cap, who'd ordered a meatball sub, exchanged the bare minimum of words with Enzo, and had grabbed his sandwich to go with a can of Coke from the drink fridge, and left.

Luca was wishing he'd brought his laptop, because at least he could've done work while waiting for *anyone* to come in.

Finally, Giana emerged from the kitchen. She had a sheepish, ashamed look in her eyes as she carried out a plate to Luca.

"Meatball sub?" she asked. "Feel free to grab a drink from the case if you'd like."

He'd intended to taste the food, of course, but he'd hoped to slip in his order so Giana didn't know the food was for him. He wanted exactly what everyone else got. But he supposed, getting up, stretching as he walked to the case, he *was* getting what everyone else was getting. Store-bought bread, and frozen-then-thawed sauce and meatballs.

Luca didn't think he had the most discerning palate in the world. That was his brother, Marco, who was an incredible chef, and who managed the steakhouse so he could stretch his wings a bit. But he knew Nonna's red sauce recipe like the back of his hand—it was a Moretti tradition to learn it when your hand was just strong enough and your arm just long enough to use the wooden spoon to stir the sauce in the big pot—and he recognized it, of course.

The sweetness of the tomatoes was dulled though. Artificial, he realized. They weren't using the same tomatoes he made sure to always import from Italy. They'd added sugar in compensation, but it wasn't the same.

He could taste the difference on his tongue.

The mozzarella and provolone layering the meatballs weren't right either. Cheap quality, and a bit rubbery.

He wasn't even going to talk about how wrong the bread was.

Nonna's meatballs and sauce only belonged on *freshly* baked bread.

If Giana and Enzo weren't going to bake it, then maybe he could get bread from this Oliver guy, who owned the bakery.

Something to look into.

He bit into the sandwich, his teeth sinking into the meatball, and it probably wouldn't be immediately recognizable to anyone else, but he tasted the freezer on it. The lack of freshness in the meat. How it *had* been fresh, and then frozen.

Disappointing.

It was a fine sandwich. Just fine, though.

Not Nonna's quality.

He ate it though, because he wasn't going to throw food away, even food that was just fine.

The lunch "rush" came and went.

Two more people showed up. One person got the chopped salad. Another an order of the eggplant parm to go.

Three people, even in this small town, in early March, on a Wednesday, was pathetic. He understood now why they were struggling.

"It's usually better than this," Giana said—Giana *lied*—as she approached Luca's table to pick up his plate. It was so empty in the restaurant she should've whisked it away the moment he was finished. Nobody wanted to come in and sit down around dirty dishes.

Luca added another mental note to the other hundred he'd made today already.

"Is it, though?" Luca questioned.

The mediocrity of this establishment coupled with the fact that *his* Nonna's name was above the door had dismissed the last of his awkwardness about setting them on a better course. And if they couldn't, if they wouldn't make the changes required to turn this business around, then he would rather they closed. Which, he had to assume, was a possibility, considering the desperation in Giana's eyes, and *three* people who had come in for lunch today.

Giana sighed. "No," she admitted. She settled in the chair opposite his. "Things were going alright until I semiretired. My back can't take the work anymore, but then Enzo . . .well, he wasn't particularly interested in the business."

The business you started for *him*, Luca thought, frowning.

"He's an artist, you see," Giana said. "On the side, of course."

"He drew the menu," Luca observed, realization dawning.

"Yes, he did. It's wonderful, isn't it?"

It was. The only wonderful thing about this place.

"But then business went bad, or went *worse*, I suppose, and I came back to help him. And now," she said, her whole face brightening, "you will fix us right up, and everything will be beautiful again. Just like it should be."

"Ah," Luca said noncommittally. He didn't want to tell his aunt it was clear—to him, at least—that Enzo had little to zero interest in the family business, and even if Luca did manage to fix Giana and Enzo's problems, it would take a long time to win over the town's trust again. This was not a matter of simple solutions, easily executable.

"How long are you planning to stay?" Giana asked.

Part of Luca wanted to say he'd be out on the first plane in the morning, because fixing the deli was impossible. Or not that fixing it was impossible, but so time consuming and difficult he wasn't sure that either of them would commit to it. But Nonna hadn't taught him the fundamentals of owning a restaurant—owning one of the Moretti family restaurants—only to have him shirk his responsibilities now.

"A few weeks," Luca said. "Maybe a month."

"That long?" Giana sounded dismayed. "But we have the same menu! The same recipes! Maybe what we need," she continued, forging ahead before Luca could broach the subject of how the menu and the recipes were executed, "is more publicity. There's a big festival in town, happening in a few weeks. The Sweethearts Festival. Maybe we could apply to be a vendor there, get some attention."

Luca ignored the ridiculous name of the festival. He wondered if they decked it out as his bed-and-breakfast was—all in pink and red and white, like a too-sweet bakery cake. Instead, he hummed under his breath. Everyone said he was so mean and grumpy, and maybe he could be, but if he truly was, down to the core, as relentless as everyone accused him of being, surely he would be more eager to tell Giana all about her problems.

But she looked so hopeful, he couldn't let her continue on like this, believing in miracles when he knew the solutions to the problems were going to be so hard: tearing everything down and starting over again.

"Not until we're confident we can turn things around. That the product we're delivering is better," Luca said gently. Probably more gently than anyone in his family believed he was capable of. Gabe, especially.

Giana recoiled. "The product is better? The *product is better*? We use the same recipes! Nicoletta gave them to me. I follow them to the letter. There's nothing wrong with our product. Enzo warned me you'd come here and try to change everything to fix it, but maybe it's not as broken as we think it is." She threw him a hard look. "Maybe you're inflexible, believe nobody can do it as right as you, just like everyone says."

It wasn't a surprise. Luca told himself it was not a surprise.

Still, it stung.

"I . . ." Luca considered explaining, in detail, how that was not true. How it wasn't that he believed his way was the only right way, though he *did* believe that, but that nobody else believed they were doing it right either, because three customers did not a business make, but then he shut his mouth.

There was no point in arguing.

Tonight, he would put together a plan. He would email it over. He would come back tomorrow, and see what Giana had to say. If his reception was as cold as her glare right now, he would just go.

Tell Mama that he tried and Giana was doomed to fail.

That maybe it was better this way, anyway, because she was growing older, and the work was hard, and Enzo was either incapable of or uninterested in continuing the family tradition.

He couldn't make people change, unless they wanted to.

He stood. "Thanks for the sandwich," he said stiffly.

She looked at him in surprise, like she hadn't expected him to be insulted at her words.

Okay, maybe he could be a bit of an asshole, but that didn't mean he didn't *feel things*.

He still goddamn felt them; he'd just gotten far too good at ignoring the pain.

"Oh." Giana hesitated. "You're welcome."

"I'll see you in the morning."

Her jaw fell open. No doubt she'd been expecting that he'd leave in a huff. Fly off and tell Nicoletta the whole thing was useless.

But *Nonna's* was still emblazoned above the doorway, so he couldn't let it go.

Not without at least trying to live up to her memory.

Luca picked up his temporary gym pass at the front desk of his bed-and-breakfast, staffed by an older woman with improbably pink hair who was typing away on her laptop. She only glanced up to give him the pass, along with a smile, and quick directions to the gym. What was with the Valentine's obsession in this town? Luca didn't understand it at all, because that holiday, more than almost any of the others, was such a commercial enterprise.

Of course, how could he complain about that, when reservations at all the Nonna's restaurants booked up months in advance for the special night? When February was, hands down, one of their best months of the year?

Still, the commitment to the theme baffled him, all the way up to his room and then back down. He was just about to head out the door as his phone beeped in his pocket. He pulled it out of his gym shorts and was reviewing the text from Marco—something about a billing issue from one of his regular meat suppliers—when he ran right into a box.

Well, someone *carrying* a box. A big white bakery box, balanced precariously on two slim but strong arms. Arms that seemed vaguely familiar.

"What the fuck," the man behind the box exclaimed. In a voice Luca swore he'd heard before. He reached out to steady the box so it wouldn't spill to the ground. It was heavy and a little awkward to balance it between them, but he managed to right it.

Then the man lowered the box, and Luca realized why he'd been feeling dejá vu since the moment of the collision.

It was the same man from the car.

The man he'd not wanted to find attractive, because he'd lectured him, unbearably, on crosswalks and how to use them, but had anyway.

Out of the car, he was even more attractive. Taller than Luca had imagined, but still a few inches shorter than him. Slim and strong. The purple beanie was gone, and a messy fringe of sandy brown hair swooped over his forehead.

"You again," the man said, clearly unhappy if his frown was anything to go by. "Do you *ever* watch where you're going?"

Luca knew he was supposed to apologize. Beg for forgiveness, maybe.

But instead he was thinking about the man making him beg for something else.

"I was—"

"Probably looking at your phone again," the man said, not letting Luca even get the rest of his sentence out.

"Uh . . ." Luca hesitated. Because he had been doing exactly that. *Again.* At least he'd been doing it on the way out of his bed-and-breakfast, and not while he was crossing the street. "Sorry. It was an important message."

Those hazel eyes, glowing and intent, swept up and down him. Taking in every single inch of his T-shirt and shorts. The bare legs and the bare arms. Luca felt naked under his gaze.

Naked *and* aroused.

"So you do know how to apologize," he said archly.

"Yes."

"Well, luckily for you, you didn't wreck the muffins. Joy would've had your head."

"Joy . . ."

Luca was not used to men leaving him this tongue-tied. He could be charming. He *could*. But he felt like he was still catching up from the first time they'd met, and now this occurrence had set him back even further.

"She owns the Sweetheart Inn?" The guy shook his head. "You really are kind of clueless, aren't you?"

"Not usually," Luca managed.

"Oh?" An eyebrow went up.

Luca liked sex, though he'd always assumed he had pretty vanilla tastes. But the idea of this guy hovering just out of touch, completely naked, as Luca groveled and begged for any scrap of attention, turned him on beyond belief.

But it was so foreign. So strange. So utterly unlike anything he'd ever imagined wanting that he shut that thought right down.

"Trust me, it's not usually an issue," Luca said, more firmly this time.

"See that it isn't," the guy said. He re-arranged the box, gripping it with one hand as he shoved a hand through his hair. "I'm thinking maybe you need a proximity alert, so I can avoid all potential accidents."

"You're saying you don't want to see more of me?" Luca grinned.

Luca felt the heat in the glare directed his way. "I'm sure that's not an issue you typically have."

Okay, so they'd each noticed the other was attractive. That wasn't crazy. Lots of people thought Luca was attractive. If he wanted a date, he never had trouble getting one. It was the second date that typically didn't go well.

And the guy? Luca had thought he was attractive in the car, lecturing him, but out of it, he was *really* attractive, so no, it wasn't exactly a shock.

"No," Luca agreed calmly. He wasn't going to apologize for being good-looking. Or pretend he wasn't. That would be stupid.

"You staying here?" the guy asked.

You wanna come up to my room and see? The question was right on Luca's tongue, and he was debating on whether it would be insane to ask it, but after he nodded, the guy plunged ahead.

"Then I'm sure I won't be able to avoid you," he said. "See you around."

While Luca was still gaping at the cool dismissal, trying to marshal his thoughts, the guy skirted around him and walked deeper into the lobby, still balancing the white bakery box in his hand.

He was half-tempted to go ask the lady at the front desk—*Joy*, he told himself, *you know her name is Joy now*—just who that was, and why it would be impossible to avoid him in the future, but there'd been a delightful chaos in their meetings so far. Maybe making them deliberate would ruin the magic.

After all, he *had* said he'd see Luca around. That might be true, because the town itself really wasn't all that big.

So maybe engineering a meeting truly wouldn't be necessary. Maybe tonight, when he ran out to grab something for dinner, or maybe even tomorrow morning, when he came down the stairs for breakfast, his mystery man would be standing there, by the coffee station, greeting everyone with a friendly smile.

Of course, he'd have a smile. For everyone but Luca.

And goddamn it, that shouldn't turn him on, but it did.

Chapter Four

"Who's that new guy staying here?" Oliver asked, as he deposited the box of muffins on the desk, next to his mother's laptop.

"You're going to have to be a lot more specific," Joy said, barely glancing up from her work.

Along with running the Sweetheart Inn, which as far as Oliver was concerned was basically a full-time job, she also wrote romance novels on the side. So successfully, he knew, that she could've left the management of the Inn to someone else, or even sold it.

But she hadn't.

Working hard, that runs in the Billings family, she said to him whenever he argued she had too much on her plate. *Not like you aren't putting in crazy hours either. Just how early are you getting to the bakery these days?*

She wasn't wrong, which was why he didn't try to convince her to slow down anymore.

"The tall, hot guy. Little stern. Lot egotistical. Always on his phone. Wears a suit like it was tailored just for him."

"Oh, that one," Joy said, glancing up finally. "You would like him, wouldn't you?"

Oliver rolled his eyes. "I don't *like* him, I've nearly hit him with my car and then just now, he almost sent your batch of muffins to the floor."

"Oliver," she said patiently.

"Okay, I said he was hot. He *is*, it's practically a fact, not even an opinion."

Her gentle glance told him he was protesting too much so he shut up.

"He's Giana's nephew. Luca Moretti."

"Wait, that's Giana's *nephew*? Seriously?"

"Yes, that means he's Enzo's cousin."

"Right." Definitely not the best person for him to be attracted to, but there'd been such alive and interesting speculation in those dark eyes. Was he smug? Too confident? Also, true. But he also wouldn't be staying.

Oliver wasn't usually the kind of person who enjoyed casual hookups, but he would absolutely enjoy a hookup with Luca Moretti.

"No doubt Enzo's been filling his head with doom and gloom about you," Joy said unhelpfully. "I told you not to go out with him."

"Mom, it was *once*." He tried hard to be open-minded and kind to everyone. Treat people the way he wanted to be treated, etcetera etcetera. Which was why when he'd returned to town, and Enzo Moretti had asked him out, he'd said yes, even though he hadn't really felt much interest. There was no telling, right?

"Once was enough, wasn't it?"

Oliver couldn't argue with that. The date had been a complete fucking disaster and they hadn't repeated it, though he had gotten the impression Enzo had enjoyed their time together a lot more than Oliver had.

"We're two young queer people in this small ass town," Enzo had told him, "why *shouldn't* we date?"

Oliver hadn't much liked being reduced to his status or his age and had no interest in wasting his time dating someone he didn't even like, even if he was the only regular option for sex.

Usually he stuck to the defense that he was just too fucking busy for sex, but then once in a while, like today, he was confronted by someone he *really* wanted to have sex with, and all those excuses went right out the window.

"Once was definitely enough," Oliver said. "You really think he'd bad-mouth me?"

Joy shot him a look. "When has he ever missed an opportunity to be bitter? I swear to God he looks for them."

"It was three years ago."

"Now you're just trying to be too nice again," she reminded him. "You know he bad-mouths you any chance he gets, *still*."

Oliver sighed. "Yes, okay, he does. So what's Luca Moretti doing here?"

"Funny, he didn't give me a detailed itinerary," Joy said dryly. "But he *is* staying at least three weeks. Said he might need to stretch it to a month. Reservation on a corporate credit card. I think it was something about Nonna's."

"That's the name of Giana and Enzo's deli."

"Not *just* the name of Giana and Enzo's deli," his mother corrected gently. "I think it's a family name. I think they own a lot more restaurants out west. California, maybe? Giana mentioned it to me once, a few years ago, right after they opened. That all their recipes were family recipes."

"Huh." Oliver considered this. "You'd think they'd . . .well, that they'd be doing better, then. Or maybe the other restaurants aren't doing well too. . ."

"I think that's the least kind thing you've said about them since they opened." She hesitated. "No, actually, that was the time you grabbed a meatball sub from them and regretted it."

"It was . . .it was fine." That was the nicest thing Oliver could say about it.

"If you want my opinion," she said, leaning back in her chair and crossing her arms over her chest, "he's here to check up on the family investment."

"For three weeks?"

"Okay, to *fix* the family's investment, then," Joy amended. She smiled then, a little sly and a lot dangerous. "Three weeks though, that leaves you plenty of time to charm him."

"Mom," Oliver groaned, "I don't *want* to charm him. I love that you have something you enjoy but you don't have to see romance around every corner, okay? I was just curious about him. That's all. We don't get many guys coming around Indigo Bay that look like that in a suit."

He'd filled it out perfectly. Oliver could still remember the way he'd looked. Annoyed and cocky and unbelievably gorgeous.

"Or in a T-shirt and shorts," she retorted, grinning.

"Enough," Oliver said. "Here are your muffins. I threw in a few Chai Spice twists, too, for variety."

"Thanks." Her eyes, a pale blue that went surprisingly well with the pastel-pink hair she'd adopted recently, twinkled. "He loved them, you know. The muffins. Should I tell him—"

"No. For the love of God, *no.*" Oliver didn't even let her finish the question. Or ask her who the *he* was. He already knew, and he wasn't willing to risk her doing anything embarrassing in an attempt to relieve his perpetually single state.

A state, FYI, he was totally okay with. He really *was* too busy for dating. Sex . . . well, that might be a different story. But he wasn't going to talk to his *mother* about that, even if she did write romance novels with plenty of steamy scenes.

"Alright, then," Joy said, still smirking. "I won't."

"Please don't."

❧❧❧❧❧ ❧❧❧❧❧

Luca stayed up til nearly midnight, until his eyes grew dry and itchy and heavy, putting together the plan for Nonna's Deli.

It had three parts: *one,* improve ingredients and decor, and make the deli generally more inviting; *two,* prepare everything fresh; and *three,* put together a marketing campaign to invite the townspeople back to experience the new changes, and hopefully, in the process, win back the town's opinion.

Luca knew they'd be operating in the red while the changes were being implemented, but with time, he did believe the deli could turn itself around. He added, at the bottom of the plan, that during this period, he'd be suspending any capital re-payments to Nonna's Enterprises, in an attempt to improve operating expenses.

But all and any of this would take hard work and a lot of time, and he wasn't sure Giana was up for it, or that Enzo was willing to make the sacrifice.

Still, he ran his errands, and carrying the paper bag of groceries on one hip, headed toward the deli, arriving at the same time as he had the day before.

When he walked in, it was quiet and apparently empty again.

He pushed open the door and saw a note from Giana, something about a chiropractic appointment she'd forgotten but she'd be back soon. Apparently Enzo wasn't coming in today. That was the one thing Luca had hesitated to put in his report. Because he couldn't force someone to be interested in the family business if they weren't, and frankly, even if he said it as bluntly as he could, he wasn't sure Giana would believe it *or* accept it.

Luca glanced around at the clean, empty kitchen and decided there was no time like the present to get started. Even if Giana decided not to accept his recommendations, he refused to serve any more frozen and then thawed ingredients. If anyone actually showed up to buy a meal today, they would get *fresh* food.

He shed his jacket, rolled up his sleeves, and, after finding a clean apron, tied it on. He pulled out a big pot and set it on the stove, starting it to heat as he grabbed a knife and began to break down and chop the garlic.

The small grocery in town hadn't had all the Italian imported ingredients he normally used, but Luca was still sure everything he'd purchased was at least better than what Giana and Enzo were currently using.

He'd carefully selected his olive oil, his tomatoes, his basil. The store obviously hadn't stocked Nonna's specific blend of pork and veal and beef for the meatballs, but he'd picked up three different packages of ground meat, and he'd make do. Again, whatever he managed today *had* to be better than whatever they were normally serving.

When the sauce was on to simmer, he got out a big bowl and was just starting to put together the meatball mix—from memory, because Nonna wouldn't have ever stood for less—when Giana walked in.

"What on earth is this?" She did not look particularly pleased, even though Luca knew the scent of the sauce, bubbling away on the stove, must've greeted her as soon as she'd walked in the front door, and nobody who smelled that sauce cooking could ever be angry about it. "We have bins and bins of frozen sauce."

"Yes, *frozen* sauce," Luca said.

She crossed her arms. "What is wrong with the frozen sauce?"

"It *tastes* frozen. It also tastes like you're taking shortcuts on the ingredients we use at Nonna's. The tomatoes you're using aren't San Marzano. Not from our regular distributor."

"They charge a fortune," she argued. "We couldn't . . .it was too expensive."

"Maybe, but you're charging similar prices to our other deli in Sonoma and they're making a good profit, *while* using much higher quality ingredients."

"I told Nicoletta I wanted help, not for you to barge in and change everything."

No, she probably didn't want him to do that. Change was hard. But what would be even harder was losing the deli, and Luca was fairly certain that was a real possibility.

"Did you read my email?" Luca asked steadily. He'd told himself he would not lose his temper and so far his grip on it remained firm.

After all, he'd known he'd get some pushback. There was even a strong chance Giana would tell him to leave. If that was the case, then he wouldn't feel guilty—he *wouldn't*—about continuing to take their loan payment every month even though it would probably guarantee they'd ultimately end up closing their doors.

It would be a damn shame, and Luca wasn't going to take the chance that fighting might save it.

"What email?" Giana asked.

"I sent it to the restaurant email address," Luca said, still trying for patience. He cracked eggs into a pitcher, one at a time. Using the routine movement to keep his pulse steady. "Last night."

"Oh, I don't really check that," Giana said, waving a hand. "Enzo does sometimes, if he's expecting something."

You will not get pissed off. You will not get annoyed. You will not swipe this whole bowl with all its ingredients off the counter in frustration.

Luca counted to ten and then spoke. "You are the business owner. It's your responsibility to keep an eye on its pulse. Email is important. You should be checking it at least every morning and every afternoon."

Giana didn't look happy about that, but after a long moment of pointed silence, she did disappear into the little nook of an office. Hopefully, he thought, to do *something* right and read her goddamn email.

Luca moved on to chopping parsley and rosemary for the meatballs before adding the big finely minced pile to the bowl.

He added dried oregano. Salt and pepper. Then carefully began to mix.

Luca, darling, he could hear his Nonna's voice in his head reminding him, *make sure you don't ever overmix. Leads to a tough meatball, and nobody wants that. They want a meatball that melts in your mouth. Like a kiss.*

Now he was thinking about that guy from the Inn.

The one from the car.

His lips were the most kissable ones Luca had ever seen.

Not that Luca probably had a chance at any kisses after he'd annoyed the guy *twice.*

Well, it annoyed *Luca* he still didn't know his name.

And that after such a late night, when he'd walked downstairs for breakfast this morning, those lips hadn't been anywhere to be seen. He'd been so tempted to just ask who the guy was, but that made him look more than a little desperate.

You are more than a little desperate.

Okay, he was. He wouldn't be here forever. He might not even be here tomorrow. All he wanted was a chance at a nice dinner, shared between two people, and some kisses after. Oh and a nice hot romp in his Inn bed.

It was plenty big enough for two.

That wasn't asking for too much, was it?

He formed the meatballs, feeling the size of them in his hands as he rolled, placing them all on a sheet tray, then drizzling the whole lot with olive oil.

He was checking the sauce, adjusting the seasonings until it tasted perfect, just the way all the cooks at every Nonna's did every single morning, when Giana appeared in the kitchen again.

She looked a little shell-shocked.

"You want to make *all* these changes?" She shook a sheaf of papers in her hands.

Luca forced himself not to roll his eyes. Of course she had printed out his email. Probably for dramatic effect, because that was something Nicoletta might do, if she felt cornered and also felt like making melodrama out of the whole thing would improve her situation.

"Yes," he said simply.

"And you'll suspend the monthly payments, if we do."

"Yes."

Luca knew better than just about anyone else the best way to take the wind out of his family's sails: by refusing to engage.

She could take or leave the plan, but what he wasn't going to do was argue with her about it.

He'd tried so many times to argue and finagle and wheedle with Gabe, and all that had gotten him was estranged from one of his brothers.

Maybe Nicoletta would be angry he hadn't tried harder, but this was a two-way street, Luca reasoned. If Giana wanted to be fixed, she had to be *open* to the idea of being fixed.

"What if we make only some of these changes?"

"No," Luca said.

"But—"

"No," Luca repeated, more firmly this time. "I can't guarantee your business will recover, Giana. I'm not a genie. I don't grant wishes. I don't see the future. But I do know how to run a successful restaurant. I think you can turn things around. That's my assessment that you're waving around so dramatically. Our final offer, so to speak."

He wiped his hands off on a towel. "Call Enzo," he added. "Bring him in, because he should be part of this conversation, even if he doesn't want to be part of this business, and make a decision. I'm going to go get some coffee, and I'll be back in half an hour."

She gaped at him. "Half an hour? You're going—" She hesitated. "And what do you mean about Enzo?"

Luca removed his apron. Rolled his sleeves back down. Grabbed his jacket. It felt like putting his armor back on. "Giana," he said in a warning tone, "I've been nice about this. I've tried to be understanding. I've given you leeway. I've let you argue with me, even though you called *me*. But do not, do not ever, mistake my temporary kindness for niceness. I'm not here to be your sweet nephew. I'm here to fix what's broken."

And he walked past her and out the door.

He knew where he was going from the moment he'd decided to give Giana some time to consider the proposal.

Because *one,* he could always use another cup of coffee, and *two,* he was undeniably curious about the busy and inviting bakery, and *three,* if Giana actually agreed to make the necessary changes, they were going to need to find fresh bread somewhere because the deli was not capable of baking it daily.

The bakery was only a few blocks down the road but positioned on the corner of the two biggest streets, Main and Hydrangea, and it had big wide spotless windows with the name *Sweetie Pie's Bakery & Cafe* emblazoned across them in a swirly bright magenta script, with little heart-shaped pies dotting the glass.

Luca pulled the door open and was immediately greeted with the scent of rich, dark coffee and cinnamon and butter, with a deeper, richer tang of sausage swirling through.

It was exactly the experience he wanted visitors to Nonna's to experience—just with their red sauce.

This guy Oliver knew what he was doing.

Not that Luca had really doubted it.

His location was prime. It was inviting. Then you walked inside and you never wanted to leave, because the scent was an intoxicating and nostalgic combination of your grandmother's kitchen right after she pulled bread out of the oven and the best coffee shop you'd ever visited.

"Hello there," a lady with bright red hair said as he approached the counter.

The actual sitting area wasn't large—only about a dozen small tables, old-fashioned and spotless, with a tiny glass vase filled with fresh flowers on top of each one—and Luca assumed that the majority of his square footage was reserved for the bakery in the back. About half the tables were occupied. One older gentleman was typing away on his laptop with two cups beside him, like he'd been there all morning already.

"Good morning," Luca said, about to order a large black coffee, but then he looked to his right and was lost.

He'd eaten breakfast before starting the day, but just glancing over at the spotless glass case, stretching across nearly the entire width of the café and filled with a plethora of delectable-looking options, had him changing his mind.

"Interested in trying anything from the case? We can heat it up, to order, if you like," the red-haired woman said with a wink that told Luca just how many people came in here only for coffee and left with coffee *and* something sweet and delicious.

"Uh," Luca said scanning the contents. There were the savory pastries—little hand pies, with perfect crimped edges, in flavors like sausage, brie and cranberry, and also white cheddar, egg, and bacon—and then there were the sweets.

Chai spice twists and cinnamon buns and butter pecan hand pies.

Cherry and apple tarts.

And a few empty white plates, with muffin markers next to them. Apple cinnamon pecan crumble sounded suspiciously like what he'd enjoyed just this morning.

"Want a recommendation?" she asked cheerfully.

He looked up and no doubt he was wearing an expression of fervent gratitude, because how did one *choose*?

He wanted to try one of everything, especially if this baker was the one who'd crafted the muffins he was devouring, calories be damned, every single morning he'd been in Indigo Bay.

"Yes, please," he said. "And tell me, does this bakery make the muffins I've been eating every day at the Sweetheart Inn?"

She smiled. "Yep, Oliver bakes for a lot of the bed-and-breakfasts in town, for sure. But the Sweetheart Inn, definitely, cause his momma owns it."

"Oh?" Luca was interested. Only because anyone this talented in the kitchen was always of interest to him. Even if there was no way he could possibly lure him away from this successful business and convince him to move to Napa and work for Nonna's.

But the fantasy was nice.

"I'm surprised Joy hasn't told you all about it," the woman said, "but then she's on deadline, so she might've had her head in the computer. But if you want a recommendation, you can't go wrong with the chai spice twist. It's fall in a bite."

Luca raised an eyebrow.

She laughed. "Yes, I know, it's not even really spring yet, but trust me, you'll love it."

"Sounds great. I'll take that and a large coffee, too."

"Sure thing. I'll just heat it up."

"Is Oliver here, by any chance?" Luca asked. "I was hoping to chat with him about a business proposal."

"Oh yeah, he's in the back. I'll grab him. Just a moment."

As the woman poured his coffee and set his pastry into a small warming oven, he looked up at the big menu board that stretched out above the counter. There was a short list of sandwiches, mostly cold cuts and a chicken salad, with two hot paninis, all listed as available on four different homemade breads. A single soup every day, that the menu noted was provided by a local company, not even made in-house.

Really, Sweetie Pie's Bakery and Cafe was more of the former than the latter, and there was absolutely no reason why it should be competing with Nonna's. Nonna's served a full menu for lunch and early dinner. People came to Sweetie Pie's for coffee and baked goods and occasionally a quick lunch.

Now, clearly, this business had the inviting factor down, and the far more appealing location, but that was it.

"Honey?" the woman called out. "Your coffee and pastry's ready. Oliver's just finishing something up, but if you don't mind waiting for a few minutes . . ."

"No problem," Luca said and picked up the cup and plate from the counter and took it to one of the empty tables. Settled down, and from the moment he took a sip of coffee and a corner of pastry, popping it into his mouth, fell headfirst into bliss.

This was really, *really* good coffee, rich and dark roasted and yet without any bit of burned aftertaste. And the pastry? Unsurprisingly, it was one of the best things Luca had ever put into his mouth.

He was just brushing the crumbs off his suit when a voice startled him.

"You again," it said. The inflection was familiar. Luca would have recognized it anywhere.

And just as he'd expected, when he looked up, there he was. The guy from the car. And the Inn. Wearing a purple apron that matched the beanie from the other day, emblazoned with Sweetie Pie's logo and there in one corner, was a name embroidered on it.

Oliver.

At least, now he knew the man's name. And that he baked so well he could make angels weep.

"Yes, it's me again," Luca said. He stood and extended a hand. "I'm Luca Moretti."

"Finally, huh? Oliver. Oliver Billings," Oliver said and shook his hand. Briefly. Luca only got a moment to feel the calloused, capable hand in his own before it was gone. "I guess you figured out where I was."

"Actually, no. This is embarrassingly accidental," Luca admitted. If he'd known *the guy* was also Oliver, who owned the bakery, he'd have approached this differently. Less formal. Less like a business proposal. A lot more like a date. He waved at the opposite chair. "Do you have a few minutes?"

"A few minutes," Oliver allowed, tilting his head. "I've got some dough rising."

"So late in the morning?" Luca questioned as they sat.

"I make rolls for one of the local restaurants in town. In exchange for their soup," Oliver said with a grin. "Know a lot about the baking business, do you?" He gave Luca a leisurely head-to-toe perusal, setting his nerves alight. "You don't look like you do."

"All our restaurants back in California bake their own bread fresh daily," Luca said. *Don't be a haughty, arrogant asshole. Don't do it and fuck this up. This is your one shot.*

Oliver's eyebrows rose. "Really? You're here for Giana and Enzo, though, and I know they don't."

"No, they don't." Luca took a sip of coffee. "Which is what I wanted to discuss with you."

"You want me to bake their bread for them." Oliver stated it, one corner of that beautiful mouth twisting into a wry grin. "That's an irony."

"It is?"

"Oh, just . . .*Enzo*." Oliver cleared his throat. "Your cousin . . .he's your cousin, right?"

Luca nodded. Though he didn't personally see much that he and Enzo had in common. Their dark hair maybe. And he supposed that someone might consider Enzo attractive. Personally, Luca didn't find sulking and underachieving particularly tempting, but still. Someone *might*.

"Okay, well, he doesn't mind telling everyone shit about me." Oliver said it frankly, without heat or accusation. "So he's not going to be very happy about this."

Like he didn't mind, it was just a statement of fact: Enzo talked shit about him.

Luca thought back and realized that when Oliver *had* come up the one single time, Enzo had definitely not let the chance go by to sneer about him.

"I don't have an issue, but *he* might not be so keen on having me bake their bread," Oliver continued, leaning forward a bit.

That's right, Luca thought with satisfaction, *get closer*.

"What Enzo wants is immaterial," Luca said. "I'm here to assist in improving their business."

"Ah, they sent the fixer out." Oliver sounded amused again. "I can see it. You're definitely more of a fixer than a baker."

Luca shrugged. "I run my family's four restaurants. They do not typically need *fixing*." *Don't be arrogant, don't be arrogant.* "But Nonna's Deli here, it is . . .an investment of ours. Not directly under my control. So I'm not here to order changes but to . . .suggest them. *Nicely*."

"Which is how they've managed to underperform all these years," Oliver said with another of those smirks. They shouldn't have been so frustratingly attractive. But Luca felt them deep down, stirring him up in a way he hadn't expected.

Oliver was definitely a very attractive package, one he'd love to unwrap.

Would he be as sweet as promised? Or a little salty too? Maybe even a bit spicy?

"You could say that," Luca said. "Part of the proposed changes are aligning the menu more directly with our other restaurants. And that includes fresh bread, daily. Nonna's here doesn't have the staff, the resources, or the equipment to do this, but you do."

"I do," Oliver conceded. "My schedule's already pretty packed, but I suppose I could fit you in. French bread? Sourdough bread? Focaccia? Rolls? Loaves? How many dozen per day?"

Luca liked every part of Oliver he'd seen so far. He was charming and sweet and undeniably adorable. Then there was how goddamned sexy he was when he got down to business.

"I'm not sure yet," Luca said. "In fact, they may not need any at all. Giana and Enzo have my proposed changes, but they are not required to accept all of them—or any of them, actually."

"You must hate that, not being able to actually impose your control over them." Oliver said it casually, like a true control-freak business owner, like he *understood*.

How did Oliver know how much he hated it? Was it that obvious? Was it written all over his face that he'd love nothing more than to march down the street and *tell* Giana and Enzo exactly what to do?

"Yes," Luca admitted.

"Nonna's isn't just an Italian affectation, is it? Was there actually a *Nonna*?" Oliver asked.

"My grandmother."

"Ah, well, there you go." Oliver leaned back, grinning. Luca wanted to chase him, but he stayed on his side of the table, with what he thought was pretty admirable restraint.

"So why *does* Enzo dislike you so much?" Luca asked.

"That's a long story. And I've got to tend to these rolls. If they overproof . . ." Oliver shrugged. "I'm a perfectionist, what can I say?"

"If he supposedly turns against you every chance he gets, what's he going to say," Luca said, deploying the most persuasive smile in his arsenal, "when he finds out I want to hire you to bake our bread? I need the insider info. Need to be able to convince him it's a good idea."

"It's not going to help you, *and* you're not going to like it," Oliver said. "Though, you sorta look like there's plenty of things you don't like."

But I like you. "You're not wrong." It was hard to admit it, but there it was. He was particular, okay? Particular and more than a little arrogant about his particularity.

Maybe it was good Oliver knew that now, even if all they ever had was a date and a night—though even that was still up in the air.

"We dated," Oliver said. His watch beeped, and he stood, just as he'd left Luca speechless for another long moment. "Well," he amended, with a cute little shrug. "It was one date. But still. He wanted to continue. I did not. And that's the story."

"That wasn't a very long story," Luca managed, and was he trailing after Oliver in his own bakery like a lost puppy looking for his owner? Yes, he was, a little.

Oliver shrugged. "I don't like to talk about it, even if he does, still."

"Sounds like you could be a little less nice to him." Luca certainly would've been.

"Yeah, but . . ." There was that lopsided, entirely charming grin again. Luca understood exactly why his cousin would ask Oliver out on a date. Because he wanted to, as well. Maybe they wouldn't have more than one, either, but it wouldn't be for a lack of desire. "I'm a nice person. Ask anyone."

"There's such a thing as *too* nice," Luca said.

"Yeah, but that's what guys like you are for," Oliver said with another smile. He turned the corner, removing himself from Luca's reach.

Frustratingly. Annoyingly.

"I guess." Luca frowned.

"Well, good luck," Oliver said. "My rolls are calling. I'll see you around."

See me tonight, he almost called out, but then he didn't.

Why?

Because of *that's what guys like you are for.*

He'd said it. *You're more like a fixer than a baker.*

He was. He'd had to learn to be tough and to be sure, to preserve his family's legacy. Was that all he was? Luca didn't like to think so, but then, he also couldn't remember a time when Nonna's hadn't consumed him.

Now it was doing it again. He'd come here with a promise to his mama that he'd take some time for himself, but what was he doing? Obsessing about Nonna's and how to fix it.

And, he thought, *I'm obsessing about Oliver.*

Chapter Five

Oliver tried all afternoon not to think about Luca Moretti.

The way he'd looked, savoring every single bite of his chai spice twist. The look of bliss on his handsome face, losing that hard edge when there wasn't anyone to argue with or to impose his will upon. It convinced Oliver that the glimpses of flirtatious, charming man he'd seen under that tough mask were the real Luca.

But, he reminded himself, *it doesn't matter who the real Luca is, because he's not staying around for you to find out. He's going to fix Giana and Enzo, or he's gonna try, and then he'll be gone, and it won't matter that you found him nearly irresistible. Even when he was being arrogant and a little bit obnoxious. But even more when he's trying to be sweet. When he lets himself be sweet.*

"You're pacing."

Marjorie looked over at him as she finished counting up the cash for the day from the drawer.

Oliver stopped in his tracks. He *had* been pacing.

"Why so tense?" she asked casually, like it wasn't unusual for him to be anxious. But it was. He was laid-back; always took things as they came. He'd had to learn to exist that way to stay in one piece when he'd worked at the high-end restaurants in Charleston, and then coming back here, and becoming a business owner? Same deal.

"I'm . . ." Oliver hesitated. He'd nearly just told Marjorie, frankly one of his oldest friends, that he wasn't tense, when he very much was. And lying to her, even when he was doing it for what felt like a good reason, was more alien to him than any rogue anxiety he was feeling. "Remember that guy who came in this morning? Before lunch? Tall, dark, unbearably handsome?"

Marjorie shot him a look. "Of course I remember him. You don't see a guy like that wearing a suit like he does all that often. I remember him." She paused. "You talked to him. I thought it was about business."

"It was." Oliver twisted his beanie in his hands. "Sort of. Kind of. We never . . .he didn't . . ."

"Ah." Marjorie didn't have to say anything else, only the single syllable. And okay, it was obvious. What he was twisted up about was Luca.

"He wouldn't stay. He's not staying. He's some big hotshot restaurant exec back in California," Oliver explained.

"And?" Marjorie retorted, raising an eyebrow. "Does that mean you can't enjoy him while he's here? Because if he'd given me even a *fraction* of the looks he was giving you, I'd take plenty of advantage."

Oliver rolled his eyes. Marjorie was sixty, at least, and proclaimed loudly, to anyone who would listen, that most men weren't worth the air they wasted.

"Don't be ridiculous," Oliver said, but while he might be able to dissemble with Marjorie—though not well, if her incredulous expression was any indication—he couldn't with himself. He *was* tempted.

"Just because something's temporary doesn't mean it's not worth doing," she said. "Like your time in Charleston. You learned a lot. You grew as a person. You figured out what you liked and what you didn't. Not everything has to be a lifelong commitment, Oliver. You *know* that."

"But . . ." Oliver hesitated. He knew she was right. So why *was* he still hesitating?

"Don't tell me," she added sternly, "you still need the birds and the bees talk, Oliver."

"No, no, no, definitely not." He'd casually dated in Charleston, hadn't he? Sure, none of those guys or those relationships, if he even wanted to use that word, had a big fat expiration sticker slapped on them, the way Luca Moretti did, but why did that matter?

"You like him, tell him." She was adamant.

Maybe the kind of adamant he needed.

"I don't even *know* if I like him yet." Though that was a lie. He did like Luca. Maybe there wasn't a good reason why he did already, but he'd felt drawn to the man, even as he both annoyed and frustrated him, since he'd nearly hit him with his car.

"Well, what are you waiting for then? Go find out if you like him." Marjorie finished counting the money and zipped it up in the pouch. "I'll take the bank deposit and you take yourself down to Nonna's and talk to that nice handsome man."

"Was he *nice* though?" Luca Moretti seemed like a lot of things, but nice probably wasn't in the top five—which Oliver *liked*, because he had plenty of niceness to go around. It was like biting into a pie, thinking it would be sweet and discovering it was salty and savory and maybe even a little spicy. Unexpected, yes, but the *good* kind of unexpected.

Marjorie smacked him in the arm. "You aren't even dating him yet and here you are already complaining about him." She grinned. "Seems like love at first sight to me."

"Oh please," Oliver said, rolling his eyes. "It's not anything like that. I just nearly killed him accidentally and then there was the time he ran right into me at the Inn."

"You even had a meet-cute!" Marjorie crowed. "What are you still doing here?"

"We did not have a meet-cute," Oliver retorted.

"Did you flirt with him?"

"Have you *seen* him?" Oliver shoved his hands into his pockets. "Of course I flirted with him."

"There you go," Marge said. "If there's flirting, no way it's not an official meet-cute. Those don't happen all that often in Indigo Bay. It's practically a crime if you don't take advantage."

"How would *you* know?" Oliver asked, in a tone of disbelief. He had no idea Marjorie was this much of a romantic. Or this much of a matchmaker.

Maybe it was like a disease and she'd caught it from his mother. Oliver shuddered. He didn't need more than one person haranguing him to find love and settle down.

Though . . .it wasn't like he *could* settle down with Luca. In a few weeks, he'd go back to the west coast, and hopefully, he'd remain a warm—maybe even a hot—memory.

That made up his mind.

He was going to date Luca Moretti and enjoy him while he was here, and *not* fall in love with him, and then when he left, he'd be totally fine with it.

"I know more than you realize, boyo," Marjorie teased. "When I was in Italy one summer . . ."

"No, no, no," Oliver said, covering his ears. "I don't want to hear it. Especially not details, okay?"

"Okay."

Oliver thought the fact she stopped meant she'd capitulated, but he also didn't miss the sly look in her eyes as he pulled off his beanie and ruffled a hand through his hair, using the shiny, spotless front window as a mirror.

"You got the deposit?" he asked casually.

"Yep, I've got it," she said. "I'll lock up. You do . . .well, whatever it is you're planning on doing." There was that sly, knowing look again.

"Alright. Have a good night," Oliver said awkwardly. He should be used to this town being so interested in everyone's personal life because they had none of their own, but nope, he wasn't. Not even remotely. On one hand, it could be annoying and intrusive. On the other . . .there'd been a cold anonymity about the big city that he hadn't liked. He'd felt so alone there, like if he fell off the face of the earth, nobody would notice or actually care.

But here? Here in Indigo Bay, he was woven into the fabric of the town's existence. He was an integral thread.

Oliver let the door shut behind him, the tinkling of the bells hanging from the corner sending him off with his own soundtrack.

It was still mid-afternoon and the sunshine was warm on his back as he walked down the street toward Nonna's.

When they'd first opened three years ago, he'd worried that the deli might cut into Sweetie Pie's business, but after going there twice, he'd realized it wasn't going to be an issue. Giana was sweet and meant well, but she wasn't really a business owner. And Enzo? Well. Oliver had only had to go on one date with him to realize he had zero interest in developing their business into something that could rival Sweetie Pie's.

He barely had any interest in the business at all.

It had been at least two years and eight months since he'd been inside Nonna's, and as he pushed the door open, he realized not much had changed.

It wasn't an inviting setup, though this time at least, the moment he opened the door, the most delicious smells hit him square in the face.

Rich tomato. Garlic. Basil. The unctuousness of roasted meat.

The change in aroma had to have come from the man sitting at one of the tables, one leg propped on a knee, his jacket tossed on the back of a nearby chair, a pained expression on his face like he was rapidly developing a headache.

Oliver realized something else, a second too late.

He'd walked right into the middle of an argument.

Three sets of eyes swiveled toward him.

Luca looked surprised, pleasantly so.

Giana looked annoyed.

And Enzo's expression, as he leaned against the front counter, could best be described as murderous.

Shit.

"Uh," Oliver said. "Hi. I thought I'd just stop by to follow up with Luca about . . .uh . . .about the bread."

He hadn't really envisioned what he'd do once he got here. In a dim, poorly lit fantasy, he'd imagined walking in, just seeing Luca here, his coat off and his sleeves rolled up, revealing those strong, capable forearms rippling with muscle, and asking him, straight out, if he'd like to have dinner tonight.

He had *not* predicted that he'd walk into the middle of an argument.

"Are you fucking kidding me?" Enzo spat out. "You asked *him*?"

Luca made a frustrated noise in the back of his throat.

Oliver had just told Marjorie that Luca wasn't really nice. And he wasn't. He was arrogant and blunt and a little overconfident of his own certainty. But Oliver realized now just how much he was holding back.

Luca had left Sweetie Pie's at nearly eleven in the morning.

Now, it was almost three.

Had they been arguing like this for four hours?

Surely not. Surely they'd had a lunch crowd to feed.

Okay, so they'd only been arguing like this for . . .at most *two* hours.

Still.

Oliver had tolerated a two-hour dinner with Enzo once, and he'd wanted to strangle him heading into hour one, and *he* didn't have a temper.

He had a feeling Luca had one. Tightly leashed, yes, but it existed.

He could see it flare in those intense dark eyes now.

"I asked him because he is capable of doing what needs to be done," Luca said. And Oliver could hear it too, in the tight control of his voice. He turned toward Oliver, and something in his face softened. "As you can see, we're still . . .debating the best course forward for Nonna's."

Oliver hadn't been afraid of him before—Luca was too controlled for even the leash on his temper to loosen without him choosing to let it go—and he certainly wasn't now. Also, he had a feeling Luca's bark was worse than his bite . . .though he wouldn't mind a little bit of Luca's biting, if he was being totally honest.

"I can see," Oliver said.

"Luca, be reasonable." Giana inserted herself. She looked desperate. "Let us make some of the changes and see what happens. I don't want . . ." She trailed off.

"You want a successful business," Luca said inexorably. "You asked me to come here and help you turn things around. This is how you do it. Not by half measures. Not by limping along for another few months, which is all you'd be buying yourself. Another few painful months before the inevitable occurs."

He stood and gestured to Oliver. "I need some fresh air," he said, and as Oliver followed him out the front door, he felt the confused bewilderment of Giana's gaze on his back and the venom of Enzo's.

Luca leaned against the brick wall of the building and let out of a gust of a sigh.

His eyes fluttered shut, and unobserved like this, Oliver could really look at him.

He looked tired. Worn down by an afternoon of fighting for what he believed in. A day's worth of dark scruff shadowed his jaw and with it and without his jacket, the pristine white shirt rumpled and its sleeves rolled up, he looked more human than ever before.

"That sounded . . .rough," Oliver said hesitantly.

Luca's eyes fluttered open, and there was that dip at the bottom of Oliver's stomach as their gazes met.

"I've spent better afternoons," Luca said. "Cleaning out the deep fryer at the restaurant. Getting a root canal. Untangling the mess my father made of the books with a forensic accountant."

"Ouch."

Luca sighed. "The biggest problem is Giana wants something that won't ever happen."

Oliver didn't need him to tell him what it was. "For Enzo to give a shit about the business."

"She wants it for him," he said, and there was an agonizing pain in Luca's voice. Oliver could *feel* it, the pride in his family's name, in the success they'd created from nothing. The difficulty of facing someone who had not only rejected it but didn't *understand* it. "And he doesn't want it at all. But she won't see it. Or acknowledge it. Until that happens, she's not going to want to change anything or fix it, because she's hoping that *he* will."

"He won't."

Luca didn't seem like the kind of guy who'd flinch away from difficult truths, so Oliver didn't bother to sugarcoat it.

"Is that why there was only one date?" Luca asked after a long silence.

Heat rippled along Oliver's spine. Even the word *date* felt loaded between them. It was clear what they both wanted; the only question was whether they'd reach out and take it.

Oliver could practically taste the frustration on his lips, even now, even though they hadn't kissed yet.

But we will. You know it's inevitable. Even if it's just for one night. Even if he leaves tomorrow morning, he's not going to leave without kissing you.

"That was one of the reasons, yes," Oliver admitted. "But there were many. Starting with we had no chemistry whatsoever." *Nothing like us. We've got enough to start a fire, right here, crackling right between us.*

"I can see that," Luca said, his voice deep and rumbling. "But you still went out with him."

Oliver shrugged. "I'm a nice guy, what can I say? He asked, and it seemed like worth . . .trying."

"Is it that easy?" Luca asked, sounding amused now.

"Sometimes," Oliver said, swallowing around a suddenly dry throat. He felt like they were edging to the point of no return. He was both desperate for them to get there and throw caution to the wind and terrified of what might happen when they *did* get there.

You're not going to fall in love with him. You're going to enjoy him and then send him on his way.

It was an important reminder. Because every time he was with Luca, he felt like falling headfirst into the mystery of him, the deep, hidden parts of him that Oliver could only catch glimpses of before they disappeared.

But he couldn't.

"What is this festival Giana keeps going on and on about?" Luca said, abruptly switching subjects, like he too needed the reminder not to fall too deeply in.

"The Sweethearts Festival? It's uh . . .well, it's our town's one claim to fame," Oliver explained. "Half an excuse to buy a bunch of clearance Valentine's Day items and actually use them, and half a tribute to the town's history."

Luca raised a questioning eyebrow.

"It's kind of a long story," Oliver added.

Luca waved around them. "Giana and Enzo are going to be arguing for hours. I've got time."

"You really think so?" Oliver was surprised.

"Deep down, Giana realizes she has only one choice. I *designed* it so she'd only have one choice. But she's a Moretti, thus she doesn't like being directed down a certain path, and so she'll fight it every inch of the way." Luca sounded darkly amused by this.

"Is that how you are, too?"

"I'd fight it tooth and nail," Luca admitted. "Unless it was the right thing to do for my family, and then I'd swallow my pride and do whatever it took."

There was another one of those dark places, illuminated, just for a second.

"You think she'll accept your offer of changes."

"I told her that for the duration she won't have to pay back the loan the family made her, so yes, she's desperate enough, I think she won't have a choice."

"That's . . ." Oliver hesitated. He didn't want to say callous or cruel or calculating, though he could see why someone might think Luca's plan was all those things. But it was generous too. Especially if he knew how Giana was and what might persuade her to take help she really needed. "That's really brilliant, actually."

It was, Oliver realized. It was perfectly executed to direct her exactly where not just Luca but *she* needed to go, if only Giana could get out of her own way.

Did Luca flush at the compliment? He had deep olive-toned skin, and it was hard to tell, but he seemed like he did.

"You think so? You don't think it's . . ." Oliver knew Luca was thinking of all the words he'd considered. *Callous. Cruel. Calculating.*

"No," Oliver said with certainty.

"Ah." Luca looked surprised. Like he'd been expecting to be condemned for the plan and couldn't quite believe he hadn't been.

"I mean, she's not going to be happy with you in the interim, but once it starts to pay off, once the business begins to improve, she'll thank you. She'll be everlastingly grateful."

"Maybe not *that* grateful," Luca said with a little bit of a smirk. "She's a Moretti, and we tend to hold grudges."

"Stubborn, huh?" Oliver didn't find that unattractive, surprisingly.

"Excessively," Luca admitted.

"Well, clearly, cause you still haven't asked me to dinner," Oliver said. "Even though I know you want to."

Luca's eyebrows shot up. "I can see I'm not the only one sure of myself."

"Not even remotely," Oliver said. "Go to dinner with me, and I'll tell you the history. I said it was a long story. Seems right we fortify ourselves during it."

"Seems like a reasonable offer."

Oliver raised *his* eyebrow. "Do you not want to?" The last thing he'd expected was for Luca to quibble about this. He *knew* he wanted. Marjorie was right; he knew what those looks Luca had been shooting him from under his lashes meant.

"Oh, I want to," Luca said. "I just . . .you do know I'm not sticking around?"

"I know," Oliver said steadily.

"I may not even be here tomorrow," Luca warned. "I don't predict Giana telling me to fuck off, but it *could* happen."

"I bet not many people tell you to fuck off," Oliver said, grinning.

"Not too many *dare*," Luca agreed, and he was smiling too, and *God,* Oliver could feel himself drifting closer into Luca's orbit. Like he was a planet, and Oliver couldn't help but feel pulled in.

"How about this? I don't mind if you *do* fly off tomorrow. As long as we get tonight." Oliver felt desire, the exquisite ache of it, settling deep into his stomach.

"And what if I stick around?"

Oliver shrugged. "Trust me, I'm particular about a second date. We'll see."

To his surprise, Luca's hand, big and strong and capable, settled around his waist and squeezed, just a little. Just enough for him to feel it, the warmth sinking through his T-shirt and so much deeper. "Trust me," he said softly, "you're going to want that second date."

Oliver swallowed hard. "I will?"

"I know, because I'm going to want one," Luca said seriously. "But we'll see."

Oliver knew it was a lot, but he couldn't hold back the words that spilled out. "Even if Giana does tell you to fuck off . . .your family couldn't do without you for a week? Just . . .because?"

Luca grinned, baring all his perfect straight white teeth. He was so dizzyingly gorgeous, Oliver could barely believe this was happening.

He'd been nearly sure, after almost hitting him with his car, that he wasn't real, but a fantasy conjured to life.

But now Luca was touching him, and he *felt* real. The most real Oliver had ever felt.

"If you knew them, you'd know the usual answer to that question but . . .we'll see."

"Alright." Oliver didn't like it, but he'd take it.

The front door to Nonna's swung open. Luca's hand dropped from his waist.

"What?" he barked, not even bothering to look at who'd interrupted them.

"I need you," Giana said. "We have another counter-proposal."

Luca's eyes fluttered shut and Oliver could nearly hear his internal groan of frustration.

"One moment," he said.

Then his eyes were open again, and they were focused intently on Oliver.

"Please tell me where and when so at least I have that to look forward to," Luca said softly.

"I go to bed early, cause I'm up early," Oliver said. Felt the rush of heat through him at the way Luca blinked when he said *bed*. "So dinner will have to be early. Five? At Rudy's, down the way? He makes a good steak."

"Sounds perfect."

Then Luca was pressing a hot, hard kiss to his forehead and was gone, sweeping inside Nonna's again, leaving Oliver dizzy with the possibilities.

Even possibilities for just tonight.

Chapter Six

When Nicoletta had made him promise he would try to enjoy himself while in Indigo Bay, Luca didn't think she'd had in mind him dating the cute local baker.

But that was exactly what he was going to do.

Well, he was going to go on *one* date, at least, with the cute local baker.

Giana and Enzo were still arguing about whether they were going to take his offer—though he was grateful that at least they'd realized he wasn't willing to compromise, after they'd spent several, incredibly frustrating hours trying to convince him to alter his *all-or-nothing* stance.

At that point, he'd told them it was ultimately their decision, and he was out of it.

He'd left, as Giana and Enzo continued to debate what to do.

Their biggest problem was exactly what he'd told Oliver: ultimately Giana wanted Enzo to give a shit about the business, and he wasn't going to, no matter how successful it became, and deep down, she knew it.

She could throw herself against reality all she wanted, but it wasn't going to change.

Luca had managed to escape that increasingly uncomfortable situation with just enough time to fit in a workout, and then jump in the shower back at the Inn before meeting Oliver for dinner.

Now he was debating putting another suit on . . .or . . .being casual and wearing one of the pairs of jeans he'd brought with him on a whim.

It wasn't that he didn't wear jeans. He did. Occasionally.

When he was cleaning his townhouse. When he was doing yard work. When he somehow got roped into going to see one of his nephews play softball.

Not on *dates*. But then all the dates he went on were usually to expensive restaurants where jeans weren't even allowed.

He had a feeling this Rudy's place, where Oliver said they could get a steak, wouldn't be fancy. In fact, he'd done some brief market research and there weren't really any fussy places in Indigo Bay at all.

You had to go to Charleston for those.

Luca put the jeans on but drew the line at a T-shirt, which he usually only wore to the gym, and threw on a dark blue button-up, leaving an extra button undone and rolling up his sleeves.

The walk to Rudy's was short, but the afternoon, even in late February, was still unbelievably mild. He didn't even need a jacket.

The weather reminded him a little of Napa, but definitely with less spring rain to worry about.

Rudy's was a small restaurant, but already packed, going by the way the lobby had a few older couples waiting when he walked in.

The decor was Southern rustic, like a Cracker Barrel had thrown up inside, but he could smell the food, and the aroma was not only fantastic, it had a strong meaty edge to it, which was always a good sign for a place that sold steak.

Plus, there was the fact Oliver had suggested it, and Luca had a feeling, no matter how much of a food snob he was, Oliver was *worse*.

Anyone who baked that well wouldn't tolerate crap.

The young girl at the hostess stand took him in head to toe and before he could even say he needed a table for two, she said, "You must be that guy Oliver said he was meeting."

For a split second, Luca wanted to ask her what adjectives Oliver had used to describe him to make her so sure, but that would not only be awkward, it would completely give his crush away.

You yourself totally gave it away, when you couldn't stop staring at him like he was the best thing you'd ever seen, Luca reminded himself.

"I'll show you to his table," she said, efficiently leading him away from the lobby deeper into the restaurant.

The floorboards were worn pine, but scrubbed clean, same as the walls, and the booths were high backed and made of logs.

It wasn't a big place, and it didn't take very long to get to Oliver's table.

"Here you go, enjoy your dinner," she chirped as Luca took in his first look at Oliver, *date-style*.

He was wearing jeans, too, but the beanie was gone, and his hair was styled, swooping over his forehead. He needed a haircut, Luca thought, but he shouldn't get one. His polo shirt was pale green and brought out the hazel in his eyes, fitting him tightly enough that Luca was reminded again of how solid his biceps were for his size.

"Hey," Oliver said, the corner of his mouth tilting up into a sweet smirk as Luca slid into the booth. "So you *do* know what jeans are."

"Everyone knows what jeans are, Oliver."

"Yeah," Oliver said, leaning over the table, eyes twinkling, "but I thought you might believe they were only for mere mortals like myself. I'm happy to report I was not only wrong, but you fill them out *very* nicely."

"Thanks," Luca said dryly.

He took a sip of water, because his throat *was* dry. He was already imagining messing up Oliver's hair. Stripping him out of that polo shirt. What his skin might taste like.

It wasn't like his arousal could possibly take him by surprise, because he'd been attracted to Oliver from the beginning, but he *was* astonished at how horny he really was.

Yeah, you dummy, that happens when you don't make time to have sex.

Cause now that he was thinking about it, he couldn't remember the last time he had.

Or who it was with.

But he had a feeling he wouldn't be forgetting Oliver anytime soon, even if they only had one night together.

"So," Oliver said, "did Giana and Enzo come to a decision?"

Clearly he wasn't the only one wondering if this one night was going to be all they were going to get.

"Not yet," Luca said. He sighed. "They were still arguing when I left."

Oliver raised an eyebrow. "You waved the white flag, finally?" He sounded surprised.

"No," Luca said. "I just got tired of them trying to change my mind about the terms."

"Ahhhh," Oliver said, picking up his menu. "So, you didn't give in."

"Did you think I would?"

Oliver laughed. "No, not really. But Giana and Enzo's endlessly circular arguments could probably convince a pretty tough person to change their mind."

"So you don't just know Enzo," Luca said as he looked over his menu. It was simple food. Steaks and chops and roasted chicken. But he found something he thought would suit and resolved to ask Oliver what he thought about his order before he put it in.

Luca *knew* Oliver, for all his sweet, kind exterior, would be beautifully and brutally honest about food.

"Oh, Giana worked for me for a bit. Six months, maybe?"

Luca was not usually surprised by things. But he was about this.

"Really?"

"It was right before she wanted to open the deli," Oliver said, "and someone—I think I can probably guess now who that was—told her that even though they were lending her money, they wanted her to have experience in the restaurant industry before she opened."

Luca had forgotten about that.

If he hadn't, he would have reminded his aunt that she should *know better*.

Especially if he'd known the experience she'd gotten was at Oliver's bakery.

Clearly he wasn't the type to cut corners.

"It was right after I had expanded some offerings, and I needed just another pair of hands. I knew she wouldn't be sticking around. And then, right before she left, I picked up Aaron, who's my assistant baker and a hell of a lot more than just a pair of hands."

Luca was digesting this new piece of information when the waiter appeared at their table.

"Oh, Oliver, I haven't seen you in a while," he said, shooting both of them a large friendly smile. "And this is new."

Oliver rolled his eyes. "Andrew, don't."

"Hey, you show up here with a date, a date who looks like *that*, and I'm not supposed to ask?"

Oliver leaned in, catching Luca's eyes. "Sorry, Andrew here is the biggest gossip in about three counties."

"Is that a problem?" Luca wondered. He honestly wasn't sure. He'd never once been on a date with a waiter who was unapologetically interested in what was happening at the table. But the last thing he wanted Oliver to be was uncomfortable.

"No, not at all, if it isn't for you." Oliver turned to Andrew. "This is Luca Moretti. He's Giana's nephew, and he's here to help her. Consult, so to speak."

"Hello, Luca Moretti." Andrew grinned. "What can I get you two cuties to drink?"

"I'll have a water and a sweet tea," Oliver said.

Normally, Luca would've already been examining the wine list, discussing its high and low points with his date, silently judging if they weren't able to keep up with sommelier lingo.

But he hadn't even glanced at the list at the back of his menu yet.

"A glass of your house red," he said, realizing he didn't even care what it was.

The only thing he cared about was sitting across from him.

"Sounds good. I'll give you two a minute to . . ." Andrew paused. "Peruse the offerings."

"Thanks," Oliver said wryly as he departed.

"Alright," Luca said, before Oliver could apologize again, "I have to ask: do you know *everyone* in this town?"

"Sort of," Oliver said with a chuckle.

"Seems like more than sort of," Luca observed. "It's just . . . not what I'm used to. Well, I *am* used to my family constantly interfering, so I imagine it's kind of like that, isn't it, except with a *whole town* instead."

"Yeah, kinda," Oliver said, shrugging.

"You don't mind it."

"Most of the time, no. It's actually . . ." Oliver hesitated. "It's actually kind of nice. It's why I came back here, instead of staying in Charleston."

"First, before you tell me what you did in Charleston, and I get totally blown away by how ridiculously cute you are," Luca said, and Oliver shot him a lopsided grin, "tell me if I should be ordering this roasted chicken."

"What would you think if I told you everything here is good?" Oliver teased.

"I'd tell you that you were a dirty, filthy liar."

"Fair, fair. The chicken's fine. Get the roasted pork chop, if you don't want a steak. Make sure to get the stuffing on the side and the

Brussels sprouts. They're fresh, not canned. But the green beans? Not so much."

"Ugh, okay." Luca mentally revised his order.

"You're totally one of those people who researches a restaurant online, reads the menu, reads the reviews, before you ever go, aren't you?" Oliver observed, no judgment in his tone.

Normally, Luca wouldn't ever be uncool enough to admit it. But he nodded.

"I get it, you just want to make sure you get a good meal," Oliver said. "You all set now?

"Yes, thank you."

"As for your question, I went to Charleston for pastry school," Oliver said. "And that was great. Working in some of the big restaurants there? Little less great. The experience was worth it, but I didn't want to stay. I thought I would, because like you know, it can be a little claustrophobic with so many people in your business all the time, but it turns out I kinda like that people care about me."

"I stayed a lot closer for school," Luca said. He hadn't even realized how he felt about that until he'd started talking about it. "I kind of wish I had gone farther away, but my Nonna, she wasn't doing well, and I didn't want to be too far."

"Family's really important to you," Oliver said, after Andrew had dropped off their drinks and taken their food order, with a maximum amount, Luca was sure, of winking. "I can tell."

"Do you think he has something in his eye?" Luca asked, somewhat amazed.

"No," Oliver laughed. "He's just like that. If you would believe it, Enzo also tried to date Andrew."

Luca couldn't imagine his sullen cousin with the bright ray of sunshine and incessant winking that was Andrew. "Really?"

"To be fair to Enzo, there aren't many queer guys in this town," Oliver said. "But yes, he did. I think they made it two dates."

"Ouch." Luca hesitated. "And yes, family is important. The most important." Usually after he said this, the guys he dated would grow colder around him. Like they realized nothing they did could ever replace the position his family held in his life.

But Oliver didn't.

"My dad died a few years back, cancer. But my mom and I are really close, and frankly, I know so many of her friends, it feels like I've got about ten moms at any given time. So I get it." Oliver laughed a little self-consciously. "I didn't mean to . . .I don't know . . .bring the mood down. I guess I find it easier to talk about it than to *not* talk about it."

"You didn't," Luca said with certainty. "I'm used to men who aren't interested in family and don't understand that my whole life revolves around them. Around our business."

"Of course it does." Oliver frowned. "They don't like that you're a smart, responsible guy who commits, who takes care of what he loves *and* loves hard? That's so weird. Honestly, I think that makes you *more* attractive?"

"Oh. *Oh.*" Luca didn't know what to say. He took a sip of wine to try to hide his speechlessness but there was no hiding from the fact that he *was*.

"Sorry." Oliver shot him a lopsided smile. "I clearly haven't been on a date in a while."

Luca cleared his throat. "It's alright. It's . . .it's more than alright, in fact. Most people just don't see that side of me. They see . . ."

Clearly *he* hadn't been on a date—or a good date he actually gave a shit about—in way too long, if he was about to give Oliver a laundry list of all the faults people usually saw in him.

"They see someone too exacting, someone difficult and arrogant because he knows what's best and doesn't suffer fools. That about right?"

"If you weren't a baker, you could've been a psychologist," Luca grumbled.

"I like to think I could've been a lot of things, but the stomachs in this town would've missed me too much. So tell me more about your family's restaurants. How many are there?"

"Four," Luca said. "Not counting the food truck my brother and my cousin run together in Los Angeles, though they technically *own* that outright now, so . . .I guess it doesn't count. And then there's Giana's deli, of course."

"Food truck?" Oliver perked up. "That's really neat. I always wonder if there would be a market here for a food truck."

"Gabriel is . . .brilliant. Difficult. But brilliant. Knows it, of course, because he's a Moretti."

"Of course." Oliver grinned.

"He was really angry with me over how the whole food truck thing went." This was another subject he should *not* be broaching, but there he went anyway, because Oliver was so goddamn easy to talk to.

"Really?" Oliver's expression turned sympathetic. "I don't have any brothers—or sisters—so I can't say for sure, but I think they're kinda a blessing and a curse, yeah?"

"I have six, so you're free to borrow a few of mine," Luca said wryly.

"*Six?*"

"Yep."

"And you're the oldest?" Oliver sounded incredulous.

Luca nodded. "It's really not so bad most of the time. Unless Gabe is picking fights, which he likes to do, or Marco's decided to be difficult on purpose. And don't get me started on Ilaria, who went to school and then refused to come home and *then* convinced Chiara to join her." The more he kept talking, the more it *did* sound bad most of the time.

"Gabe is the one who owns the food truck?"

"Yes, with our cousin Ren, and I should've known, the two of them in LA together . . ."

"What happened?" Amazingly, Oliver actually looked interested in this family drama.

"I tried to hold on too tight. Tried to push too hard. And then he was his usual difficult self about it. About *everything*."

"I can't imagine that," Oliver teased.

"He paid back his loan, and he and Ren do whatever they want now. Though . . ." Luca sighed. "It's not like that isn't just as successful as I hoped they might be. It is. Maybe even more. But now he hates me."

"He doesn't hate you."

Luca raised an eyebrow.

"Well, okay, maybe he *thinks* he hates you, but only because he thought his big brother didn't approve of what he was doing. That hurts."

"Really, how are you so good at this?" Luca was a little mystified. Nicoletta and Matteo had been trying to talk to him about Gabriel for *months* and had never made as much simple sense as that.

Oliver shrugged. "I think of a baker kind of like a bartender. We have a lot of repetitive tasks and so we end up listening a lot to people's troubles, and it turns out, I'm really pretty good at listening."

"I can tell," Luca said. It was one of the things, besides Oliver's attractiveness, that had drawn him to the guy in the first place.

"I think you should call Gabe. Text him. Just let him know you're thinking about him." Oliver held up a hand when Luca began to protest. "No, I know you are. You wouldn't have brought him up if you weren't. And sometimes, you gotta be the older brother, you know? Reach out. Be the bigger person."

Luca hadn't reached out before, because he'd been worried Gabe might not respond, or might respond negatively, and their whole relationship might get worse. Already Nicoletta was pissed at him for Gabe leaving for Los Angeles and now essentially refusing to come home.

He didn't need any more flack.

"I'll think about it," Luca said.

It didn't feel like it had been so long since he'd actually been on a date—far, far longer since he'd been on a good one, for sure—but he never remembered conversation flowing this easily.

Usually it was stilted. Difficult. Awkward. Luca had to search for things to say. Navigate around all the things he *wasn't* supposed to say.

But with Oliver, it was so easy. After Andrew dropped off the bread basket, which Oliver said *he* provided, so Luca didn't bother to even prevaricate—he immediately grabbed one of the hot rolls—he knew *just* what he wanted to say.

"So, your mother owns the Inn I'm staying in, huh?"

Oliver nodded. "It's been in our family for four generations."

"But you didn't want to run it?"

"I don't know, someday I'm sure I will. But the bakery? It's my first love."

"I can tell. I could tell the moment I walked in that it was. Actually," he corrected, "I could tell before that. The moment I tried one of your muffins at the Inn, I knew you were special."

"Like my muffins, do you?" Oliver said with a teasing grin.

Luca couldn't deny it; he was having an actual *good* time just talking to Oliver, but there was also that desire to get his hands on him, to kiss him, to feel his body pressed against his own.

"Actually, yeah," Luca said, and he was smiling again, so much his face hurt.

But then how often did he have chances to smile back at home?

It felt like he was always dealing with a disaster with the restaurants—which . . .he supposed it was a minor miracle nothing had happened in the last few days—and it wasn't like any of his dates ever made him smile, nevermind laugh out loud.

But Oliver did it easy as breathing.

"It's alright." Oliver leaned forward, the corner of his mouth quirking up like he had a particularly tasty secret. "I like yours, too."

"You two are really too adorable for words."

Luca was finally forced to look away from the potent heat in Oliver's eyes by Andrew's timely—or rather untimely—interruption.

"Sorry," he said, completely without self-consciousness, "I thought you might want your dinner ASAP, so you can get out of here." He winked again.

Luca might normally be really annoyed by the insinuation he could barely wait to finish eating before sex, but maybe it was a little bit true.

Only a little bit though, because he *did* really enjoy talking to Oliver.

"Andrew, you are absolutely incorrigible," Oliver said but didn't exactly look disappointed either as the waiter set their plates in front of them.

"Hey, I know you get to *bed* early," Andrew teased. "Anything else I can get you? Refills? More rolls? A condom?"

"Oh my God," Oliver cried out, his face flushed. "*Please,* stop."

"Thanks, we're good," Luca managed to say, embarrassed despite himself.

After Andrew departed, Oliver looked over at Luca from behind a partially covered face, still red. Still adorable, frankly. "I'm so, *so* sorry," he said.

And okay, yes, Andrew was embarrassing. But maybe they were the embarrassing ones, fawning all over each other, when everyone who even looked at them had to know what they *really* wanted to do, which was rip each other's clothes off.

"Don't be," Luca said.

Maybe back in Napa, he might've been a little more stunned by Andrew's comment, but honestly, that *never* would have happened in any of the restaurants he frequented with his dates.

Hadn't he smiled more tonight than he had in forever? He could chalk almost all of that up to Oliver being amazing, but some of it was the more relaxed atmosphere. The lack of pressure. He wasn't auditioning someone to be his husband, or long-term partner, even, or to help him lead the Nonna's empire. No, he was just spending the evening with someone because *he* wanted to. Not because it was expected of him, or because he genuinely expected it to go anywhere.

He was doing it because Oliver was too compelling a person to *not* spend time with.

"Really, you're not mad?" He waved around. "This must not be like any other date you've been on."

"No, no, it hasn't been." Luca had to be honest. "But I like it better because it's different. And because it's you."

Oliver flushed again. "Stop sweet-talking me; you already know I'm a sure bet."

Luca raised an eyebrow. "You are?"

"Well, not a *sure sure* bet, but um . . ."

"How about this? Let's enjoy our dinner, and see what happens after?" Luca asked.

Oliver nodded. "I like the sound of that."

Chapter Seven

Earlier today, Oliver had told Marjorie that kindness wasn't in Luca Moretti's top five attributes. But he was slowly revising that analysis.

Was it a dominant characteristic? No, not really.

But Luca was kind when it mattered, like when Oliver was feeling vulnerable, after Andrew was his normal obnoxious self.

He should've told Lucy *not* to sit them in Andrew's section, because he should've realized the waiter would be way more interested than he needed to be in Oliver and his dining companion. Not just because Luca looked like Luca, but because the last honest-to-God date Oliver had been on had been the Enzo disaster, and he knew everyone was hoping (perhaps even rooting) for him to bounce back from that particular mess.

As usual for Rudy's, his steak was perfectly cooked, the roasted potatoes on the side crisp with their parmesan garlic crust, and the Brussels sprouts delicious.

Luca seemed to be enjoying his meal as well, specifically thanking Oliver more than once for guiding him in the right direction and theorizing how they managed to keep the pork chop so moist.

"I have it on good authority they brine the chops," Oliver said.

Luca had been fascinated by that, and they had a long, involved discussion about one of the recipes at Luca's restaurants, where he'd been trying to adjust one of his Nonna's recipes to be more consistent. Brining, Luca thought, might be a way to guarantee that.

Watching Luca talk passionately about his grandmother's legacy, her recipes, the responsibility she'd given him, and how he'd not only taken it on without complaint but with a commitment to carry it out to the best of his ability, only made him more interested in the man.

Was he interested in the man underneath the clothes?

Absolutely. Andrew had not been wrong about that.

You'd have to be dead not to think about Luca Moretti naked.

But Oliver was also really enjoying hearing him talk. He was deeply interested in food: how it was made, how it was prepared, how it was served, and that was a topic of conversation Oliver could talk about forever.

He'd meant it before when he'd said Luca was *more* attractive because of who he was, that fierce intensity he carried with him, the love he showed for his family through the care he took with his birthright.

They finished eating, Luca taking one last sip of wine before leaning back in the booth with a deeply satisfied smile on his face.

A glance at his watch told Oliver it was almost six-thirty. An hour and a half before he needed to be in bed—though he could stretch that, if absolutely necessary.

And to truly enjoy Luca's company, he had a feeling it might be absolutely necessary to go a little short on sleep tonight.

"That was a great meal," Luca said.

"I'll pass your compliments onto Rudy," Oliver said. "And tell him how meaningful they truly are."

"There's actually a Rudy?" Luca asked in surprise as Andrew—thankfully almost silent this time, apparently chastened by Oliver's embarrassment—dropped off the bill and picked up their plates.

"Hey, let's walk a bit; it's a nice evening," Oliver said, after he let Luca take care of the check. Luca was clearly well-off. He could afford it, and Oliver decided it wasn't worth arguing about. If Luca wanted to buy him dinner, he was not going to overthink it. He'd let Luca take care of it. Take care of *him*.

In every possible way.

"Sounds good to me," Luca said. "It's warm here, for spring."

"Wait til you're here in the middle of August," Oliver said as they stood and began to make their way out of the restaurant.

Luca froze in front of him and then his own muscles tensed up the moment he'd realized what he'd said.

"Of course, you won't be here in August, which let me tell you, is actually a blessing," Oliver said hurriedly, feeling stupid for broaching the one subject he'd promised himself they wouldn't touch, which was how short whatever this thing was between them would be, no matter how good it was.

"That hot, huh?" Luca asked as he pushed open the door, letting Oliver walk through it first.

That was the other *nice* thing about Luca. He was a gentleman. Respectful. Conscientious. Didn't expect anything, even though Oliver had practically thrown himself at him.

Had even said, *let's see what happens after*, like he had hopes and aspirations but not expectations.

Enzo had expected that he'd kiss Oliver and also that Oliver would like it. He'd expected they'd sleep together, because he'd paid for dinner.

It was all those things, *plus* absolutely zero chemistry, that had guaranteed no second date.

Luca was supposed to be the arrogant one, but he didn't seem particularly arrogant now. Enzo's cousin felt like an entirely different story, especially in the dark, just his face lit by the streetlamps as they strolled together down the sidewalk.

The first time Oliver had ever seen him, he hadn't believed he was real, and there was a part of him that *still* didn't think he could be.

"I can't remember the last time I ever went on a date," Luca confessed, into the still evening air as they headed toward the park at the center of Indigo Bay, "and actually wanted there to be a second one." He glanced over at Oliver.

There was no way around it. Oliver *yearned*.

Maybe Luca Moretti wasn't everyone's idea of a fairytale prince, but he seemed to fit the fantasy man bill pretty well for Oliver. Even just a little spicy underneath, the way he hadn't realized he liked, but he *loved* about Luca.

"Well, the last date I went on was with your cousin, and we *know* I didn't want a second date with him," Oliver teased. He expected Luca didn't normally do this, but it felt natural to reach out and take his hand, intertwine their fingers together and squeeze.

Luca looked surprised and then smiled, softly, squeezing Oliver's hand back.

"Please tell me I'm at least doing a little better than him," Luca said with a smirk.

"Loads better," Oliver said. "But honestly, don't think I'm comparing."

They'd meandered through the park now, and they were standing near the statue of Eliza. The groundskeepers in town always did an extra special buff to her bronze exterior whenever the Sweethearts Festival came around, and this year was no exception. She was glowing softly in the light from the streetlamps dotting the park.

Luca stopped next to her, glanced down at the plaque identifying her. "Eliza Billings," he read.

"You wanted to know the obsession with all things love, and the Sweethearts Festival, and I said I'd tell you the story, but maybe," he added with a tiny smirk, "we don't have time for the long version anymore."

"Oh?" Luca raised an eyebrow. "Why would that be?"

"I'd rather spend my evening doing something else." There was no point in prevaricating, or even pretending they didn't both want the exact same thing: to end the night getting hot and heavy in a bed somewhere. In Luca's room in the Inn, or even in his room, in the tiny bungalow he'd bought two years ago.

"Me too," Luca said with a chuckle. "So give me the short version. And *Billings*. Eliza Billings. She's your ancestor, isn't she?"

"Yes," Oliver said, nodding. "Eliza was one of the first children born to the new inhabitants of this town, when they settled it in the early

1800s. She grew up with Nathanial Billings. They were childhood playmates I understand, but then Nathanial went to sea, like so many teenagers did back then."

"They were sweethearts, then, Eliza and Nathaniel."

"If they were, then this story would be like any other town's story," Oliver said with a grin, "and we wouldn't be celebrating it every year with an explosion of red and pink you're never really prepared for."

"So what happened?" Luca looked intrigued now.

"Nathaniel was engaged to a woman named Betsy when he went to sea. They were sweethearts, and when he came back from his long sea voyage, they were to be married. But when years passed and he never returned, Betsy stopped waiting, and married someone else. But Eliza? Eliza waited." Oliver sighed, a melancholy sigh, because sometimes he knew how Eliza had felt, back then, not necessarily because he'd been in love with someone his whole life and had been waiting for those feelings to be returned, but because it felt like he was always *waiting* for something, he just never knew what.

"For how long?"

"Years. She'd climb to the highest point on the coast—this is South Carolina so it's not *high*, but it's high enough to see the ocean, as far as the eye can see. And she'd wait. Wait for him to come home. Everyone else, his parents, Betsy, everyone else, they believed he was dead, his ship lost, never to return, but Eliza? She never stopped believing."

"She never stopped loving him." Luca's voice echoed soft and wondrous. Like he couldn't imagine that kind of steadfastness. And for a man who rarely went on even a second date, that made sense. But the wonder was surprising. Like he'd never even considered that kind of love before, but surely he'd seen it? His family was large, by his own admission, and he cared deeply for them.

How was his love, his protection, his dedication any different from Eliza's loyalty to Nathaniel? It was familial love, yes, and not romantic, but still, Oliver wasn't sure there was any difference.

"Never," Oliver said. "She never stopped loving him. She never forgot him. She never married. Ten years went by, and she kept going up to the high point, to watch and to wait. The town began to say she was crazy. Delusional."

"Why?"

"Well, this *is* a small town," Oliver teased. "We like to be iconoclastic, especially to outsiders or to anyone who's different. And Eliza was different. Because she didn't just wait for him; she refused to believe he was dead."

"This has to have a happy ending, or else there wouldn't be a red and pink explosion happening every year," Luca said grumpily.

"Just wait," Oliver said. "Eliza became the town pariah. Everyone thought she had lost her mind. There was talk of bundling her off to a sanatorium in Georgia, of sending her to relatives in Boston. But she refused to leave. She said she had to stay here, and be here for Nathaniel, not *if* he came back, but *when*. Then one night, a terrible storm blew in. Like the hand of God, they said, touching the space between the land and the sea."

Luca squeezed his hand. "You're good at telling this," he said.

Oliver nodded. "My mom actually wrote the history of this. Her first book was Eliza and Nathaniel's love story. So I think I get it from her."

"I think it's also you," Luca said. "You believe."

He supposed Luca wasn't wrong. He did believe. In love and loyalty and steadfastness beyond common sense. He believed in pie for breakfast and delicious coffee and in putting love into his food so that not only could everyone taste it, they could *feel* it.

"After the storm cleared," Oliver continued, "the residents of the town could see that a ship had been dashed on the rocks, and floating on a big spar in the bay, all among the wreckage, was a man with long dark hair and a big bushy beard, and blue eyes that everyone recognized. It was Nathaniel."

"I knew it!" Luca crowed with delight. "But Eliza loved him, only Nathaniel didn't love her. He loved Betsy."

"But Betsy was married with three children now. He came to her little house she'd lived in with her parents and there was no room for him there."

"And then he fell in love with Eliza?"

"I told you it was a long story," Oliver said with a grin. "But yes, eventually, he did. She took care of him, nursed him back to health, physical *and* mental, and as winter turned to spring, he fell in love with her, too. They married a year later and had five children, one of whom is, yes, my ancestor. The anniversary of their marriage is the date of the festival each year."

"What prevented him from coming home for all those years?" Luca wanted to know.

"Their boat had sunk off a tiny island in the Caribbean and they'd been stranded there for years. When they'd been picked up, he headed to England, because that was where the ship was going, and it took him ten long years to make it back."

"He expected Betsy would wait for him, didn't he?" Luca sounded mad she hadn't.

"Of course he did. Because he'd waited for her. But he discovered his love for her wasn't as real as he'd believed. Not as real as his feelings for Eliza."

"She was standing in front of him all along."

"Yes," Oliver said with a satisfied nod. "Yes, she was."

"That's actually . . ." Luca looked surprised again. "Actually a great story."

"Worthy of a festival?" Oliver asked slyly.

"If any story is," Luca agreed, his tone begrudging. "It's still a *lot* of pink and red."

"Which is why I went with magenta and purple for my bakery colors." Oliver grinned. "Gotta mix it up. Can't be too expected."

"It's okay, I think the rest of the town has got you plenty covered." Luca paused. "I have to say I didn't expect that story."

"Did you think a story that inspired an entire town to obsess about love wouldn't be romantic?" Oliver teased.

"No. But you know what *did* surprise me?" The corner of Luca's mouth tilted up in a sexy smirk. "How it made me want to kiss you even more than I did before."

"Oh." Oliver was sure he looked at least semistupid right now, his mouth falling open a little right before Luca leaned down and captured it.

Oliver had only been thinking—and okay, *dreaming*—about kissing Luca since he'd nearly mowed him down. Would it be a hard kiss? Fierce and intense like Luca was a lot of the time, or sweet, like Luca's soft secret underbelly he'd kept under wraps until tonight?

The kiss was neither.

Luca cradled his cheeks in his palms and devoted himself to the kiss. It was sweet and passionate and gentle and intense, all wrapped up into one unexpectedly incredible package.

Oliver groaned as Luca tilted his head and their tongues brushed.

"God, I knew you'd taste like this," Luca said breathlessly as they broke apart.

Probably better, Oliver thought, his head spinning with a surge of lust and affection.

He was so goddamned charmed by this man.

"Taste like what?" Oliver said, licking his lips and nearly reaching a hand up to fist in Luca's collar so he could drag him right back where he belonged—that big hard body pressed against his own.

"Sweet, like sugar." Luca dipped his head down and stole another brief kiss. "But a little spicy too like cinnamon. Like cardamom. Like nutmeg."

"I didn't . . ." Oliver didn't get the rest of the sentence out, before Luca was there, intoxicatingly big and warm and present, pressing their lips together again.

"I know," Luca said, and the look in his eyes said it all when the kiss ended. "It's just you," he added helplessly. "Like it's in you. Like it's just *you*."

"Well, there's more of me, too." Oliver couldn't help himself. He angled his body against Luca's, felt his sharp intake of breath. Felt something else, too. Something insistently hard and hot. Something he couldn't deny any longer he wanted desperately. "I think you've got to check me out, top to bottom. Maybe part of me won't taste so good."

"Not possible," Luca swore under his breath. "Not even fucking possible."

"But you're not *sure*," Oliver said in a low voice, fluttering his eyelashes in what he hoped was an enticing way. "Let's go back to your room and make sure. Gotta do your due diligence, right?"

"You're such a tease," Luca said roughly.

"Exactly the idea," Oliver said. "Come on, the Inn's only a few blocks out."

"That wouldn't bother you?" Luca paused. "You know, cause your mom . . ."

Oliver raised an eyebrow. "Are we really going to talk about my mom right now?"

"Trust me, I don't want to, but she *does* own the Inn," Luca said.

"And? It's not like people don't have sex there *all the time*. Like really, *all the time*. You don't even want to know the shit they find in the rooms sometimes. Sweethearts Festival, right?"

"Makes sense." Luca swallowed hard, his Adam's apple working. "So you wouldn't mind if I took you back to my room and . . ."

"And?"

Luca leaned in. Oliver could smell his cologne, or maybe the sharp lemon tang of him was just his skin. It made Oliver's mouth water.

"And took all your clothes off. Made you feel good. Anything I want. Anything *you* want."

"We could . . ." Oliver stuttered a little over the words, because he wanted that so much he was nearly burning up with it. "We could do that."

"Then what are we waiting for?" Luca grinned at him. "Let's go."

<hr>

It was highly possible Joy was still at her desk, working, since it wasn't quite seven yet, and she *was* on a deadline. So Oliver took them in the back way, typing in the code to the back door, and up the old servants' staircase.

A minute later, Luca was letting them into his room with his keycard.

He'd left a light on in the corner, and as Oliver glanced around, he wasn't surprised at all to see Luca's clothes were tucked away in the dresser and the wardrobe in the corner, and the bed made neatly.

This was not a man who enjoyed chaos.

But maybe Luca might enjoy a little bit of *sexy* chaos.

Before he could say a word, or dictate everything—which, Oliver could acknowledge was probably how he normally had sex—he reached up and tugged Luca down, kissing him as he pushed him toward the edge of the bed.

Luca went, to Oliver's surprise, as pliant as anything, kissing Oliver back like he was starving for it.

Touching him like it, too, those big, capable, competent hands feeling him everywhere. His chest, his waist, and finally his bare skin, Oliver shivering as Luca's fingertips brushed the line of his spine.

Oliver reached for him, thumbing open one button at a time on his shirt.

Luca groaned, rough and deep, nearly a growl of desperation, his kiss growing more passionate as Oliver wrenched off his shirt and took a step back, breathing hard, to admire what he'd done.

Luca's eyes were pitch-black with desire, his hair mussed from Oliver's hands, and as he leaned back, his smooth, toned olive muscles bunched up. He was thick and solid and *built*, with honest-to-God abs Oliver couldn't wait to touch, to *taste*.

"How do you look so . . ." Oliver swallowed hard. "Your family is famous for *pasta*."

But Luca just shrugged. "I like to work out. It . . .it helps."

Oliver wanted to know what it helped with. Restraint? Controlling his temper? The fact that he was probably practically living like a monk because he worked so goddamn much?

Just like you, his body reminded him firmly, *and this whole celibacy thing is gonna come to a screaming, wonderful end.*

But he wasn't about to stop any of this to have a conversation about why Luca looked like a freaking Roman god brought to life.

Instead, he was going to *enjoy* it.

Pressing a palm to the taut muscles of Luca's chest, he trailed his fingertips down, feeling Luca quiver with anticipation when Oliver finally reached the button of his jeans.

Oliver could see the hard outline of his cock, and now he wanted to feel it. Licking his lips, he popped the button open and lowered his zipper, tugging his jeans down, as he sank to his knees.

"Oh, *fuck*," Luca swore and both his arms and his glorious thighs flexed when Oliver ran a teasing fingertip down his hard cock, encased in a pair of tight black briefs that would probably focus heavily in every single fantasy he had for the rest of his life.

If Oliver had known he looked like *this*, he'd have forgone any of the lecturing about crosswalks and teasing about dates and just dragged him back to any available room with a lock the first time their eyes had met.

"Do I need to beg?" Luca asked in a low, rough voice. "Because I will. No shame. I want you to touch me so much I can barely . . ."

Oliver's pulse thrummed, and he felt it everywhere—his cock, his heart, his head—as he leaned forward and mouthed at where Luca's dick twitched beneath the black fabric.

He didn't answer—Luca didn't need to beg, because Oliver's self-control might be pretty good, but it wasn't great—just finally tucked his fingers under the waistband of his briefs and tugged them down toward his jeans.

His cock was just as gorgeous as the rest of him. Long and thick and flushed a beautiful pink color. Oliver wrapped his hand around the base and his tongue around the head and sucked, the sound of Luca moaning joining the echo of his own desperate heartbeat thundering in his ears.

"That's it." Luca's voice cracked. "Suck me, baby. Wrap those pretty pink lips around my cock and suck."

Oliver had had a decent amount of sex in his past, and he *enjoyed* giving head, but he'd never been as eager to do anything in his whole goddamn life. He slid Luca's cock into his mouth a little at a time, sucking hard, loving every time Luca groaned. Loving every time Luca pushed him further, harder.

Luca's words and Oliver's position might make someone think the former was in control, but Oliver knew better. He could feel the twitch of Luca's dick as he teased it with his tongue, could see the flex of his arms and the desperation in his eyes whenever he glanced up. Could taste his precome as he grew closer to orgasm.

But Oliver didn't want it to end. He wanted this to go on and on and permanently imprint on the backs of his eyelids.

Still, he was not expecting the harsh whisper of, "Wait."

Or for Luca to drag him up by the arm and with a neat show of strength, deposit him on the bed.

"I want," Luca said, hovering over him, eyes wild, "to taste you. You promised me."

Oliver licked his suddenly dry lips. Overwhelmed in the best way possible. "I did?"

"Yes."

The tough, indomitable Luca was back, and maybe he shouldn't have been as sexy as the putty-in-Oliver's-hands Luca, but he *was*.

Basically, every single bit of Luca drove him insane.

Luca made quick work of his clothes and then he was leaning down, his lips brushing against Oliver's stomach leisurely, like he had all the time in the world.

"Still sweet," he breathed out unsteadily, as his lips moved lower and then lower still. "So goddamn sweet."

Oliver was past words. He'd never been harder in his life and Luca hadn't even touched him yet.

When he did, Oliver couldn't help it. He shook with the pleasure of it as Luca's tongue leisurely licked up him with a confident mastery that would've made Oliver's knees weak if he'd been standing.

Then Luca's mouth moved lower, tongue flicking out to taste both of his balls, making Oliver bury his mouth into his arm so he wouldn't scream.

"See?" Luca's voice was so deep, it was practically a rumble. "Still sweet here. But—" He hummed against Oliver's sensitive skin, making him see stars. "—how about here?"

Oliver's vision totally whited out when Luca's tongue meandered even lower still, brushing up against his hole.

"God, I knew it," Luca boasted. "So fucking sweet. Turn over, baby. Let me make you feel good."

His knees wobbled but he managed it, Luca's hands a hot brand against his thighs, his ass, as they took possession of him, angling Oliver exactly the way he wanted.

He felt consumed, *owned*, as Luca's tongue found him again. Licked lazily, casually, even as Oliver buried his head into the covers and screamed.

It had been way too long since anyone had done this, and it hadn't been anything like the confident way Luca moved his tongue, as if he knew just what Oliver would like, and he felt sure he could make him come just like this.

"Oh yes, you *love* that," Luca said with satisfaction as Oliver twitched, unable to help thrusting back against his tongue.

Way too soon, Luca's hand brushed his balls. Then his cock, and Oliver trembled right on the edge.

But didn't tumble off, because Luca kept him there instead. A breath away from the best orgasm of his life, until he was groaning and crying and begging for it, for more of his tongue, for more of his fingertips, slicking up his cock with his dripping precome.

"You ready to come, baby?" Luca asked. But then instead of waiting, not that Oliver was even remotely capable of coherent speech at this point, he twisted his tongue in, hot and insistent, just as he fisted his whole hand around Oliver's cock, and he came in an explosion of pleasure so radical he nearly blacked out, pulsing over and over into Luca's hand.

"Shit," Oliver said, collapsing to the bed, knees so wobbly they could no longer quite hold him up.

"Turn over," Luca said and there was that undeniable steel in his voice again. "Let me see you."

He turned over, because he couldn't do anything else, and was greeted with the incredible view of Luca, mouth wet and red, hand fisted around his own cock, pumping it hard, his biceps flexing with the motion, his eyes wild and desperate.

And then he was coming too, stripes of come all over Oliver's chest.

Luca orgasming was a sight like nothing Oliver had ever seen, and he'd been wrong before. *This* was what would occupy every single goddamn fantasy for the rest of his life. Luca, undone.

When his hand finally slowed and his eyes fluttered open, signaling it was over, it didn't *feel* over, because the warmth in Luca's gaze was like a flame against his skin.

"Wow," Oliver said softly, because that was still all the words he had for what had just happened.

Luca grabbed a few tissues and cleaned his hand and then cleaned Oliver before tossing them into the trash and collapsing on the bed next to him, grinning. "Right?" he said.

They weren't exactly *cuddling*, but they were both lying there, arms barely brushing, and there was a quiet, companionable silence Oliver didn't really want to break.

He knew he should get up, finish cleaning them both, and head home to his own bed. His alarm went off insanely early, and he was fairly sure Luca—he of the "never a second date"—would not be particularly interested in him spending the night.

Also, in Oliver's experience, as brief as it was, most people were not interested in matching his sleeping habits.

But then Luca shattered every expectation. "Stay," he said quietly, his gaze meeting Oliver's. "You should stay."

"Really?" Oliver knew how dubious he sounded. "You know I'm going to have to go to sleep in a bit." He yawned as a punctuation to the sentence. The incredible orgasm Luca had given him made him loose and languid and suddenly sleepy.

"I know," Luca said. "I might not, but I can be quiet."

"Then . . ." Oliver wanted to ask *why*, then. Why ask him to stay?

Was that a blush making its way up Luca's cheeks? Oliver was pretty sure it was, not just the dim light in the room. "Maybe I don't want it to end," he said. "Even if we don't get a second date."

"Nothing from Giana?"

Luca shook his head. "I was so sure she didn't have a choice."

Oliver was currently in a sex-drunk haze, but he was also a realist. "I imagine that's not something she enjoys," he pointed out dryly. "What would you do if someone backed *you* into a corner?"

"They wouldn't dare." Luca's confidence was nearly arrogance, but again, Oliver didn't find it unattractive, when on any other person it would have been.

"But what if they did?" Oliver persisted though, because while he might not be a Moretti, he wasn't exactly a slouch either. Hadn't he been forged in the hell of some of the best kitchens on the east coast? Hadn't he started his own business and seen it through those first few tough years when it had always felt like there was too much to do and not enough hands to help?

He had.

Luca rolled his eyes. "I would destroy the corner."

"You would," Oliver agreed. "She's probably trying to find a battering ram as we speak."

"Really?" Luca sounded surprised.

"Oh come on. She might look like a sweet older lady, but does that make her any less of a Moretti? Did it make your *Nonna* any less of a Moretti?"

"No," Luca admitted guiltily. "No, not even close."

"Then don't underestimate her," Oliver reminded him.

Luca sighed. "That means I may have to *still* convince her, then, and honestly, dealing with her means dealing with Enzo, and I want to wring his neck." His smile was so warm. "How did you even deal with him for one date?"

"The good news is my standards are much improved," Oliver teased. He brushed his hand more fully against Luca's, and to Oliver's surprise, his smile deepened even further.

"So you'll stay, then?" Luca sounded so hopeful, what could Oliver say?

"If it won't bother you, truly, that I go to bed early. Or that I leave *really* early."

"Of course not. I figured you would."

Oliver could see that he meant it, *and* it wasn't as if someone like Luca Moretti would ever judge him for working too hard, or for too many hours.

He'd understand, every single step of the way.

"Uh, alright. Well, I'm gonna . . ." Oliver motioned in the direction of the bathroom. "Get cleaned up."

He got up and went into the bathroom, shut the door, and stared at his reflection for a long moment.

It wasn't the first time he'd had this feeling—the, *I wish you didn't live on the other side of the country* feeling—but it was the strongest it had ever been.

Oliver didn't just want a second date. He wanted dozens of dates. He wanted to do this all the time, not only tucked up into a third-floor room in his mom's Inn, but together in his own little house, in the comfortable bed he'd picked out.

He wanted to come out of the back of the bakery and see Luca eating one of his pastries and drinking his coffee.

Even though he knew that wasn't in the cards, he still wanted it.

Maybe the smart thing to do would be to wash up and come out of the bathroom resolved to *not* spend the night, because Oliver wasn't stupid or naive. Staying here was only going to intensify these feelings.

But when he finished and walked out, Luca was still lounging on the bed, totally naked and totally glorious, without an ounce of shame, but he'd tugged the blankets back and he'd pulled out his tablet, flipping through something on it, and he'd also put on a pair of dark-rimmed reading glasses.

Luca with one of those perfectly cut suits on was a marvel.

Luca naked was stunning.

Luca naked with those glasses?

Oliver stopped in his tracks, pretty sure his jaw was hanging open.

"You alright?" Luca asked, barely looking up from what he was reading.

"Yes," Oliver said, amazed that his voice didn't shake. He'd just had the orgasm of a freaking lifetime, and he should've been satisfied, but his blood already felt hot again.

"Alright, good," Luca said. "I thought I'd do some work. Do you need the light off to go to sleep? Me to turn the brightness on my screen down?"

Kindness, Oliver decided, was definitely in his vocabulary. But maybe it was more than that. Luca was conscientious. He *thought* about other people. Now, sometimes you might not like the thoughts he had or the resulting fallout from them, but it didn't mean he didn't consider others.

"Uh, sure, yeah, we can do that. Turn the light off. And if you can just angle it away?"

Oliver pulled on his briefs, climbed into the bed, and tugged the sheet up, despite the fact that he'd just made his mind up to go, not to stay.

But even if Luca Moretti broke his heart, it would be worth it. This would be worth it.

"Sure." Luca pressed his fingertip against the screen after Oliver flicked the bedside lamp off. "This okay?"

"Yeah, yeah."

"Good." Luca sounded very pleased about that.

He wasn't the only one either; Oliver definitely made a pleased sound as Luca tucked an arm around him, pulling him a little closer. "And this?" Luca asked quietly. "Still okay?"

"Yeah." Oliver looked over at his screen. "What are you looking at?"

"Income reports from the last few nights at the restaurants," Luca said. "Usually I go through them every night, but I've been . . ." He smiled, teeth bright white in the darkness of the room. "Preoccupied, we'll say."

"With Giana?"

"Sure," Luca said.

Oliver fell asleep like that, Luca's arm warm and sturdy around him and the realization in his heart that Luca hadn't meant Giana at all.

Chapter Eight

JUST BECAUSE HE WAS used to getting up at the ass crack of dawn didn't mean Oliver always *liked* it.

It was hard enough getting up with the alarm when he was alone in his nice warm bed.

It was ridiculously tough when Oliver opened his eyes and saw Luca's handsome face, barely visible in the darkness of the room, relaxed and sleeping, tilted toward him like he'd wanted to fall asleep looking at him.

Of course he didn't, Oliver ordered himself to believe. *This is just . . .*

Well, he didn't know what it was.

Maybe it didn't have to have a label or an identifier. Maybe it just *was*, for as long as Luca was here in town.

He gathered his clothes silently, let himself into the bathroom, and brushed his teeth with the extra toothbrush he knew his mom kept in every guest room. He'd always stored extra T-shirts at the bakery, so he could just throw one on and his walk of shame wouldn't be *that* obvious.

Aaron might guess, and Marjorie definitely would, but he wasn't really ashamed. He'd taken what he'd wanted and it had been even better than he'd anticipated. Where was the shame there?

He wanted to press another kiss to Luca's forehead, smooth and relaxed in sleep, but he didn't want to wake him up, so he pushed the desire down and let himself out of the room.

The Inn was still quiet, because it was too early even for people to be stirring. So instead of heading directly out the back door, Oliver pushed open the swinging door to the kitchen and stopped right in his tracks.

He'd meant to pour himself a big iced coffee to go, because his mom kept cold brew in a big jug in the industrial-sized refrigerator.

But the light was on, and there she was, rolling out scone dough on the counter. The pale expanse of it was dotted with dried fruit and nuts. He'd told her a thousand times he'd be happy to bake her scones at the bakery, but she'd resisted, said she liked working with the dough herself. Had even reminded him, firmly, he got his affinity for flour and sugar from somewhere.

"Oliver," Joy said steadily as he tried to unstick himself from the doorway. "Up early?"

He'd told himself this wasn't a walk of shame, but he also hadn't anticipated facing his *mother* on it, either.

"Uh, yes," Oliver said. He passed by her on the way to the fridge. Grabbed himself a plastic cup, filled it up with ice from the bin on the counter, and found the jug of cold brew in the fridge.

"Oliver, you *can* look at me," she said. And when he turned around, she had her hands on her hips, leaving flour dusted down her apron-front.

He steeled himself for her disappointment and finally met her gaze.

"It's . . ." But he couldn't finish the sentence any better out loud than he'd been able to finish it in his head.

"I know," Joy said, patting him on the shoulder, trailing flour as she went. "Besides, I can't say I'm surprised."

"What?"

"Marge texted me last night, said I should expect it. But I kinda thought you'd go to your place."

Maybe they *should* have.

"I have to be up so early . . ." It was a terrible excuse but the truth was he hadn't wanted to walk all the way to his own place, and the Inn had been so much closer—but he couldn't tell his mother they'd been too eager to wait.

"Uh-huh." She was smiling now. "Well, can't say you don't have good taste. He's very handsome, isn't he? Giana's nephew, and apparently *very* successful, according to Marge."

"And doesn't live here." Oliver forced the words out to remind both of them this wasn't going the place she thought it was.

She shot him a chiding look as she returned to her scone dough. "Since he's staying here at the Inn, I *did* assume that."

"Oh."

"You work too hard. Always have. You get that from me, too. This might be good for you."

"You're not going to . . ." Oliver trailed off, flushing with embarrassment.

"Lecture you about sex?" Joy laughed. "Oliver, I am not naive. Not even in the slightest. I'm just glad you didn't give in to Enzo. You deserved better than someone who believes you should just settle."

"Thanks," Oliver said dryly. "I think so too."

"Do you think Giana should listen to him?" Joy asked as she floured the cutter she used on the scones. Heart-shaped, of course.

Oliver reached back into the fridge and pulled out the milk. Stirred some into his coffee. "Yeah, actually," he said. "He's smart. He's got a plan. And well . . .we both know Giana doesn't."

"Bless her heart," Joy said. "Her plan is for Enzo to somehow, miraculously, develop both an interest and an aptitude in the business, but we both know that isn't going to happen."

"And it won't save it," Oliver said bluntly.

"No." Joy's sigh was reluctant.

"So why are *you* up so early?"

"Couldn't sleep," she said, placing her cut-out scones on a parchment-lined baking tray. "I'm stuck on the end of this book and I keep going round and round, trying to fix it, but it won't be fixed."

"Don't they just . . ." Oliver waved his hands. "Fall in love and live happily ever after?"

Joy smacked him on the arm, leaving more flour behind. "You know it's more than that."

He did, but it was fun to work her up anyway. At least he'd made her at least half as agitated as he'd been when she'd found him sneaking out.

But, he considered as he took a long drink of coffee, maybe it was good she knew. He wasn't trying to hide it. Not really.

He could have offered to fix dinner for Luca at his house, if he'd wanted to keep it a secret. Instead, he'd met him at Rudy's, which meant the whole town probably knew now.

"I gotta get to work," Oliver said.

"Can't wait around for a fresh scone?"

"No, I've got bread I've got to get started." Oliver was a little disappointed because he *was* a little hungry now that she mentioned it, and her scones were famous for a reason. "Just don't make him squirm too much, okay?"

Joy shot him a look. "Have you seen him? He's not really the squirming type."

Oliver thought about Luca's tough outer shell and then the surprisingly soft interior. The interior he kept hidden. The one he'd shown Oliver because maybe he couldn't help himself.

"You'd be surprised," Oliver said.

"Maybe I would." His mother's face softened into a warm smile. She gave him a quick hug as he passed by her on the way out the door. "Have a good day and don't work too hard."

Oliver rolled his eyes, but there was a smile on his face as he headed out into the pre-dawn dark.

Luca had known when he woke up Oliver would be gone.

He was prepared for his alarm to go off, and roll over to a cold, empty spot where he'd been last night. He'd mentally bargained with himself that it was fine. It was the trade-off he'd made when he'd asked Oliver to stay.

Which . . .he still didn't really know why he'd done that. It was not his usual MO, at all, because typically he liked his own space and his privacy, but something about Oliver had plucked at a feeling inside him he hadn't felt in forever.

He hadn't wanted him to go, because he didn't know how much time they would have together —and it felt safe to ask, because it wasn't like either of them believed this was going someplace it wasn't.

They knew he lived in California, and that fact alone would keep this from getting too serious.

Still, even though he'd known he wouldn't wake up to Oliver, he hadn't anticipated he'd wake up to a phone call at six in the morning.

Luca rolled over with a groan and fumbled for his phone. "Yes?" he growled as he hit the screen to answer it.

"Yes," Giana said. She sounded annoyed.

Probably not as annoyed as Luca was.

"Yes *what*?" Luca barked.

"Yes, we will make the changes. But I want in writing, signed, that you're discontinuing the payments." Her voice was prim.

Luca scrubbed a hand over his face. "I already had something written up," he said. "I'll send it over to you. To your email. That you'll be checking."

"Yes," she grumbled.

"I want you and Enzo there at eight sharp today."

She started to grumble more, but he interrupted her. They were going to do things his way—she'd just agreed—and he was really tired of arguing. "No," he said. "You agreed. And you're awake, you just called me at . . ." He checked his watch. "Six a.m. We're definitely both awake, so we might as well get started on the work at the restaurant."

"Fine." She didn't sound happy, which confirmed for him the only reason she'd chosen to call him this early had been as punishment for forcing her into a corner.

Guess this was battering ram Oliver had referred to.

She was going to take it to him, instead.

Well, if she tried, she was going to find out just how indestructible he was.

It would take more than a few early phone calls to disturb him.

"With Enzo," Luca said firmly. "Not just you. You *and* Enzo."

There was a long silence. "Okay," Giana finally said.

Honestly, Luca thought as he hung up and flopped back into the bed, the sooner his aunt came to terms with the fact his cousin was never going to want the business, the better.

Maybe he would eventually buy it back from her, after it was back to Nonna's standards, and it would give him an excuse to come here a few times a year.

To see Oliver.

But didn't they both deserve better than a few stolen days a year?

Luca knew Oliver did, but it hadn't stopped him from pursuing him anyway.

As for him, he wasn't quite sure *what* he deserved, but enjoying Oliver definitely felt like pressing his luck. Still, that wasn't going to stop him while he was here.

He knew if he wanted to get a workout in before he met Giana and Enzo at the restaurant, he'd need to get up now. But he still stayed in bed for another five minutes, and if he rolled over and sank into the sweet scent of Oliver on the other side of the bed, well, nobody knew but him.

Luca was not surprised when Giana opened the door for him at eight on the dot.

He was also not surprised when she glared at him when she did it.

"Good morning," Luca said, because his Nonna would've had his head for being rude. It was bad enough he'd backed Giana into a corner, though if he knew Nonna at all, she'd have approved of that particular move.

"Is it?" Giana said, crossing her arms over her chest.

"Yes," Luca said crisply. It was, though not for the reasons she thought.

Oliver was down the street, probably just pulling loaves of bread out of his ovens, the sweet smell of yeast swirling around him. It was hard for it not to be a good day, when he could walk a few blocks down and see him and sink his teeth into another one of those delicious pastries.

He pulled out his phone and began to take pictures of the small dining room.

"What are you doing?" Giana asked, following him around as he documented every mediocre inch.

"Taking pictures and sending them to my sister," Luca said. "She's got a flair for this kind of thing. She helped remodel our own restaurants a few years back, and the difference was astounding."

"And where are we going to get the money for this?" Giana asked archly.

"Just trust me on this," Luca said, as he snapped pictures of every angle of the sign. "Can Enzo do more of these?" He paused. "And where is he? I thought he was supposed to be here."

"He'll be here."

"Tomorrow, he'll be here *on time*," Luca said firmly.

Unlike his family, which worked late at the restaurants, his sisters Chiara and Ilaria, who lived and worked in the Bay Area, got up early because they served coffee and pastries every morning.

He attached the images to an email to Chiara and then, after telling Giana she'd better find out quick where Enzo was, stepped outside to call her.

"Big brother," Chiara said, actually answering his call, to his surprise. He'd expected to just leave a voicemail explaining the email and pictures and asking her to get back to him with what she thought they could do with the space. "You're up early."

"No, it's just past eight here," he said. "Didn't Mama tell you? I'm with Giana for the next few weeks, helping her out at the deli in Indigo Bay."

"You mean you're fixing her deli," Chiara said slyly. "But that makes sense."

"What makes sense?" Luca's spidey senses were immediately alert. "What's going on?"

"Nothing," Chiara said. "Just surprised you were up so early, that's all. What do you need? Make it quick, we're about to open the coffee shop."

"I sent you an email with a bunch of pictures of the deli," Luca said. "When you get a minute, if you could take a look, maybe figure out a way we could spruce it up a little."

"How much?" Out of all the Moretti children, Chiara was the most like him, endlessly pragmatic. Which he really liked about her.

However, even if he'd liked that about her, apparently he'd still driven her off, or so his mother liked to tell him—and Gabriel too, when he gave her the chance.

He couldn't help it. He was who he was. Exacting and arrogant and particular.

"Not as much as we spent. A lot less, hopefully."

"The deli's doing that badly, huh?" Chiara asked.

Luca didn't like to admit it. It felt like a personal failure, even though he'd hardly been involved up til now. "We're going to turn it around."

Her tone grew sly. "How much does Auntie Giana hate you right now?"

Luca glanced in one of the big picture windows and saw her on the phone, expression filled with frustration and annoyance—talking to Enzo, then, probably. "A lot," he admitted.

"You do know what's best though," Chiara said thoughtfully. "Whether she likes it or not."

"Thanks," Luca said dryly.

"How about I send a two-part plan," Chiara said. "Some cheap-ish sprucing up for now, and bigger plans for later, when the business is better off."

"Perfect," Luca said. "I knew I could count on you."

He could practically hear her eye roll through the phone.

"Once a Moretti, always a Moretti," she said. "I gotta go."

Ten minutes later, while he was going over the documents he'd had his lawyer draw up making the new arrangement official and binding, Enzo showed up.

He looked even sulkier than before, if that was possible.

It astounded Luca that he'd actually had the nerve to take Oliver out and then *alienate* him.

How stupid could you be to have a man like that and let him slip through your fingers?

Well, you'd have to be very stupid, and Enzo was clearly feeling that acute stupidity now, because the first thing he said—or sneered—to Luca was, "Did you have fun last night?"

"Enzo," Giana chided.

"It's none of your business, but yes."

"I warned you about Oliver."

"No," Luca said steadily. He didn't want to engage Enzo about this, but if they didn't put it to rest, he'd never be able to attempt to focus and listen. "No, you did not warn me. You offered your own poor experience, and I decided to improve upon it."

"Oh," Enzo said, tilting his head, "like you improve *everything*, huh?"

"Yes." He wasn't going to make excuses for being the best at what he did. He definitely wasn't going to apologize for it.

Enzo rolled his eyes. "You're such a fucking cold asshole, I'm shocked you didn't give Oliver frostbite."

"Enzo," Giana hissed under her breath.

"Let me be very clear," Luca said, trying to rein in his temper. It usually wasn't very hard, but Enzo pushed all the buttons. "I said it before, but maybe I wasn't clear enough: it is *none* of your business, and if you continue talking about Oliver that way, or Oliver *at all*, I'm going to make you stop."

Enzo opened his mouth, then snapped it shut again. Probably because he knew Luca could absolutely make him if he set his mind to it.

It wouldn't be very hard, Luca theorized, *and* it would be very satisfying to wipe that semipermanent smirk off his cousin's face.

"Guess he was pretty good, huh?" Enzo said it under his breath and Luca snapped, before he even had a prayer of controlling himself.

He grabbed Enzo's collar and pushed him back against the counter, terror widening his brown eyes. He heard Giana's panicked gasp from behind him, but he didn't let go. Enzo wiggled, but he still didn't loosen his grip. They might be nearly the same height, but Luca was strong. Easily strong enough to deal with this worm.

"What did I *just* say?" Luca asked in a low, furious voice.

"Fine, fine, do whatever you want with him. It's not like we were going to date anyway."

"No shit," Luca said. Finally let go and took a step back. Took a short, deep breath. "Now, on to actually *important* business."

"What?" Giana looked shocked, eyes wide. "But—"

"Keep up," Luca barked. It wasn't just Enzo's stupid crap causing his temper to bubble up, but the fact that he'd been having a spectacular morning and it seemed both Giana and Enzo were determined to destroy every bit of it with their bullshit. "We're trying to save your business here."

"Right."

"As I was saying before Enzo decided to grace us with his presence, these documents," Luca said, gesturing toward the contract Giana had printed out, "will protect both of us."

It was the kind of contract Matteo and Nicoletta should have had her sign from the beginning, if they were going to lend her their money and the recipes. They should have protected themselves. Protected the brand.

Luca wasn't all that surprised he had to clean up the mess now; part of him had come to expect it.

Giana signed. Enzo signed, because Luca insisted on it, even though according to Giana she had yet to officially give him any part of the business. Someone, Luca decided, had to make him give a shit, and apparently that was going to be him.

At least Enzo kept quiet, but the sulkiness in his expression was more intense than normal. Luca ignored it.

He agreed that they would use the rest of the frozen meatballs and sauce this week. Next week, starting Monday, they would be making fresh every day.

"And the bread," Luca added. "I'll contract with Oliver to make it." He shot a hard look at Enzo, daring him to say anything. But he still stayed sullenly silent. *Thank God for small blessings.*

"I don't know if we can afford that," Giana argued.

"I'll make sure you can," Luca said. "I'll be going over your financials with a fine-tooth comb this morning, while you and Enzo prep for the lunch crowd today."

He'd been afraid she'd argue with him, but she just looked relieved.

Maybe happy someone else was going to be taking on the financial burden, at least for a little while.

God knew Enzo had never given her a break.

But as he settled down in the little office off the kitchen with Giana's laptop and booted it up, Luca found he couldn't quite focus.

It wasn't the very healthy dose of distraction Oliver provided.

It wasn't how he'd sincerely wanted to beat Enzo's face in and hadn't been able to.

It was the way Chiara had said, *that makes sense*. And the false note in her *nothing* that had followed his question.

He'd let it go, but it was bothering him still, lingering in the back of his mind.

He'd been in Indigo Bay for four days now and he'd barely heard anything from California. The regular reports had been uploaded, of course, and he'd reviewed them last night, as Oliver had slept next to him in bed.

But there'd been no emergencies or problems or even minor panics. Luca had worked at the restaurants for years—for basically his entire life—and he knew how unusual that was. There was always *something*, and surely everyone back home knew to contact him in case something came up. Not just because they thought he should be informed, but because typically, Luca was the only one who could truly solve anything.

He liked it that way.

Loved having his finger on the pulse of every single one of the restaurants.

And there'd been nothing. For *four days.*

Luca pulled his phone out of his pocket, trying to ignore the way his heartbeat had increased with the beginnings of his own panic, and sent two texts.

One to his father, who was the world's worst liar, with a simple question about how everything was going.

Another to Marco, asking if he'd heard about the veal price increase.

And since he hadn't quit thinking about what he and Oliver had talked about last night, a third, before he could change his mind, to Gabe. He didn't think he'd respond, but it was worth trying. Worth reaching out. Oliver had said so, and he seemed to have a very solid head on his shoulders.

Maybe it was time to really put things in the past, between him and Gabe.

He couldn't quite settle down until he got responses, at least from Matteo and Marco, but it was still really early in California and really, *really* early for anyone who worked in the restaurant business. He probably wouldn't hear for a few hours, but at least he'd reached out.

And, Luca reasoned, if something catastrophic had happened, they *would* have told him. They wouldn't have been able to keep it a secret.

It wasn't quite the reassurance he wanted—he wouldn't get that until his concerns were alleviated—but it was enough to settle him down and let him lose himself in the numbers on Giana's laptop.

Chapter Nine

A FEW HOURS LATER, Luca stretched, his back popping as he exhaled hard.

At some point, Giana had brought him a salami and provolone panini, and he'd eaten it with one hand while he'd read the screen, trying to figure out the solution to Giana's financial conundrum.

She could, he believed, barely afford the changes they were making.

But in the end, if business increased because of the improvements, it would make all the difference.

Luca glanced at his watch, surprised it was almost two p.m.

The bakery closed at three, and he wanted to talk to Oliver about the bread before that.

They hadn't made plans for today, but then Luca hadn't been sure he'd even be here today.

He checked his phone and realized, even though it was eleven a.m. in California, he hadn't gotten an answer from his father. Marco had merely texted back that yes, he knew about the veal increase, but he didn't think it necessitated a pricing change on their end.

And like he'd expected, nothing from Gabe. It shouldn't have hurt, but it did, anyway.

Luca made a frustrated sound in the back of his throat as he grabbed his suit jacket and headed out into the restaurant.

He passed by Enzo, who was washing dishes. Enzo glared, but didn't say anything.

Giana was out in the front, cleaning tables.

"I'm going to see about the bread," he told her.

"Are you really sure Oliver's the best choice?" Giana asked. "We could just keep getting bread from—"

"Yes, and *no*," Luca said firmly.

"But—"

Luca raised an eyebrow.

"It's just that he's our competitor, should we really be giving him business?"

"Actually, he's not," Luca pointed out dryly. "His lunch menu is limited, and frankly, I think he makes most of his money from his commercial baking enterprise. You should know that, Giana. You worked for him."

"Not for very long," she defended.

"Still," Luca said.

"It's just . . . *Enzo*," Giana said, and then she was wringing her hands. "Oliver puts him in such a bad mood."

"That is one hundred percent Enzo's problem. If he wants to sulk like a child over someone who isn't interested in him, that's his choice. But this is business."

"So you aren't going to buy Oliver's bread because . . ." Giana hesitated, no doubt aware she was beginning to cross over into uncertain territory.

Because she was.

Luca felt his temper flaring again, hot and wild inside him, at even the insinuation he was buying Oliver's bread because he was *Oliver*.

"No."

She threw up her hands. "I'm just saying—"

"No."

Giana didn't say anything for a long moment. "Fine. If it has to be Oliver, then it has to be Oliver."

"Unless," Luca replied in a silky voice, "you decide we can hire a part-time baker to come in every morning to bake fresh bread, yes, it has to be Oliver. Trust me, after spending the morning with your books, you do *not* have the budget for that."

"I know I don't," she said stiffly.

"Then it's settled," Luca said. "I'll see you back here at eight tomorrow."

"So early?"

"So early," Luca retorted and let the door close behind him.

He was so fucking tired of arguing with her. Tired of dealing with her ass of a son. But they were still family, still *his* family. They were *Morettis*. Why had he dedicated himself to this family if he was going to just reject them the moment they began to annoy him? How many times had he fought with his parents? Or his siblings? Too many times to count. They'd gotten past it—at least mostly, if he was counting Gabe here—but that didn't mean it didn't happen regularly. But he still worked hard, *this* hard, because he cared. Because he loved them.

He didn't know Giana and Enzo enough to feel the same way, but in the end that didn't matter, because they were still Morettis. He wasn't going to give up on them, either, just because they had an undeniable knack for pissing him off.

But the moment he pushed open the door to Sweetie Pie's, that same delectable scent of sugar and butter and cinnamon wrapping around him like dejá vu, to his surprise, Luca discovered all his anger and frustration began to melt away.

"Hello." The red-haired lady was back at the front counter, and her smile today was especially bright.

No doubt another person who'd discovered he'd taken their town's favorite baker out on a date the night before.

At least she looked happy about it.

"Hi." Luca found smiling back at her was surprisingly easy. "I'm Luca, by the way. Luca Moretti." He extended his hand across the counter, and she shook it.

"So you're Giana's nephew," she said. "I'm Marjorie. We worked here together for a bit, before she opened Nonna's."

"That's what I hear," Luca said.

"Coffee?" she asked. "And another spice twist? Or I think we might have a cranberry walnut scone left. Oliver made those special this morning. Think he had a hankering for them."

The way Marjorie was eyeing him made Luca wonder if there was some mysterious connection between a night of good sex and a desire to make scones the next morning. He would have to ask Oliver.

Speaking of Oliver . . .

"Coffee, yes, and—" He'd intended to say no to both the pastry and the scone, but with the aroma in his nostrils it was proving to be tougher to resist.

Kind of like the man who ran this place.

"And the scone," Marjorie finished with a knowing grin. "They're very good. Joy's recipe, you know, but Oliver has a knack even she doesn't have. Which . . ." She mimed locking her lips with a key. "You did not hear from me."

"Naturally." He hesitated. "And Oliver, if he's free?"

She shot him a knowing look, which he'd fully expected. "I think he's working on some testing in the back, but I can't see why you shouldn't go back there."

Luca raised an eyebrow. "That's allowed?"

"Normally? Absolutely not. But," Marjorie leaned over the counter, her voice lowered, "I think he'd make an exception for you."

"Okay."

She turned, filling his coffee cup from the carafe behind her, and he went to pull out his wallet, but she waved it away. "On the house," she said.

Luca frowned.

"Specifically, per Oliver's instructions," she said.

Sipping the coffee, he was not surprised to discover it was just as good as it had been yesterday.

"Well, I'll have to thank him," Luca said.

The corner of her mouth quirked up. "You sure will. I'll heat up your scone and drop it off in the back when it's done. Just go around the side; I'll let you into the door," she said.

He followed her instructions, still sipping his delicious coffee, and then went through the door to the bakery.

It was warm back here, with the row of ovens at the rear of the building, and full of shiny professional equipment.

Oliver, as Luca had expected, knew exactly what he was about.

The man himself was bending over one of the tall stainless steel counters, rolling out dough with fluid, confident movements.

"Hey," Luca said. Suddenly and very weirdly uncertain. They hadn't talked about this. Well, they *had*. Sort of. They'd both expressed interest in a second date, but maybe that had just been the romance of the story Oliver had told him, the magic of the stars, and then the really fantastic sex.

The situation under the bright light of day might be very different.

Oliver glanced up, and his smile when he saw Luca standing there proved maybe it wasn't different at all.

"Hey." Oliver didn't stop rolling but the heat in his eyes as he swept Luca's body head to toe told him that he wasn't unwelcome. The opposite, in fact.

"Marjorie said I could come back . . ." Luca trailed off.

"Oh yeah, of course. I had a feeling you might stop by."

"Thanks for the coffee, by the way," Luca said.

Oliver smiled. "We can correct that to, I was *hoping* you'd be by. Optimistically, with good news."

"That I've got," Luca said. "Giana signed our agreement this morning. So not only do I need bread from you, I'll be around at least another couple of weeks. Unless you get sick of me."

"Not likely," Oliver said. "Did she continue to protest too much?"

"Yes, but that battering ram we talked about?"

Oliver raised an eyebrow. "Yeah?"

"She called me at six a.m. with her answer," Luca said with a sigh. "Her version of punishment, no doubt."

"No doubt," Oliver agreed.

"What are you making?" Luca took a few steps closer. He really wanted to kiss Oliver, but this didn't seem like the time or the place. Now that he was sticking around, he was going to get plenty of chances.

He wanted every single one of them.

"Testing some new sausage pastries," Oliver explained. He gestured toward a pan of coiled sausages on a baking tray, that looked like they'd already been partially roasted, their skins beginning to crackle. "I was thinking, caramelized onions, some grainy brown mustard, maybe a bit of sharp white cheddar, all wrapped up in a flaky package with the sausage as the centerpiece."

"Feels a bit British," Luca observed.

"That's the idea," Oliver said. "But I wasn't happy with the dough I used before. It was a variation of our savory pie dough, and it didn't work as well as I wanted. So I'm trying some puff pastry."

"You make your own puff pastry?" Luca knew Oliver was a baking god, but this was really taking it a step too far. Everyone else he knew bought theirs frozen, because that particular type of dough was tricky, finicky, and a pain in the ass to make, with all the layers and layers of butter folded in to make it flaky and delicious.

But of course, Oliver would ignore the easy way out and make his own.

Oliver grinned. "Hell yes I do. We make everything here."

"You churn your own butter? Mill your own flour? Harvest your own salt?" Luca teased.

The look Oliver flashed him was full of heat, and Luca patted himself on the back for not just bending him right over the counter and kissing him so fiercely neither of them could breathe.

"Within reason, okay?" Oliver retorted without much heat. He took out a knife and began to cut out big triangles of the dough.

Luca's phone vibrated in his pocket and he pulled it out, glancing at the screen. Hoping the text was from his father, but it wasn't. It was from Chiara, who'd clearly just sat down and looked at the photos he'd sent earlier. **Needs work**, she said, **but we can spruce it up.** And then a second message came through immediately after: **Who created that incredible menu board?**

Luca texted back: **Shockingly, your cousin Enzo.**

When he slipped his phone back into his pocket, Oliver was occupied brushing mustard on the rectangles of pastry.

"Sorry," Luca said, belatedly realizing maybe he shouldn't have been rude and looked at his phone. But what if it had been Matteo? Finally telling him what the heck was going on back home?

If anything was going on at all?

But Oliver just waved off his apology with the pastry brush. "No big deal," he said. "I get it. Everything okay?"

He considered saying *yes, everything's fine.* With anyone else, he probably would've. But instead, Luca discovered he *wanted* to tell Oliver about his worry. Because Oliver would understand? Or was it more than that?

"No," he said slowly. "Or yes. Maybe? I don't know. That's the problem. I left four days ago, and in my experience, things go wrong like clockwork and four days is the longest I can imagine without an emergency of some kind."

"You think they're not telling you?" Oliver glanced over at him, raising an eyebrow. "But don't you have your hands full here with Giana and Enzo? They know what you're doing here in Indigo Bay."

For a split second, Luca almost regretted saying anything at all. Oliver didn't understand after all. Didn't he know that only *Luca* could satisfactorily handle problems?

Of course he didn't. He didn't know how the Moretti clan routinely ran around clucking like chickens with their heads lopped off.

"But," Oliver continued in a casual tone, like Luca wasn't currently swamped with doubt and regret, "I get it. I haven't taken a vacation in five years, because I don't trust anyone to handle things the way *I* would handle things at the bakery. Especially if something went wrong. So, like I said, I get it." He paused. "Anything in particular freak you out or is it just how long you've been gone?"

Luca let out a breath. He hadn't realized how much it mattered that Oliver understood, until he had. "I talked to my sister Chiara this morning. She's got a knack for design, and I'm trying to get her to put together a plan to spruce up the deli. She remembered I was here, and then said, *oh, that makes sense.* That was weird on its own, but after that, she totally clammed up when I asked her about it."

"So it *could* be nothing," Oliver pointed out. "Surely if there was something really bad, your father would've messaged you."

"Or my brother Marco. He runs the high-end steakhouse, and when I'm not around, though it's not like that happens all that often, he and my father handle things."

"So, they're handling things now, then," Oliver said. It sounded so fucking reasonable, so why couldn't Luca believe it?

"Except my father ignored my text, and Marco sent me a total garbage response."

Luca didn't miss the glimmer of a smile playing on Oliver's lips. "Anyone ever tell you that you're a bit paranoid?"

Had they?

Absolutely. They usually weren't quite so nice about it, or quite as charming when they said it. Luca shouldn't be surprised Oliver had thought it though, no matter how kindly he'd said it. Because he *was* paranoid.

What if Carlos had had another drunken meltdown over his girlfriend? What if, even worse, he'd *quit*?

What if the wine delivery didn't come in?

What if they ran out of tomatoes? Or mozzarella? Or chicken?

What if, what if, what if . . .

Luca knew imagining all the things that could go wrong was a quick path to insanity. Yet he was doing it anyway.

"Yes," he said shortly. "I've definitely heard that before."

But Oliver's expression, as he settled the sausages into their nests of mustard and caramelized onions, was free of judgment.

"This is good for you, then," Oliver said. "Being here, in Indigo Bay, and letting them handle things."

"But—"

Oliver finished crimping the edges of his pastry and picked up the tray with flour-covered hands. Slid it into one of the free oven bays. "Listen," he said, his tone suddenly full of steel, "either they can handle it or they can't. You can't always be there, for every single thing."

"But—" Luca tried to interrupt him again, but Oliver wouldn't let him. Stopped right in front of him and without bothering to wipe his hands, placed them right on his shoulders, no doubt dusting them liberally with flour. But Luca wasn't thinking about that. He was thinking about Oliver's sweet lips and his floppy hair and the gentle toughness in his hazel eyes.

The way he'd kissed him back.

The desperate pleas he'd made as Luca had coaxed him toward orgasm.

"No." Oliver stopped him again, before he could keep arguing. "You *can't.*"

Then he reached up, and they were kissing again.

Oliver smelled sweet, but a different kind of sweet. The scent of the caramelized onions and the sausages clung to him, and it should've been a turnoff. Just like the flour all over his suit.

But Luca lost himself in it the moment their lips touched.

Oliver made a little questioning groan in the back of his throat as his mouth opened underneath Luca's, and Luca ground his hardening cock against his thigh before he could stop himself.

Before he could stop himself seemed to be an occurrence that happened a lot around Oliver.

"Oh shit," a voice echoed behind them, and suddenly Luca's arms were empty again.

It was that red-haired lady. *Marjorie*, was that her name? She was standing at the entrance to the kitchen, holding a plate.

Oh, his scone.

He took the plate from her and tried not to blush the same bright red as her hair as she shot him a knowing look.

Oliver had retreated to the other side of the kitchen, pretending to check something at the oven.

At least they'd only been kissing? Okay, they'd also been half a minute away from humping each other helplessly, maybe, but Luca believed—he *had* to believe—that both of them would've realized and stopped before anything questionable happened in the middle of Oliver's bakery.

"You enjoy that . . .scone," Marjorie said with a wink and a grin, before she disappeared through the door toward the front.

Luca broke off a piece of scone and popped it in his mouth. Couldn't help the moan that escaped him as he tasted the richness on his tongue.

"Good, huh?" Oliver was back. He still looked flushed, but whether that was from embarrassment or arousal, it was hard to say.

Embarrassment, Luca insisted to himself, because if he thought about Oliver's milky pale skin naked and flushed with pleasure, he was going to lose even *his* vaunted self-control all over again.

"My mom makes the best scones in town," Oliver said. He reached in and took a piece, too, savoring it as he chewed. "Though these are pretty good."

"Marjorie said yours are better," Luca said. *Everything you make is better.*

But Oliver just laughed. "She *would*, though Joy would kill her if she heard that."

"That's exactly what Marjorie said."

"Trusting you with town secrets? Marjorie must like you," Oliver said. Luca had an inkling from the look in Oliver's eyes that she wasn't the only one.

"Still?"

Oliver shrugged, and there was that same flush, coming back. He reached up and brushed the flour off his shoulders. "Sorry, I made a mess out of you."

"In more ways than one," Luca teased.

Oliver's hazel eyes were luminous, even in the harsh fluorescent lighting of the kitchen as he gazed up at him.

"What are you doing tonight?" Luca asked, before he could stop himself.

There it was again. *Before he could stop himself.*

"Well, I was sorta hoping *you* might be free," Oliver said.

"There's no kitchen at the Inn, but I was thinking . . ." Luca shoved the part of his brain that kept yelling how he didn't do this, not for anyone, not ever before. "Hoping, actually, that I could cook you a meal."

Oliver raised an eyebrow. "You want to make me dinner?"

That sounds serious, the unspoken end of that sentence, echoed between them. Maybe it wouldn't be with anyone else, but they both cared so deeply about food. It was an intrinsic part of their lives. Oliver must know Luca didn't cook for just anyone. But Luca didn't look away, didn't flinch.

It is, he wanted to say in silent response, but he didn't.

Because that would be totally crazy, and he was Luca Moretti. He didn't do crazy things. He was steadfast and certain and *cautious*, more than anything else.

"Yes," Luca finally said. "Yes, I do."

"I suppose I could always invite you over to my place," Oliver said.

Luca had a sudden and terrible feeling he'd overstepped. "But of course, you don't have to do that, not unless you want to," he said quickly.

"But I do," Oliver promised, and he was smiling again, reaching up and patting Luca's cheek. No doubt getting flour all over him again. Luca, who normally *hated* mess, discovered his feelings about it greatly depended on who was making the mess. "You wanna come over tonight? Cook me dinner? Seduce me in my kitchen?"

"All of the above, *yes*," Luca said.

"Now that important thing is settled . . ." Oliver hesitated. "Did you want to talk about the bread order?"

"Oh, yes, we should." Luca, who never found himself getting distracted from business, discovered he'd completely forgotten about his supposed purpose in coming to the bakery.

That's because it was never really why you came.

The truth made Luca squirm as Oliver walked over to a small room tucked away from the kitchen and grabbed a clipboard. He was flipping through some pages when Luca leaned over and read some of the notations.

"You're still using paper?"

"Just for this," Oliver said, jabbing him lightly in the ribs. "Don't give me shit. Some of us like our paper. Don't worry, there isn't a big overflowing box full of paper receipts in my office."

"I'm relieved," Luca said dryly. "And so is your accountant."

"How much bread do you need? And what kinds?"

"Sourdough loaves, maybe thirty a week? At least at first? Maybe fifty after a month?"

Oliver scribbled that down. "What else?"

Luca hesitated. He wanted to add a few things to the menu, items that had done well in their deli in Napa, but for the paninis he needed focaccia.

In the Napa deli, they baked it fresh every day from Nonna's recipe. But Luca had practically sworn a blood oath to never give one of her recipes to a non-family member.

What would Giana say if he shared it with Oliver?

Would she tell Nicoletta and Matteo? That seemed very likely.

He could already imagine their disappointment, the painfully sympathetic tinged with betrayal look on their faces that said they understood he'd lost his head to a cute guy and betrayed the family.

"You make focaccia?" It wouldn't be *Nonna's* but it was Oliver's so it could hardly be bad.

"Yes," Oliver said. "Not on the regular, but I can. How many pans?"

"Two, every other day," Luca said.

He told himself that he wasn't betraying Oliver by not sharing the recipe. He was not betraying Nonna and his *family* by keeping the recipe a secret, the way it had always been.

"Sure thing," Oliver said, making more notes on the schedule on his clipboard.

"What are you topping yours with?" Luca asked.

"Rosemary, or thyme? Roasted garlic? Just sea salt? There's options. It's up to you."

"Rosemary and sea salt, please," Luca said. He shouldn't be so surprised to see the business-focused Oliver. He knew that version of Oliver existed. There was no way Sweetie Pie's was as successful as it was without focus. Luca should know. But he was still surprised by Oliver's sudden brisk professionalism.

"Delivery early or late?" Oliver glanced up when Luca didn't answer right away. "Do you want to ask Giana?"

"Early," Luca said firmly. "She's not going to like it, but it's what she should do." Bread, even well-wrapped bread, could turn stale overnight. And that was exactly what they were trying to avoid.

"You gonna get more five a.m. bludgeoning phone calls?" Oliver asked, setting the clipboard on one of the bare counters.

"It's possible," Luca conceded. Giana was not happy, and if it was possible, Enzo was even more pissed off.

"I bet Enzo wasn't particularly pleased either, cause I'm sure Andrew told the whole town who he served last night," Oliver said. "Did he make things hard for you?"

Luca rolled his eyes. "No, he couldn't possibly. He's more of an annoyance than anything else, but the way he keeps talking about you pisses me off."

"Oh, he's been that way forever," Oliver said, dismissing it with a casual wave of a hand. "It's no big deal. It doesn't bother me."

"It bothers *me*," Luca said slowly. "He was a jerk and you should be *allowed* to not go on a second date with someone."

"Well, *yeah*, but explain that to Enzo," Oliver said with a chuckle.

"I did."

"Really?" Oliver sounded surprised. Maybe not at his admission, but at the steel in his tone.

"Really. I'm not happy with how he keeps talking crap, and I let him know I'll be extracting a pound of flesh for every time it happens again."

Oliver looked at him, jaw dropped. Then he threw his head back and laughed. "Oh my God, I'd have paid good money to see you threatening him. Did he shit himself? Did Giana freak out? She seriously babies him, you know. It's a problem."

"Metaphorically, of course, *yes,* he totally shit himself," Luca said with a fierce grin he couldn't hold back—and didn't even want to. It had been satisfying to wipe that sulk off Enzo's face, even for a moment. "And yes, Giana freaked out. I think she believed he wouldn't stop, and I'd make good on my threats."

"Would you have?" Oliver asked speculatively, glancing up at Luca from under light brown lashes.

"I'd have made him regret it for sure." Violence was definitely not the answer, but he'd have done something, Luca knew that much.

He really didn't like how Enzo harassed Oliver.

Or how Enzo had the nerve to be annoyed about Luca taking Oliver out instead.

"Just wait til he finds out you're getting a second date."

"I'm looking forward to it, though frankly, I think he's already guessed."

"I'll have to make your deliveries myself and make sure to give you a nice big wet kiss right in front of him," Oliver said, a determined look in his eyes.

"Any time you want to give me one of those, I'm never going to complain," Luca said.

"I'll have to keep that in mind," Oliver teased. "What time do you want to come over tonight?"

"Five is good, again." Luca was already thinking of the food he'd cook Oliver. *His* food in Oliver's mouth. It filled him with a savage sense of satisfaction.

"I'll text you my address," Oliver said pulling his phone out of his pocket, and laughed, , probably realizing he didn't have Luca's phone number.

Luca took the phone, added his number in, opening a text window so Oliver could send him his address.

"You know—" Oliver nudged him. "—now that I can bother you all the time, I probably will."

"Anytime," Luca said and realized as he left the bakery ten minutes later, Marjorie's knowing smile still lingering in his vision as he'd said goodbye, that he meant it.

Oliver could bother him *anytime.*

Chapter Ten

Oliver headed home just after four, after he'd finished cleaning up his empty bakery.

Marjorie had insisted, again, on taking the deposit by the bank, because, as she put it, he had "*another* hot date tonight."

He did. He really, really did.

There was a flare of excitement in his stomach at the thought of Luca here, in his house, as he walked around, picking up the random clutter that always seemed to gather during the week, when he was at work more than he was ever at home.

It didn't take him long to tidy up and then he moved onto the bedroom.

New sheets, definitely. He threw the dirty ones in the wash and pulled out the nicer high-thread-count set Joy had gotten him for Christmas that he never used because it seemed silly to bother for just him.

But it's not just you, tonight.

After making the bed, he moved onto the kitchen. Because he was a pro and there was nothing worse in the universe than a dirty kitchen, his was spotless. There was nothing to be done there, except lean against the counter and imagine Luca in here. Imagine what kind of delicious dinner he might prepare for him.

Definitely something Italian. Definitely something from one of his Nonna's recipes.

In any other situation, Oliver might think he was pressing his luck. Surely, someone like Luca might save a *Nonna* meal for someone he really, really liked.

But Oliver wasn't blind. He could see the light in Luca's dark eyes whenever he glanced in his direction. The *how* and *why* still baffled him a little bit, but he knew Luca liked him a lot, and the sentiment was, without question, returned.

Sure, he'd been horny and Luca was attractive and he was attracted to him, but Oliver didn't think he'd be doing this if that was all it was.

If that was all it was, he'd have suggested dinner out again. Or just meeting up later in Luca's room, for a quick, yet totally satisfying, fuck.

This wasn't just about sex.

Oliver knew it, and maybe that knowledge should fill him with apprehension, but it didn't.

It filled him with excitement, instead.

He headed to the shower, wondering as he washed every inch of his body if Luca would still say he tasted sweet.

Or if the soap and water scrubbed away all the aroma from his day at the bakery. It hadn't yesterday, and Oliver felt the burn of anticipation as he dressed.

Precisely at five p.m., there was a knock on the door.

Of course Luca was on time, exactly. Oliver should be relieved he wasn't *early*.

He opened the door and Luca was standing outside, carrying a paper bag full of groceries and wearing a T-shirt and jeans. Oliver had never seen him look so casual, but he looked amazing.

So freaking good in fact, Oliver was proud he didn't immediately suggest he remove Luca's clothes with just his teeth.

"Hey," Luca said.

"Come on in," Oliver offered, opening the door wider. "I realize I should've asked you if you needed anything . . ."

"No," Luca insisted with a bit of a smirk as he walked into the house. "I wanted to surprise you, anyway."

"With?" Oliver asked archly as the door closed behind Luca. "I know you texted me if I liked mushrooms, and *yes*, as I said, I do. Chicken marsala?"

The smirk spread into a wide smile. "Like I'd *ever* be that predictable," Luca said.

"Kitchen's through here," Oliver said, leading the way. He hopped up on the counter, letting his legs swing as Luca set his grocery bag down. "You just let me know what you need."

"I'm sure I'll find whatever it is." Luca glanced around. "This is a nice house."

"Small," Oliver said. It *was* small, probably much smaller than any of the houses Luca was familiar with. He'd done a little digging on his break today, and yes, the Morettis ran a set of *very* successful restaurants in Napa. There was also a branded line of pasta sauces and antipasto spreads, sold in specialty markets and gourmet stores. The

Moretti family was, without question, definitely well-off, and even more so now that Luca had taken over the management.

"But it suits you," Luca said, beginning to lift items out of his paper bag, starting with a bottle of wine.

"This was actually my parents' first house," Oliver said. "I was born here. We moved a few years after that, to a bigger house, but when it came up for sale, I thought buying it was a nice full circle feeling. Of course, I changed some things."

"Like the kitchen," Luca said, sounding amused. "You have an opener? Glasses?"

"Opener in this drawer," Oliver said, sliding open the drawer underneath him and pointing, "and glasses up in that cupboard."

It was sexy as hell to watch the utter competence in Luca's movements as he opened the bottle of wine and poured some into the glasses.

"Yes, I did have the kitchen remodeled. And a few of the non-load-bearing walls removed. Paint. And new flooring. The seventies kind of owned this house before I bought it," Oliver said, taking one of the glasses from Luca's hand. The wine was a rich, deep ruby color, and he had a feeling it would be really good. Because Luca wouldn't tolerate anything less.

"Well, I like it," Luca said, like he was daring someone to argue with him. "Especially the kitchen. It's not big, but it's . . .well designed."

Oliver lifted his glass and Luca met him halfway. "To a guy who knows how to give a real compliment," he said. "Cheers."

After taking a sip of the wine, he wasn't surprised at all at the deep fruity flavor that bloomed across his tongue.

"This is really, *really* good. You got this here? In the land of sweet wine and muscadine?" Oliver raised an eyebrow, craning his neck to see the bottle's label.

Luca flushed. "Well, to be honest . . .no."

"No?" The second sip of wine was usually better, but in this case, it blew the first one right out of the water.

"I . . .uh . . .shipped some wine here from Napa," Luca confessed.

"You *shipped* wine here?"

"In my defense," Luca said, finishing unloading his bag, "I know there isn't good dry wine here, and I didn't know what I'd find in the stores, *and* I was planning on being here a few weeks. It's sort of a habit—maybe a bad one?—to enjoy a glass of wine at night, as I review the books from the day."

"It's not bad," Oliver said. "Especially not when you share your wine with *me*."

"I can do that," Luca said, tilting his head. Regarding him. "You like wine, then?"

"I like *good* wine," Oliver corrected with a grin. "So, you gonna tell me what you're making me yet?"

"Mushroom ravioli with a tomato sauce," Luca said. "And a salad to start. You like fennel?"

"Love fennel. We don't get a lot of gourmet cooking here, but in Charleston . . .that was the one thing I loved about it. The food."

"I've never been, but it sounds like a great place to go."

"Ugh, it was great for that. Not so great otherwise, and I don't really miss it. But to be able to go to a really good meal every once in a while? That would be nice."

"Rudy's is it, then?" Luca asked as he opened a bag of flour, labeled as special for pasta.

"Wait," Oliver said, "you're going to make your own pasta?"

Luca shot him a look. "What do I look like? Someone who *buys* it?"

"Fair, fair, I just—"

"You literally just made your own puff pastry today, when everyone else I know gets it from a store." Luca sounded amused as he scooped flour onto the counter.

"Apparently I'm not the only perfectionist in town now, but really, homemade pasta is the best."

"I know." He sounded smug now, and maybe if Oliver didn't know him as well as he was getting to, he might've been turned off by all that arrogant certainty. But he knew more about Luca now. He knew there were depths to him. And it wasn't like Oliver actually disagreed with him.

Plus, competence porn was totally a thing.

He settled back on his counter perch with his fucking fabulous wine and prepared to be turned on, just by watching Luca make pasta.

His hands were sure as he cracked eggs, sprinkled in salt and then, after whisking the wet ingredients together with a fork, began to slowly work in the flour using just those same strong, confident hands.

Oliver remembered the way they'd felt on his body last night, and he shivered a little, even more turned on than he'd expected.

Luca glanced up.

"You have great hands, that's all," Oliver said, aware of how inane and utterly crush-struck he sounded. He wasn't even really ashamed of it.

"That's *all*?" Luca teased. "You can't just say that and nothing else."

"You just . . .know what you're doing."

Oh, boy, did he.

"I'm not the only one," Luca pointed out dryly as he continued to knead the bright yellow dough in slow, confident movements, the muscles on his forearms flexing in the most distracting way.

"You cook often?" Oliver asked. Wanted to picture him in his restaurants, at his kitchen at home. Wondered what it would look like, what *Luca* would look like, in it.

He knew he'd never see it, not in person, so maybe it would be enough to imagine it.

"Not as much as I'd like, honestly," Luca said. "Though the week before I came here, our head chef at the main Nonna's location . . .he had a bad breakup, got drunk on the Marsala, and I didn't have a choice but to sub for him the whole night."

"You cooked on your line all night?"

Luca grinned, all those white teeth flashing a bit like a wolf's. "I was definitely out of practice. But no, I'm . . .I hate to say it, but I'm too busy to really cook the way I used to. The way I want to."

"You're welcome."

Luca glanced over at him.

"For giving you an opportunity tonight," Oliver teased.

"A generous soul," Luca teased right back.

That was the problem, Oliver thought, as he watched Luca set the pasta dough aside and pull out a pan—for the mushroom filling, he said—he could not only imagine Luca in his own kitchen, making dinner for both of them, but he could see him like this, six months from now, even six years from now.

He'd tried not to dwell on the fact that whatever this was between them had a time limit, but at moments like this, it was hard not to resent it.

It was so fucking unfair that he'd finally found someone he couldn't get enough of, and they lived on the opposite side of the country. Oliver didn't even bother thinking about the possibility that Luca might move here. His whole life, his business, and his *family*, who he clearly loved, were all back in California.

There was no point in even thinking about it, because nothing was going to change.

Enjoy this moment, because it's all you're gonna get.

"You alright?" Luca asked.

Oliver shook off his sudden melancholy, realized that Luca had been talking to him the whole time, as Oliver's chef knife had flashed and decimated a whole container of mushrooms, two shallots and several cloves of garlic.

Whether Luca cooked often for himself or not, he had exceptional knife skills.

Oliver's surprise must've shown on his face, because Luca said, "My Nonna never would've tolerated if we didn't know how to chop properly."

"Of course," Oliver said, dredging up a smile. "Come here."

"But—"

Oliver reached out a hand and hooked it around Luca's waist. The kitchen really wasn't that big, and that made reeling him in possible.

Made it possible to tug him closer, then frame Luca's face with his hands and kiss him.

The sudden rush of anticipated pleasure was almost enough to lose the rest of his bitterness. *You can have this now.*

And so he did. He kissed Luca sweet and hard and a million shades in between and reminded himself that he was living in the moment.

Not in the future.

When Oliver finally lifted his mouth off Luca's, his eyes were glazed over and unfocused.

"What was that for?" Luca asked, voice low and rough.

"Because I could," Oliver said. Which was truth enough.

"Do you . . ." Luca hesitated.

"Want to go to bed now?" Oliver asked the question and then considered it. He hadn't kissed Luca for that reason, but there was no denying the arousal thrumming through his veins, or his hard cock, straining against the zipper of his jeans.

He definitely wanted him.

But anticipation was part of the pleasure too, and they were grownups, weren't they? Surely, they could sit through making dinner and eating it, first.

"We . . .uh . . .we can have dinner. We *should* have dinner."

Oliver told himself he wasn't disappointed as Luca turned back toward the stove, but he could see the tight line of his back through the cotton fabric of his T-shirt and Oliver had a feeling he wouldn't be the only one struggling to focus on what they should be doing, instead of what they *wanted* to do.

You're going to make the filling, then the sauce, then roll out the dough, and you're going to make raviolis so good the angels would weep, Luca told himself forcibly as he turned toward the stove. He was not going to cut this short and convince Oliver to go to bed with him now, no matter how much he wanted to.

You're a gentleman, he added, as an additional reminder.

Because the last thing he wanted was for Oliver to think this was just about sex.

It really couldn't be anything like what he wanted it to be, but it could be *something,* still.

Fond memories Oliver looked back on, when Luca was long gone, at least.

He took a deep breath and then another one.

Reached for the knob to flick the burner on the stove on.

But instead, at the last moment, gripped it instead.

He turned back to Oliver. Still sitting on the edge of the counter. His hazel eyes were wide, pupils blown.

Luca recognized the look on his face, because he was feeling the exact same way.

"Fuck *should do,*" Luca said and in two steps was back in front of Oliver and they were kissing again, and this time it wasn't so much sweet as it was desperate.

Oliver half-gasped, half-moaned into his mouth and wound his legs around Luca's waist, pulling him in close, until he could feel his cock press against Oliver's.

"Shit," Luca swore, between life-altering kisses, heart thundering as Oliver rubbed against him.

"Bedroom," Oliver ordered and then his arms were around Luca's neck and he was a surprisingly light weight in his arms as Oliver fastened his mouth to his neck and led him, between bone-melting nibbles to his ear, so he'd head the right direction.

Not that it was particularly difficult. The house, as Luca had told Oliver earlier, was small.

So was Oliver's bedroom, but the bed was big, definitely big enough for both of them. He set Oliver down on the edge, on the bright blue quilt, and pulled back for a second.

Tried to slow his labored breathing.

Not from carrying Oliver.

But from how desperately he wanted him.

He'd never felt like this before, half-insane with the need to shed all his clothes, strip the ones from Oliver, and press their bodies together.

Oliver pulled off his shirt and was already wiggling out of his jeans.

Luca swallowed hard as more and more of Oliver's gorgeous skin was revealed.

"Come on," Oliver said enticingly, and that was all the encouragement Luca needed to push his worries to the side.

He stripped his T-shirt and jeans off, and it was so easy to fall right into Oliver's big soft bed, caging him in. Oliver grinned up at him, lifting a hand to trail through his hair, tangling in the short strands near his neck and pulling him down.

"I like this," Luca said softly, before their lips met again.

He did. He couldn't remember ever feeling so light.

Was it the wild, carefree look in Oliver's eyes? The way he didn't try to change him, just accepted him the way he was? Or was it the way Luca's blood surged whenever he looked at him? The sweet taste of his skin, the only sweetness it felt like he'd indulged in, in forever?

Whatever it was, Luca wanted more of it.

He wanted *all* of it.

He leaned down and kissed him, letting his body drop farther down, rubbing his cock against Oliver's, until they were gasping into each other's mouths.

"Please," Oliver begged, eyes wild. "God, *please*."

"You need more, baby? I can give you more."

Oliver nodded wordlessly, and Luca slipped down his body, tasting him here and there. Luca's tongue curling around a nipple, then a nip on his belly. Oliver's abs tensing as Luca's mouth moved lower. How was he still so fucking sweet? Luca would go to the grave not understanding how it was even possible, but loving it nonetheless.

He tugged Oliver's briefs down and slicked his tongue up his cock, giving both of them just a little taste. Oliver uttered a string of garbled praise and begging, so he kept his tongue slow and leisurely, straining against the teasing of his mouth.

Slicking up a finger with his tongue, he slid it down, past Oliver's balls, lower still, circling his hole for a second and then pushing it in, just as he enveloped his cock in his mouth and sucked hard.

Oliver's cries grew louder, and Luca could tell he was close, so he went a little faster, trying to draw his pleasure out as much as he could.

He felt the beat of his own pulse in his head, his blood as hot as it had ever been, his dick a hard, insistent line in his boxer briefs, but he forced his focus to stay on Oliver.

Make him feel good, make him feel the best.

Luca pulled him back from the ledge once, then twice, slowing his movements, just giving him little teasing sucks and pulling his finger out, just tantalizing him with the idea of it, until he was flushed all the way up his chest, to his cheeks. Then Luca finally let him fly, swallowing his cock down and finding that spot inside him with his finger that made him swear.

Oliver shook and pulsed for what felt like forever, Luca dragging it out as much as he could, as he sucked him dry.

When it was finally over, Luca let his cock slip from his mouth and worked his way back up, feeling the little shudders of Oliver's body as he found sensitive spots all over his stomach and chest, then his neck.

His cock rubbed insistently against Oliver's soft belly, even as he tried to avoid it. But he was too hard, too aroused, too close to coming undone himself, just from the pleasure he'd given Oliver.

Oliver's eyes flickered open. That bright hazel drowning him.

"Come 'ere," he said roughly and slid a hand between their bodies, gripping Luca's cock, his tantalizingly brief strokes convincing him to move.

He straddled Oliver's chest, pulling himself upright, but then Oliver shocked him by not just firming his grip, moving it more insistently, pleasure shooting through him at the touch, but raising his chin and licking at the flushed, swollen head.

"Shit," Luca swore, as the two very different touches, one brief and light, the other insistent and forceful, pulled him right toward his orgasm.

Then Oliver's other hand was there and it was tugging on his balls, and Luca dug his fingers into Oliver's chest and bellowed as he came hard.

A stripe of come landed on his chin and then his cheek, and Luca couldn't help the savage sense of possession that rocketed through him at the sight.

Oliver's not yours, he reminded himself, when he could think straight, when he was already reaching for a tissue to help him clean himself up.

But that didn't feel quite right either.

You want Oliver to be yours.

It was never going to happen, because Oliver lived here, had lived here his whole life, had come back here because he'd missed it, had built his business here. He not only knew the story of the town; his family *was* the story of the town.

And Luca had his own obligations. He didn't always enjoy them as much as he wanted. He didn't always feel as secure and *home* as Oliver felt here, but that definitely didn't change anything.

Didn't change the promises he'd made to his Nonna. To Nicoletta and Matteo. To his brothers and sisters, even as they resented him for the work he did to fulfill them.

Luca flopped down on the bed next to Oliver, who turned over, curling into him.

He didn't do cuddling normally, didn't have the time or the inclination, but he pulled Oliver in closer, running a hand down his bare back, reveling in the feel of his soft skin, the firm muscles under his touch.

"That was…great," Oliver said with a happy sigh. "I'm glad we have absolutely no self-control whatsoever."

Luca chuckled, the laugh pulled out of him by the wonder in Oliver's voice. Like he'd truly believed they could resist and was pleasantly surprised they couldn't.

"I suppose I was trying to be a gentleman," Luca said.

"It's more fun that you're not always," Oliver said slyly.

That was the worst of it, wasn't it?

Here was someone, *finally*, who liked Luca for exactly who he was, didn't want to change him, didn't want him to behave differently, and wasn't attracted to him for what he could bring to the table.

He's not for you, Luca reminded himself again, but it was getting harder and harder to believe that was true when it felt so much the opposite.

"If that's the kind of result I get from not being a gentleman, I'll ditch the manners more often," Luca said. To his surprise, meaning it.

"You still going to cook me dinner?"

Luca frowned. "Of course I am."

"Then," Oliver said, draping himself more firmly across Luca's chest, "I see no issues. Gentleman in the kitchen—"

"Do not say freak between the sheets," Luca ordered firmly, but Oliver was already laughing, and it was so easy, so goddamn easy, to just join him.

Twenty minutes later, they were back in the kitchen.

Oliver had returned to his perch, but wearing only his briefs and Luca's T-shirt, which he'd stolen, without much protest from Luca himself.

Luca shot him a look as he turned the knob, lighting the gas flame on the burner. "You look good in it," he said, even though it was, yes, kind of drowning him.

Honestly, the way Oliver looked in his clothes made him want to drag him back to bed all over again.

But he couldn't, because now he really needed to make dinner.

"And you look good without," Oliver said, sticking his tongue out as he picked up his wine. "Real good."

"Thanks," Luca said dryly. He normally wouldn't ever do this, showboat in front of someone and try to cook with just a pair of jeans on—and his Nonna would be undeniably aghast at even the thought of it—but he'd never met anyone he liked as much as Oliver before.

And, well, he wanted Oliver to like him back.

Even if it was a terrible idea. Even if this whole thing had a built-in expiration date, he still wanted it.

So he basked, maybe a little bit too obviously, in Oliver's admiration as he moved around the kitchen, cooking and preparing the filling and then beginning to roll out the pasta dough.

"So tell me more about this festival," he said, as he worked. "Why does Giana think getting into it as a vendor will make a difference for the business?"

Oliver, still perched on the edge of the counter, one side of Luca's T-shirt sliding off his shoulder, rolled his eyes. "Because she's delusional. The vendor applications for the festival closed ages ago. She knows it too. She just thinks she can ask and I'll give in."

"Would you?" Luca hadn't gotten the impression Oliver had a particularly soft spot for his aunt, but maybe he'd read the situation wrong.

"If she had actually sent in a proposal instead of just . . . *please, Oliver, help me, because I need you to,* maybe. As for the festival itself, yeah, it's a pretty big deal. Lots of vendors. Food and local arts and crafts. That type of thing. Plus, lots of very silly love-themed events during the day, like a kissing booth and the dating game. We get a lot of tourists during the weekend."

"So it *would* help," Luca said, trying to approach this from a purely business angle.

"If things were better . . .yes, it might convince some people to try the food who might not normally," Oliver acknowledged, but he didn't sound very certain. "Don't tell me she's got her heart set on this. It's less than two weeks away."

Luca tested the thickness of his pasta and sighed, grabbing Oliver's rolling pin and continuing to roll his pasta. What he wouldn't give for a real pasta maker right now, but he could hear his Nonna's voice in his ear, telling him that back in the old country, they'd always done it by hand and he should stop being so lazy.

"She keeps mentioning it," Luca acknowledged.

"Sounds like Giana," Oliver said ruefully. "Once she gets an idea in her head, it's hard to dissuade her. You know, I tried to convince her not to open the deli?"

Luca couldn't say he was surprised.

"Let me guess, she wouldn't budge."

Oliver nodded. "Wouldn't even *listen*."

"Sounds like a Moretti," Luca said wryly.

"And you're all like this? *All* of you? All seven of you?"

"It would be great if there were only seven of us," Luca said with regret. "It's actually more like twice that. Marcella's married with kids, Dario's engaged, and I know he wants a family. Plus my parents, plus Ren's parents."

"Growing up, I always wanted a big family." Oliver's voice was wistful. "But it was just the three of us and then there were only two of us."

"You're close to your mom, though?" Luca had seen Joy Billings around the Inn a few times since he and Oliver had started dating, and there'd been a part of him that had wanted to introduce himself as more than just Giana's nephew, but he'd stopped himself, because this wasn't like that.

Maybe if he was staying . . .

But he wasn't.

He knew he wasn't.

"Oh yeah," Oliver said, and the melancholy edge of his smile melted away. "Always. She's the one who taught me how to bake."

"And you've apparently eclipsed her," Luca teased.

"It's just easier for me to bake for her, though she still does some things at the Inn herself."

"Uh-huh," Luca said. Not convinced at all, but undeniably charmed by the fact Oliver was the only one in town who didn't realize he'd become better than his teacher.

"So what's the sauce you're going to put these with?" Oliver said, and Luca let him change the subject.

He understood how prickly family could be, even when you were close. Even when you loved them without reservation.

He felt that way about his family all the time.

Which . . .it weighed on him that Matteo still hadn't texted him back, and that Marco had been so close-lipped about everything.

What was going on? The sales for the last few days had been as expected, so it wasn't *that* kind of disaster.

But there had to be one, Luca knew. They wouldn't be so cagey otherwise. But then, he'd never expected them to keep whatever kind of mess they'd made to themselves, either.

"I thought we could go the typical route," Luca said, "and pair the raviolis with a browned butter and sage sauce, but I decided to make my Nonna's famous fresh tomato sauce. It's the best."

"That sounds amazing," Oliver said, sipping his wine. "Did you hear from your dad, by the way?"

"No," Luca said heavily.

"I'm sure everything's fine," Oliver said. But he didn't sound particularly convinced.

Luca was definitely not convinced.

"I just don't get it," he said, putting a big sauté pan on the stove and drizzling olive oil in. To roast the tomatoes, he needed medium heat and lots of garlic and fennel. He added everything to the pan and then tossed it as it began to sizzle. "When I'm home, they can't come running to me fast enough."

"Doesn't that get old though?"

Luca considered this. "Yes, sometimes," he admitted. "But it's . . .it gives me purpose, too, you know?"

"Do you feel like you don't have a purpose if they're not running to you constantly to fix everything?" Oliver asked, tilting his head.

Luca didn't want to think about this, but Oliver was making him do it anyway.

"I'm just saying," Oliver continued, his voice softening—*God*, how was he so damn sweet? Luca wasn't sure he deserved it, at all, not when just a second ago, he'd resented him for bringing it up. "You've got plenty of purpose here."

"Yeah, arguing with Giana about every single thing," Luca grumbled. "Not much of a purpose."

"It is if you save her business," Oliver pointed out. "That's what you came here to do."

Luca shook the pan again, seeing the cherry tomatoes begin to blister and break down.

"So, if she asked really nicely . . .*would* you put her in the festival?" Luca asked. Because Oliver was right, he was here to save her business—and the upcoming festival was the best chance to get the word out that Nonna's had made some significant changes.

Oliver shot him a look. "Really?"

"What if *I* asked you very nicely?" Luca teased as he moved to start slicing his fennel for the salad.

"I'd think about it," Oliver said. "It's not like these things are *very* official, but there are limits to what I can do."

"Somehow, I find that hard to believe," Luca said. "Everyone in this town practically worships you. The festival is about *your family*."

"I'll think about it," Oliver said with a sigh. "I know she could use the help and I do want to give her that."

"Even though you didn't want her to start it in the first place?" Luca arranged the thin slivers of fennel on two plates, along with segmented orange, parsley, and a drizzle of olive oil.

"I just knew Enzo wasn't interested in the business and she was starting it mostly *for* him."

"It's a problem," Luca agreed. One he had yet to figure out how to solve.

But he would.

Ten minutes later, they were sitting cozily on the corner of Oliver's small kitchen table, sharing the food he'd prepared. Oliver hadn't bothered to put pants on, but he'd returned Luca's shirt and found his own.

"This is delicious," Oliver said, as he savored each bite.

They were all Nonna's recipes, of course, the nostalgia and history of them rich in Luca's mouth as he chewed and swallowed, but now, there was something new, too.

Was it Oliver? Was it the slightly different ingredients here?

He wasn't sure.

"I'm so glad you're enjoying it," Luca said, meaning it. He reached out and squeezed Oliver's bare knee.

Felt himself wish that things were different.

Felt himself accept that they just were.

"You've got no idea how much," Oliver said with a grin.

Chapter Eleven

LUCA WAITED THREE DAYS and four more unanswered texts to his father before he finally broke down and called Gabriel.

"What?" his brother barked into the phone, like he hadn't wanted to answer, had felt obligated to, and now wanted to exact his revenge, one annoyed word at a time, on Luca for making him feel too guilty to click decline. "I'm busy."

"Aren't we all?" Luca retorted.

"Well, it must be important," Gabe said, "or you wouldn't be calling me."

That was true.

Though he'd texted him the other day, just because he wanted to, and Gabriel hadn't responded then, either.

It stung. It shouldn't, because Luca had a pretty good idea of why his brother never wanted to talk to him, but that didn't make it ache any less.

"Have you talked to Dad recently?" Luca asked, tamping down his own temper, his own hurt feelings. They'd only make things worse, and as much as they both disliked it, he *needed* Gabe right now. He'd even considered the timing of his call, waiting until it was after five here in Indigo Bay, when the lunch rush at the food truck would've passed.

Oliver was at a festival meeting so he was on his own tonight, and he'd grabbed a salad from the corner store and poured himself a glass of wine while opening his laptop.

He was not missing Oliver. He absolutely was not. They'd just spent a lot of time together in the last few days, that was all.

"Haven't you?" Gabe retorted. "Aren't you there, in his pocket—or maybe he's in yours?—all the goddamn time?"

"No," Luca said shortly.

"No?"

"I'm not in California, you idiot," Luca said. "Didn't anyone tell you? I went to help Giana. I've been here for over a week, and nobody is telling me a fucking thing."

Gabe was silent for a long moment.

"I didn't know, actually," he said. He sounded like he regretted that. Or maybe that was just residual guilt.

That was the thing about being a Moretti. They certainly never lacked guilt; there was always extra to go around.

"How is it?" Gabriel asked, his sentence rushed like as soon as he started saying it, he'd regretted it.

"Indigo Bay? Small. Quiet."

"I meant the deli," Gabe said in a wry voice. "And Giana."

"A mess, and argumentative," Luca admitted. And like the word vomit was contagious, he kept going. "I'm really fucking grateful I never had to come down to LA and fix you."

"Like you'd ever need to," Gabe scoffed.

"Exactly," Luca said with finality.

Gabe was quiet again for a very long moment. For so long, Luca almost asked him if he was still there.

"We're both Morettis, aren't we? Ren and I?"

"And how is our darling cousin Lorenzo?"

"Glaring at me, though I think that's more you by proxy."

"Lovely," Luca said dryly. "I miss him a lot too."

Gabe cleared his throat. "Do you want me to call him? Dad, that is?"

"If you have the time . . ." Luca trailed off, like this hadn't been exactly the reason he'd reached out in the first place.

But had it been?

Or had he just wanted to hear his little brother's voice again? Without him being angry or yelling or arguing with him?

I'm sorry, I fucked it all up.

He wasn't insane enough to say that, but he hoped it was there, unspoken between everything he'd actually said out loud.

"I think I can find the time," Gabe said.

"Good."

Silence fell between them again.

It was time to hang up, before things got really awkward, but crashing into Oliver had changed things already. Changed *him* already. Luca could feel it. Could feel himself trying to be different, even if he wasn't quite sure he could get there.

But damnit, he was going to try anyway.

"Everything good there? How's . . .uh . . .Sean, was it?" Luca stuttered over his name, hoping he'd gotten his brother's boyfriend's name right. Gabe would be pissed if he didn't.

"He's good, we're good," Gabe said, sounding surprised.

Thank God, I got it right.

"We hired some more part-timers at the truck," Gabe said. "We've been busier than ever, so it made sense since we're just now getting ready for the spring and summer here. It'll be a crazy season, for sure."

Luca took a long sip of wine. Discovered he was actually enjoying himself and there wasn't a single ounce of guilt to be found.

"I'm really glad," Luca said, and meant it.

"When are you gonna be back?" Gabe asked casually.

"Oh, not for another two weeks at least. There's this big festival thing here, and Oliver thinks he can convince the food vendor committee to consider Giana's last-minute application. I won't want to miss that, because she'll need the help."

"Oliver?" Luca was three thousand miles away, but he could *hear* Gabe's eyebrows hit his hairline.

"Oh, he's . . .uh . . ." Luca stammered. Why *had* he brought up Oliver? And why couldn't he just say who Oliver was, without making it weird?

Because he couldn't help himself.

His brain was one long sentence of *Oliver, Oliver, Oliver,* and it was a serious problem.

"He's what?" Gabe asked slyly.

"Just uh . . .a guy here. Who owns a bakery."

"Didn't know you had a sweet tooth," Gabe said. He sounded deeply, seriously amused.

"I don't," Luca said shortly.

"Seems otherwise," Gabe teased.

There was a scuffle on the other side of the phone and then suddenly there was Ren's voice in his ear. "Did you finally find someone to unbend you? Remove that enormous stick from your ass?" Ren demanded to know. "Cause if you did, I wanna send him a nice fruit basket. He'll deserve it."

"I date," Luca said defensively. A hell of a lot more than Ren had, at least before he'd finally found himself a boyfriend.

"Sure you do," Ren said.

"It's not . . .not anything," Luca said. Not quite believing it himself. *Because it could be something, if you didn't have to leave.*

But that didn't matter, because he did. The fact that his father wasn't returning any of his texts, and Marco was dodging him . . .that said it all.

He couldn't stay here, couldn't even *dream* of staying here.

"Uh-huh, you keep telling yourself that," Gabe said, chiming in.

Oh great, they'd put him on speakerphone. Now the whole food truck lot probably knew how pathetic he was.

"I suppose you knew you were in love with Sean the whole time," Luca grumbled.

"Yep, even when you showed up to yell at him," Gabe said, sounding very proud of this fact—or the fact he'd managed to weave in a reminder that Luca had acted like a total asshole.

"I didn't *yell*," Luca said. Though he probably had.

"Okay, when you showed up to threaten him. Any better?" Gabe was grinning now. Luca could hear it in his voice. He told himself he deserved this, and at least if Gabe could smile about it or maybe even laugh about it, then maybe he wasn't quite so angry anymore.

Maybe they could finally move past this.

"Better. And . . ." *Apologize now, you dumbass, the moment's begging for it.* The voice in his head sounded surprisingly like Oliver's, and so he listened. "And I'm sorry I did that. You had things under control and I barged in with my usual—"

"Attempts to control everything and everyone? To impose your arrogant Moretti conviction on the situation?" Gabe asked archly.

"Yes." It was not easy to admit it, but apologies weren't supposed to be easy. And he was Luca Moretti, wasn't he? *Easy isn't worth doing,* Nonna had always told him, growing up.

He could almost feel her now, smiling down on him, glad he'd swallowed his pride and made nice with his younger brother.

"See? That wasn't so hard," Ren said. "It's almost like you're a human being now. We really should send this Oliver a fruit basket."

"Do not," Luca ordered. The worst of it was Lorenzo *would*, because he had more of a sense of humor than his brother did. He'd easily find the one Oliver in town who owned a bakery, and a few days later some big extravagant display of fruit would show up on his doorstep and that wouldn't be embarrassing at all.

"Don't worry," Gabe said heroically. "I'll make sure he doesn't."

Now he had to be indebted to his little brother, and wasn't that just annoying as hell.

"Thanks," Luca said shortly.

"So you just want me to call Dad and ask what? Why aren't there are any fires you're making Luca put out from three thousand miles away while he's in the middle of a three-week-long argument with our aunt over her deli?"

Luca sighed. "Something a little more subtle than that, please."

"I'll see what I can do," Gabe promised. "You want me to call Marco, too?"

"No, I'm going to deal with him myself." Marco knew better than to dodge him. He *knew better*, and Luca was going to take some pleasure in reminding him of that particular fact.

"Better him than me," Gabe said.

"Tell Oliver hi for us!" Ren called out.

"I don't know how you tolerate him," Luca grumbled.

"He's actually a hell of a lot better since he started dating Seth," Gabe confided. It was just him again. "Besides, you shouldn't let him needle you like he does."

"And how am I supposed to do that?" He'd been one of Ren's favorite targets from way back when.

"Maybe try that unbending thing a little," Gabe suggested. "He teases you because he can. Because you let him."

"It's just—" Luca began to argue but then stopped. He *was* making himself a target, wasn't he? Why had he never seen that before? Every single time he got all starchy and arrogant, it just made the situation with Ren—and Gabe, too, and honestly, Ilaria and Chiara and some-times even Marcella—*worse*. "Okay, I'll try that."

"You will?" The surprise in his brother's voice was impossible to miss.

"I said I'll *try*," Luca reminded him.

"Right, right. Okay, well I'll call Dad now." Gabe hesitated. "You need anything else?"

Luca's eyebrows rose. When was the last time Gabe had offered *additional* help without being asked first?

Maybe there really was something in this unbending thing.

"No, we're good here. Well, not *good*. But managing."

"You would be," Gabe said wryly. "Giana would be stupid not to listen to you."

"But—" Luca tried to insert, but Gabe stopped him.

"No, you have a lot of good to bring to the table. It's her own bankruptcy if she doesn't want to listen," Gabe said. "You can be a real asshole, but that's mostly because you're usually right, and honestly, that's obnoxious."

Luca didn't know if he was supposed to apologize for that. Wasn't being right most of the time a *good* thing? "Sorry?"

Gabe sighed. "You just never let anyone forget it, that's all. Still, she should be arguing less and listening more. You know what you're talking about."

"Thanks." Luca didn't know what else to say. None of this was news to him, but his family—especially Gabe—certainly never said it.

They all, it felt like, resented him for the skill and the hard work he'd put in.

Maybe because he'd gotten a little too familiar with throwing it in their faces.

"I'll let you know what Dad says," Gabe said.

"Alright. Just text me, unless it's a major emergency," Luca said.

"Should I send positive thoughts to Marco right now?" Gabe teased, but it was sweeter, friendlier than usual.

Luca rolled his eyes. "Marco is going to be just fine. He's a big boy, he can take care of himself."

"Yeah, he can. Alright, I gotta go, will let you know what Dad says."

"Good. Thanks." Luca felt that surge of awkwardness again. He knew what he wanted to say to his little brother. *I love you and I miss you.* But he didn't, because this had to be enough, at least for now.

Rome, after all, wasn't built in a day.

Or in a single phone call.

But he hung up with Gabe feeling better about their relationship than he had in years. Since before Gabe had run away with Ren to Los Angeles, for sure.

During the call, Chiara had sent over some plans. Luca browsed through them, nodding in approval.

She had such good instincts, and they were, he was sure, totally wasted, running that coffee shop. But he was also sure if he told her that—or *kept* telling her that—she was going to clam up and eventually hate him. Just like Gabe had.

Luca sighed.

He sent a quick text to Marco, which just said **Call me.**

Then he sent a little longer one to Oliver, even though he was in his meeting and probably wouldn't see until after.

Talked to my brother Gabe tonight. Maybe he won't actually hate me forever.

To his surprise, Oliver texted back right away. **I have a feeling nobody could ever hate you forever.**

He was staring at the screen, trying to decide how to respond when Marco called.

"What," he barked into Luca's ear. "I'm busy."

"It's Dad's right to dodge my texts," Luca said, "but you know better. You going to tell me what's going on?"

"What's going on is you're not here and we're all having to work more, work harder. That's all." Marco could be brusque—they often took chunks out of each other—but they also *understood* each other.

And Luca knew he was bullshitting him.

"Don't lie to me," Luca said.

"Oh, so you *are* here and we don't have to work too hard?"

"No, I'm saying I know shit is going down there, and you're not telling me, and it's making me fucking antsy."

"You've got your hands full with Giana," he said gruffly after a long silence.

"Yes, but somehow that doesn't make me *less* capable of handling things back home."

"We've got it," Marco said stubbornly. "I'm not saying it's easy but you know how you are, always bailing our asses out. Maybe it should be us doing it for you, once in a while."

"Now you're just talking crazy," Luca said dryly.

"Dad said you'd say that," Marco said, confirming that this enforced silence *was* a plan. They'd shut him out on purpose. His temper surged.

"I can feel you silently raging over there," Marco continued, chuckling under his breath. "That's always when we should get scared. If you're yelling, we're probably all safe."

"Probably," Luca said through clenched teeth. "For the last fucking time, tell me what's going on, or I'm gonna come back." *Don't make me come back, not yet, not quite yet . . .*

"You won't," Marco said, which was annoying, because he was right.

He'd come out here to help Giana and he was going to stick to that. The one exception was if he saw a serious dip in the restaurants' income, and he hadn't. It was still steady, the numbers just as expected for this time of year.

Luca grunted under his breath.

"Don't be mad," Marco said, his voice gentling. "We mean well."

"You didn't think I'd freak out? *No word* for days?"

"You're getting the nightly take, you know things are fine."

"Yes, but—"

"Always a *but* with you, Luca," Marco said, chuckling.

"I hate you."

"No, you don't." Luca could hear the echo of his own certainty in his brother's voice.

"Fine, fine, keep your secrets," Luca said.

"What's this about some guy you're seeing there?"

"What." Luca heard the flat panic in his own voice. "What guy?" But of course there was only *one* guy he could be talking about.

Fucking Gabriel.

"Gabe texted me, he thinks you're like . . .unbending over this guy."

"He doesn't know what he's talking about." Unfortunately, though, he sort of did. That was the worst part of it.

"I don't know," Marco said thoughtfully, "I was expecting a lot more yelling just now. Maybe you are shifting down a little. Would that be so bad?"

"You know the answer to that." He didn't answer it on purpose. Was he more relaxed here in Indigo Bay? When he was around Oliver? He was. He couldn't deny that. But it wasn't a permanent change. The moment he was back in Napa, things would go back to normal. He knew they would. Knew they *had* to.

It wasn't that he was incapable of change; he was, like any other person.

But change meant he might be less capable of overseeing the family. Less capable of handling the stuff they needed him to handle. And neither of those options was acceptable.

"I think it would be nice. Human-like Luca." Marco hummed under his breath. "So you gonna tell me about this guy?"

"Gabe is the worst."

"That is something I'm not gonna argue with you about," Marco said, chuckling. "But he's clearly onto something."

"He's a guy who owns the bakery here. I'm having him bake Giana's bread."

"And?"

"How do you know there's an *and*," Luca insisted.

"Because you don't want to talk about him, and if there wasn't anything, you'd say so, straight out, no bullshit."

It was annoying how well Marco knew him.

"Fine, fine, we've been on a few dates. He's . . .well, he's nice."

"Nice?" Marco sounded strangled. "You're dating someone who's nice? Not a clone of yourself, for once?"

"Yes," Luca said, because he couldn't deny that either. He did tend to gravitate toward men like himself. Busy men, arrogant men, men who put their business above anything else.

The thing was, it wasn't like Oliver didn't do that, too. He did. His bakery was well-established, successful, and he worked damn hard to make sure it continued. But none of that seemed to harden him. He was still kind and sweet, and *bent*.

"Huh. Well, I'm glad for you."

"It's . . ." Luca swallowed hard. "It isn't anything, really." *It can't be anything.*

"It would be okay if it was," Marco said. "You know that."

"Not when my place is back in California."

"Hey, aren't we handling shit here? We are. Nobody's come running to you in over a week. I think that's a new record."

It was.

But that didn't mean the current situation was a long-term solution.

"I'm very proud of you," Luca said dryly.

"You should be. Hey, I gotta go," Marco said. "Supplier's here. Gotta yell at him about the veal."

"I thought . . ." Marco had said it wouldn't be an issue. Luca had checked with him and he'd *insisted* it wasn't an issue.

Luca hadn't realized he'd meant that *he'd* take care of it, because it was definitely an issue.

"Yeah, exactly," Marco said with satisfaction. "Let me handle it."

Luca hesitated. Should he? *Could he?* But then Marco hung up before he could argue.

Luca was still baffled when he set his phone down.

Perplexed too, at how this had even happened. And . . .gratified . . .that it had.

Even if it wasn't forever, it was still a break—and Luca would take it.

Oliver debated for only about two seconds before deciding it wasn't *too* late to swing by the Inn and see Luca.

He wouldn't have considered it, because even though they'd spent several evenings together, he knew how this was going to end and he'd need to live without Luca in the future, but then Luca had texted him.

Just because he could.

Like he was thinking of him, too.

And Oliver hadn't been able to resist.

Let's be honest, you didn't even try that hard.

He snuck up the back stairs, avoiding the common areas his mother might be lurking in. It wasn't like she didn't know he was spending time with Luca, but if she knew how much, she'd have something to say about it. A warning, probably.

A warning he didn't really need, because he'd already memorized his own.

Oliver knocked on the door, holding his breath a little, because maybe Luca wouldn't want to see him, after all. He wasn't supposed to be here . . .maybe he'd made a mistake.

But when Luca pulled open the door, an annoyed expression on his face, no doubt at being bothered, it immediately melted away into a surprised pleasure.

"Oliver!" he exclaimed in a low voice. "Is everything okay?"

"You mean, did I want to wring the necks of the entire festival committee for the whole duration of the meeting? Absolutely, I did." Oliver slid inside as Luca held the door open wider, then he closed it behind him.

"That bad, huh?" Luca had his glasses on, because he'd clearly been working, if his open laptop and the scribbled notes on a pad of Inn stationery were any indication. A half-drunk glass of red wine sat on the desk next to his laptop.

"Yes," Oliver said. "But it's okay. It's always like this."

One of Luca's dark eyebrows shot up. "And you still volunteer every year?"

"You said it yourself, my family's the whole festival. How can I say no?" Of course, he'd never tried either, but he could only imagine what would happen if he did.

The confusion.

The disappointment.

The various people who would be dispatched to the bakery to try to change his mind.

"Seems like I'm not the only one who has to deal with that kind of responsibility." Luca's sigh was deep.

"But you talked to Gabe." Oliver perched on the side of the bed, hoping—and also *not* hoping—Luca wouldn't take it as an invitation. He really needed to get a good night of sleep. There was a ton of work to be done in the bakery tomorrow, and he couldn't play hooky for another night, no matter how much he might want to.

Responsibility. That was a word he'd never hated before starting his own business.

Or meeting Luca, who had his own share of them.

"Yeah, I did." Luca stayed over by the desk, lifting his wine glass. "Want some?" he asked.

"No, but I'll just have a sip of yours, so I can try it," Oliver said. Luca crossed toward the bed and took a seat next to him, handing over the glass.

"It's a pinot, from a vineyard near us," Luca explained as Oliver took a sip.

It was delicious. Fruity and deep and rich.

"You have exceptional taste in wine," Oliver said seriously, then took a second sip.

Luca laughed. "So I've been told," he said.

"So, you and Gabe," Oliver prompted, passing the glass back over.

"It was . . .nice actually, to talk to him," Luca said. "Surprisingly."

"You aren't surprised," Oliver corrected gently. "You wanted to talk to him. I could tell you did."

"How are you so smart?" Luca wondered, and Oliver thought it must be a rhetorical question, because he wasn't, at all. If he was smart, he wouldn't be sitting here on Luca's bed at the Inn, sharing a glass of wine.

He'd be at home, going to sleep alone. Not unbearably tempted to throw all his rules and his *responsibilities* right out the window.

"Just observant. Baker, remember? Better than a bartender," Oliver said with a grin. Trying to lighten his own mood.

"I talked to Marco too. He confirmed they're handling stuff on their own, deliberately."

Oliver wasn't surprised. This was exactly what he'd suspected, and, he knew, Luca's worst fear.

That they could do things without him.

That he wasn't indispensable.

That he wasn't *needed*. Or even worse, *wanted*.

"And?" Oliver kept his tone really casual.

"And? *And*?" Luca totally sounded like he was panicking about this. "I mean, it's sweet, sure, because they know I'm busy here, but what if . . ."

He trailed off, clamping his lips shut.

Oliver reached over and took his hand. Squeezed it. "What if they don't need you? I think you know that's not true. They're just trying to give you a little bit of a break. You work really hard, and they know that. And maybe this is also them telling you, *hey*, we can do this, too."

"Can they, though?"

Oliver shot him a look. "I know you don't mean that."

"They just haven't ever done it before," Luca said with a heavy sigh. "I guess . . .I guess I assumed they couldn't."

"And you could."

He nodded.

"There you go. It's all okay. You're fine." Oliver stole the glass and took another sip of wine.

It shouldn't have felt so right, sitting here together and sharing a glass of wine, but it did.

"I'm . . .I'm okay." Luca admitted it slowly. Carefully. Like he was testing it out.

"Yeah, you really are." Oliver grinned. "Okay *and* fine. Especially in these." He touched the corner of Luca's glasses. "Please wear them all the time."

"Seriously?"

"They're sexy librarian glasses," Oliver said. No other explanation needed. "Maybe you could tell me to *shush* a half dozen times and then if I won't, *make* me do it."

Luca laughed, sounding a hell of a lot lighter, and Oliver didn't miss the light returning to his eyes either.

"But not tonight," Oliver continued reluctantly. "I've got to get home. Get some sleep. Tomorrow's a long day."

"I know tomorrow's our first bread delivery, but if it's too much—"

"No," Oliver stopped him before he could do a very un-Luca like thing and tell him to delay the first order. "Really, it's fine. I've got Aaron to help. Just a lot of other things I need to get done tomorrow too. I wish I could stay, but I can't."

Luca had the nerve to look disappointed. Which, in turn, stoked Oliver's own regret.

Then Luca leaned in and said, in a deep, soft voice that felt like it altered something permanent inside Oliver, "What if I tried to convince you?"

Oliver hesitated.

"Or . . ." The corner of Luca's mouth kicked up. "How about if I just gave you a kiss goodnight?"

Oliver opened his mouth to argue, to tell him it was never going to be just one kiss, but that was all the invitation Luca needed to press their lips together.

They'd only spent a handful of nights together, so the kiss shouldn't have felt so stupidly sweet, but it did anyway. Like that was truly all it was, like that was all Luca wanted from him. Just a kiss.

Luca's hand crept up and cupped Oliver's head and his touch was gentle. Had anyone ever treated Oliver like this before? He didn't think so.

Right after Luca's tongue brushed his, velvet-soft and in no particular hurry, he broke off, giving Oliver just the tiniest nibble on his bottom lip before he pulled away.

Oliver's eyes fluttered open.

He wanted to reach back and kiss him again.

Because even though it was just supposed to be a kiss, it was impossible for Luca to not light a fire—even a small, cozy one—inside him.

"There," Luca said. "You're all set now."

"Am I?" Oliver felt turned upside down.

"I'll see you tomorrow," Luca said, his voice becoming firmer. "You've got sleep to get, yes?"

"Yes."

Luca wasn't wrong.

But already Luca made him want to throw everything away.

Made him want to play hooky.

It wasn't the first time he'd ever been tempted, but the temptation had never been more seductive.

"I'll see you in the morning," Luca said. He drained the rest of the wine and stood.

But Oliver didn't.

Couldn't he sit here forever and just *look* at Luca as he walked into the bathroom, washed out the wine glass, set it back on the desk, next to the corked bottle, and turned back toward Oliver.

"You haven't moved," he said, in a deeply amused voice.

"I will," Oliver said, with as much dignity as he could gather. "I'm in mourning that you didn't try to convince me."

"I sort of got the impression you didn't want me to." Luca rubbed the back of his neck, looking rueful.

"I *didn't*, but I also did." Oliver forced himself to move, get upright. Took two steps toward the door. He wanted to tell him it had been easier to justify *this* when they were also having sex. But he'd stopped by tonight just because he'd wanted to, and Luca had kissed him just because he'd wanted to.

"Believe me, I understand," Luca said. "But I'm not a saint . . ."

He wasn't.

But he was trying, and that meant so much more to Oliver than he realized it would.

"Alright," Oliver said, "I'm gone."

"Wait," Luca said and then he was right there, in Oliver's space, pressing him back against the door. This kiss wasn't quite so gentle, but it was still so goddamn sweet.

Then Luca was gone, a few feet away, and shoving his hands into the pockets of his jeans, like he needed to control himself every way he could.

Oliver missed the pressure of his lips, but if he didn't reach for the doorknob now, every single good reason for why he should would fly right out the window.

"I'm really gone now." Oliver took a deep breath and felt for the doorknob. "Night."

The last thing he saw before the door closed behind him, was Luca's face—and the affection in his dark eyes stuck with him all the way home.

Chapter Twelve

"Giana," Luca said patiently—or at least he was *trying* to be patient—and mostly failing. "That sauce is from yesterday."

"Yes, I know," she snapped back at him. "We're going to finish it off, then we'll have the fresh. We need to figure out how to predict better how much we're going to use, because I'm not throwing it away."

"Oliver doesn't throw anything away," Luca offered mildly, leaning against the back counter, watching as Giana stirred the sauce in a pot on the stove, re-heating it.

She rolled her eyes. "Oh yes, *saint* Oliver."

"I know he gives some of his extras to a shelter down by the wharf," Luca said. "And you should know that too, since you worked with him. In the future, that's what we'll do. I'll contact them today, make sure they can use what we're giving them."

Giana's frustration softened. "That's . . .that's actually really nice, Luca."

It was like nobody but Oliver knew he could be nice.

But he could.

He was proving it one day at a time, here in Indigo Bay. And when he went back home—and that thought stung, deep down, in a place he wasn't necessarily ignoring, but that before the last few weeks, he hadn't even knew existed—he wasn't going to stop trying. He'd begun to make amends with Gabe. He'd accepted what Marco had said. He'd even listened to Oliver and decided that he would *let* the rest of the family take care of things, for now.

"That's what we do at our own restaurants, back in Napa. I know it's going to take us some time to adjust the food estimates. Especially when we're working toward a period of growth. That's always going to be hard to get it right. It's okay that it's not right now," Luca said. "We'll get there."

Giana actually shot him a legitimately grateful look.

"Thanks," she said.

"You're welcome." He heard the front door open and close, and assumed it must be their bread delivery from Oliver's bakery.

Luca straightened. "I'll get them," he said, but before he could turn to go, Giana reached out and caught his arm. "I mean it," she said. "*Thank you*. For that. And for everything."

It was the first tiny inkling he'd had that she actually *was* grateful.

"Oh. Well, you're still welcome." But she still had his arm.

"I didn't know if I even wanted this place," she said, voice bittersweet. "I wanted it for Enzo. I *still* want it for Enzo. But . . ."

"Maybe he'll come around." Luca wasn't going to hold his breath, but maybe he'd discover a shred of familial obligation at some distant point in the future.

"Maybe." But Giana also didn't look convinced. She dropped his arm. "Go see about the bread," she said.

He had an inkling their conversation wasn't over, but he was feeling at least decent about the fact that his aunt had realized what he'd tried to do for her. It was, at the very least, better than her hating and resenting him for every change he'd implemented.

When he pushed the door open, he was surprised to see Oliver standing there, a big bundle of wrapped bread sitting on the front counter.

"Oh," Luca said. "It's you."

"You thought I'd send a lackey on your very first day?" Oliver grinned.

It hit him square in the chest.

Someday, in just a week or two, you're not going to see him smile anymore.

Luca pushed the thought aside. He couldn't focus on the good—on the *very* good—that was happening right now if he was constantly worrying about the future. He wouldn't. He would just take each day as it came. Enjoy them. Enjoy *Oliver*.

"I guess yeah, I thought you might," Luca said, coming around the counter.

"Besides, I promised you a kiss," Oliver said, looking downright excited about the prospect of collecting.

"I don't think Enzo is here, unfortunately."

"That's okay," Oliver said casually and reached for him anyway.

This kiss was hotter, wilder than the one last night. Like Oliver had been thinking about it since he'd left Luca's room and wanting it more with every second that passed between then and now.

Luca lost what was left of his mind and pressed his hips against Oliver's, both of them groaning as arousal rushed through him.

Because he hadn't stopped thinking about it either.

How much he hadn't wanted Oliver to leave last night, even though he'd known he'd needed to.

It had nearly killed him to do the right thing—and at the last second, he'd almost buckled, and had convinced him anyway.

"God," Oliver groaned as he nipped at his mouth. "I want you."

Luca's fingers tightened on his hips, dragging him even closer. "Tonight?"

"Can't. Have another meeting. Longer meeting. But tomorrow? I've got the day off, and I thought maybe you could play hooky too and come hiking with me. I wanted to show you the spot. You know, *the* spot."

Luca raised an eyebrow. "Is this some kind of sex thing? Because if it is, I'm on board."

"No," Oliver said, laughing and putting a little distance between them. It was better this way, but that didn't mean Luca *liked* it. "It's the spot where Eliza went when she was missing Nathaniel, and the spot where she found him, after he came back to Indigo Bay. It's just a bit of a hike, and I thought I'd put together a picnic for us."

"Leave that to me," Luca said.

"Like feeding me, do you?" Oliver smirked.

Sue him, he totally did. And he was going to do it now, while he still could. "Yes."

"Well, then I'll allow it. Pick you up at eleven tomorrow."

Luca nodded. It was time for Giana and Enzo to be on their own for a day. He'd been working with them so closely, there wasn't time for them to prove that *they* wanted to be on this path. Though he supposed Giana's appreciation just now was the first real proof he'd seen. Tomorrow would cinch it.

He'd ordered the decor on the plan Chiara had sent over, and it was showing the shipment would be received in two days, so there was a little bit of time for him to do something else.

He'd intended on working on some of his own plans for the California version of Nonna's, but this would be better.

After all, wasn't his family always telling him to work less? Hadn't Nicoletta told him to take some time for himself while he was here?

"Alright, important things out of the way," Oliver said. "Let's talk about the bread." He gestured toward the packaged bundle on the counter. "Focaccia as promised. Do you want to try it?"

Luca knew it would be good, because Oliver wouldn't make something bad, but he nodded anyway. Still feeling that weird remnant of guilt that he hadn't passed over Nonna's recipe.

Oliver put the sandwich rolls, which were resting on the top, on the counter and pulled off the plastic covering on the pans of focaccia. They looked really good, golden brown and pitted with a sprinkling of sea salt and fresh rosemary dotting the surface.

"Looks solid," Luca said.

"Knife?" Oliver asked archly. Like he believed he had something to prove. And he did, with this, even though he didn't even know it. Which . . .there was that pang of guilt again.

Luca reached behind the counter and came up with a clean knife from one of the silverware bins. He neatly sliced a corner off, broke it in half and handed half to Oliver and popped the other half into his own mouth.

Rich, warm yeast flooded his taste buds, followed by salt and the rich buttery feel of the olive oil. It was really good bread. Exceptional bread, even.

But it wasn't Nonna's.

You are not disappointed, he told himself firmly. *If you wanted him to make Nonna's focaccia, you could've given him the recipe.*

"Yeah, that's good," Oliver said, savoring the bite with a long eye-fluttering look that couldn't help but spike a flare of heat at the base of Luca's stomach again.

Yes, he really loved feeding Oliver. Even when it was Oliver's own food.

"I thought my opinion was the one we were worried about," Luca teased.

"Of course, but if you tell me it's not good, now I'm gonna know you're full of shit," Oliver teased right back.

It was funny, even when he was trying to be snarky, he was still so fundamentally sweet Luca knew if he kissed him again, he'd taste sugar on his tongue.

"Noted." Luca smiled. "But I wasn't going to tell you that at all. It's really good. Just like I expected it'd be."

Oliver flushed, cheeks turning pink. The fact that Giana was just in the back was all that kept Luca from kissing him and *more*.

"Good."

It was time for him to go and they both knew it, but instead of saying his goodbyes, Oliver lingered.

"What are you doing for the rest of the day?" he asked, carefully wrapping the focaccia back up.

"Teaching Giana the new panini I want to make with this," Luca said. "And work. Always more work. What's tonight's meeting about?"

"We're a little over a week out, so it's to go over the main schedule, do a walk-through of the festival grounds, make final decisions about where everything's going. That kind of thing." Oliver hesitated, and Luca couldn't help but jump in.

"Final decisions?" he asked.

Oliver had to know what he was worried about.

But instead of telling him, *sorry, I couldn't make it work for Giana,* he said with an eyeroll, "And yes, saved a spot for her."

Luca shouldn't have been too surprised. This was Oliver. He had a soft spot for everyone—except maybe Enzo, and that was totally deserved—and he wasn't afraid to show it, not like Luca, who kept his own guarded and buttoned up all the goddamn time.

But he was still so pleased he'd done this for her.

That was what he told himself. *It's for Giana, because she worked for him, and he feels sorry for her. Not because you asked. Not because he wanted to do something nice for you.*

"That's great," Luca said, resisting the urge to put his hands on Oliver and thank him a lot more intimately, *again.* "That was really generous of you."

"Well, someone asked me *nicely,*" Oliver teased. "And they reminded me that I have some power around here."

"Just don't let it go to your head," Luca murmured, tucking his head closer to Oliver's. Wondering if he could get away with just one more kiss.

"I won't," Oliver promised, "as long as you give me my goodbye kiss."

Luca almost asked if they were doing that now, but he wanted to give it just as much as Oliver wanted to receive it, so it seemed very stupid to prevaricate.

He dipped his head and they were just in the middle of a kiss he was trying to keep PG when the door to the kitchen swung open and there was a distinctly male oath uttered behind them.

Well, I guess Enzo caught us anyway.

As Luca lifted his head, he couldn't even say he was sorry.

At least until he saw the punched-out look in Enzo's eyes. Like he'd just been hit in the stomach with a two by four.

Maybe Oliver didn't want that second date, but I know now that Enzo did.

He hadn't meant to be an ass about it, and if he'd known that this was more than just wounded pride, he'd have made sure not to kiss Oliver where Enzo could've caught them.

He could be autocratic and arrogant, but he wasn't an asshole.

At least he tried not to be.

Oliver glanced back over his shoulder. Saw the fury in Enzo's eyes. "I'd better go," he said, and with a last peck to Luca's cheek, had slipped out the door before Luca started toward Enzo.

"Really?" Enzo sneered. "You're really just going to—"

But before he could finish his sentence, Luca said, "I'm sorry," and that took every bit of the wind out of his sails.

The disdain slid right off Enzo's face, to be replaced by hurt.

"It's bad enough that I don't want to be here, and I am," Enzo said quietly. "Do you have to make it worse by hooking up with Oliver?"

"I can tell you honestly that you weren't a consideration when Oliver and I started dating." Because that was what they were doing; regardless of the timeframe, regardless that he couldn't stick around. It was still dating, because there was no way with his entire heart filling with so much affection it was *just* sex. "Maybe I should have, but I care about him, and I'm not sure if that would've stopped me, because I think . . ." Luca hesitated. "Because I think he feels the same as I do."

And he probably did.

Oliver had a sweet and open face, but Luca had a feeling even if he could hide it, he wouldn't.

Maybe it would be better if they didn't feel the same, because it was only going to suck in the end, but Luca was trying to believe just because something ended didn't mean it wasn't worth enjoying in the moment.

"Is that supposed to make me feel better?" Enzo demanded.

Luca sighed. "No. But it's the truth."

"So you're just going to mess with his head while you're here and then leave, huh? How is that any better?"

Here was the thing: Enzo didn't have any right to ask that question. None of this was his goddamned business at all.

But that just happened to be the same question Luca couldn't stop asking himself.

"I'm not messing with his head," Luca said gruffly. "Oliver's an adult. He knows the situation. Better than you do, anyway."

"Okay." Enzo didn't sound convinced at all.

Not surprising, considering Luca wasn't even quite convinced.

Luca decided it was high time to change the subject. "You made the menu board, didn't you?"

Enzo nodded stiffly.

"You don't need me to tell you it's really good."

"No, I sure as hell don't." Enzo crossed his arms over his chest.

"But you do need me to ask why the hell you don't do more of them."

Enzo glowered. "I do?"

"You're really talented. This is gorgeous. My sister, Chiara, you know her, right? She . . .well, she went to school for design, and she loved it."

"She the one who made the design plan my mom showed me?"

"Yes."

"It wasn't bad."

"Then you saw she wanted to know if you could make some more pieces. Maybe even do a mural for the back wall."

"I'm not trained, you know. I just. . .I just like it. Making things."

"And I'm not a trained chef, but I can still hold down the line when they need me to. School isn't everything." Luca had a feeling he'd finally uncovered the real reason Enzo was so sullen all the time. He'd wanted to go to art school and Giana had made him stay at home, with her, preparing to take over a business he had zero interest in.

Enzo looked at him suspiciously. "You really want me to paint a mural?"

"You saw the plans. Not just me, but Chiara thinks it would transform this place."

She'd also told him personally, in an email he *hadn't* forwarded, she thought he had real talent that was totally being wasted here in Indigo Bay. At the very least, she'd written, why didn't he set up his own thing, creating art pieces for other businesses in the area?

Luca hadn't been able to answer the question, though he'd suspected the truth: because Giana had kept him so tied to her apron strings, she'd sucked all the confidence out of him.

He didn't do it because he didn't think he was capable of doing it.

"Well, I guess I could put together some sketches."

"You saw Chiara's ideas," Luca suggested, more gently than he'd have believed himself capable of only a few weeks ago. "But if you have something else in mind, let's see it."

"I think . . ." Enzo glanced at the back wall. "I've got some ideas."

"Alright. Can't wait to see what you come up with," Luca said.

"You mean that." Enzo glanced back at Luca, eyeing him suspiciously.

"Lying to people isn't really my kinda thing," Luca said. "Being painfully blunt usually is."

"Yeah, yeah," Enzo grumbled. "I can see that. So you're gonna break Oliver's heart, then?"

Luca sighed. "It's none of your business, but no, I'm not going to do anything. It's just . . ."

What was it?

He didn't even know.

Could he break Oliver's heart?

He sure as hell hoped not.

But his own traitorous heart leapt at the possibility.

Because breaking it would mean Oliver loved him.

And oh *God*, wouldn't that be a thing?

A bad, bad thing, Luca reminded himself.

"Right," Enzo said self-righteously before Luca could even decide how he felt about that—good and bad and everything in between, apparently. "Don't do it, okay? He's a good guy. Nice."

"I know." Luca took a breath. Tried to rediscover his grip on sanity. "While we're at it, though, maybe you could stop bad-mouthing Oliver, because he *is* a good guy. Your words. Not mine."

"You don't—"

But Luca didn't let him finish. "I *do* believe he's not just a good guy—he's a great guy, which is why I'm sick to death of you saying shit about him. Just quit it, okay? Some things aren't meant to be."

"I bet you don't even know what that's like," Enzo complained.

"Better than you realize," Luca retorted. "You take over three restaurants, add a fourth and start a line of ready-made sauces and dips *while* wrangling six younger siblings and get back to me."

Enzo didn't have anything to say to that. Which, was that even surprising?

Still, he said as he turned to leave, "I'll do some sketches today. Send them over."

"Good. Keep your mom in the loop, too. And cc my sister, okay?"

"Chiara?"

"That's the one."

Finally, Enzo slunk out and Luca let out an enormous sigh.

His phone buzzed in his pocket, and he realized he had two texts.

The first was from Gabe.

Enjoy your break, and let them take care of shit for once, was all it said. Guess he'd talked to Matteo, and it seemed everyone was on the same page with this plan.

The second, just arrived, was from Oliver.

Don't kill him, okay? I want to take you on a picnic tomorrow, not bury a body.

First, he replied to Gabe: **I'm trying.**

Then to Oliver: **That all you want to do?**

Gabe replied almost immediately with **Try harder.**

Luca rolled his eyes. His brother was never going to *not* drive him crazy. But maybe they could keep heaping dirt on this hatchet between them.

Then Gabe sent a second text. **Ren says maybe you should ask your friend Oliver to distract you.**

Luca laughed then, out loud, unable to contain his amusement.

Tell Ren I'm touched by his interest in my love life.

Luca stared at the screen, at the words he'd typed, before he sent it.

It wasn't a lie. It *was* his love life. How could it be anything else, how could it be just fun, or just fucking around, when he felt like this?

When he couldn't imagine flying away in a week and a half and leaving Oliver here? When he couldn't imagine not seeing his smile every single day?

Maybe he should broach the idea they could do this long-distance. But the moment Luca thought it, he discarded the idea almost immediately. That would be almost harder than not having him at all. The problem with Luca was he didn't do half-measures. He knew it, didn't necessarily *like* it, but it was a cornerstone of who he was. He committed. All-in or nothing.

And all-in was not an option here.

All in would mean abandoning his family, who were managing for now, but he *knew* wouldn't be able to handle things long-term. Not with his parents growing older, Gabe down in Los Angeles with his own life, and Marco so committed to the steakhouse.

They needed help. Help he gave, freely.

He'd never resented it, but could he continue to say that, if he had to leave Oliver back here? Leave the amorphous outlines of a relationship that could've been, if he wasn't committed elsewhere?

Luca didn't know.

But what he did know was that he didn't have a choice.

This was his life.

It had been set in stone the moment he'd been born first.

He should go to the kitchen and walk Giana through the new bread, show her the panini he was adding to the menu, but before he could, his phone dinged again.

It wasn't Gabe this time, but Oliver instead.

Oh, Oliver wrote, **I've got plans. Plans not including burying a body. BIG PLANS for you.**

Luca was torn between chuckling and shoving his phone in his pocket and heading to the bakery, to tease out of him just exactly what those big plans were.

That was the problem with Oliver; he made him want to do the impossible.

Chapter Thirteen

There were many better things Oliver could be doing on his day off.

He could be working on last-minute plans for the festival. They were there, just sitting in his inbox taunting him.

Just like his overflowing laundry hamper.

Just like the pans stacked up in the sink from the last few breakfasts he'd shared with Luca.

But he left them all behind and walked over to the Inn, opening the door and letting the comforting scent of lavender and fresh-baked blueberry scones hit him.

"Oliver," his mom called over, barely raising her head from the laptop she had set up on the front desk. "Is that you?"

"It's me," he said. Regretting, immediately, that he hadn't gone in the back way and snuck up to Luca's room.

He should've known his mom would be down here.

Ready to pounce.

Ready to demand answers.

But in a very Joy-like way, which meant she'd weasel them out of him without him even realizing he'd given up the goods.

He loved her, he totally did, but she was also a huge pain in his ass. Especially about this.

There were a lot of benefits of having a romance author for a mother; this was not one of them.

"Come over here for a sec," she said. "I'm assuming you're not here to see me."

"No," Oliver admitted, his feet reluctantly carrying him over to where she was sitting. "How's the book coming?"

"Terrible, but don't try to distract me," she said. She glanced up at him. "You're meeting Luca, aren't you?"

Oliver tried to remember when he'd told Luca that living in a small town and everyone giving a shit about what you did was a *good* thing. Cause it didn't feel particularly good now.

He had a feeling he was in for a big lecture.

He even had a feeling he knew what she'd say.

"Yes," he said, because he wasn't going to lie to her about it either.

Joy's lips pursed. "You're spending a lot of time together, aren't you?"

"Well . . .he's not here for very long," Oliver reminded her.

As soon as the words were out of his mouth, he realized they were the wrong ones.

"Exactly," she said. "He's not sticking around, Oliver."

"You don't think I know that?" He sighed. "I *know*, Mom."

"Do you?"

"I know him pretty well by this point. I know he's not."

Of course knowing it and coming to terms with it were two entirely different things.

"Still." She looked concerned, which was even worse. "I write these things for a living, Oliver, and in my head, and on the page, they end differently than they do in real life."

"If you tell me in real life people leave, *I'm* going to leave," Oliver said bluntly.

"I'm not," she said, shaking her head. "I'm just worried. I thought you'd . . ."

"I'd what?"

Her voice lowered. "Spend less time with him. Keep a distance. The nights . . .those are one thing. But I heard him tell another guest you're taking him to the lookout today. *The lookout*, Oliver."

"And what?" But he knew what she was trying to say.

"It's not a place you take a guy you've slept with a few times. It's a place you take a guy—"

He wasn't going to let her finish that thought.

It was bad enough it was already echoing in his own head. He didn't need to hear it out loud too.

"It's a place you take a guy who's visiting and wants to see the sights? Yeah, I know it is," he finished instead.

Joy sighed. "I knew you wouldn't take this well."

"Then maybe you shouldn't have brought it up," Oliver suggested.

"I couldn't stand by and watch . . ." She trailed off. "Don't fall in love with him, Oliver."

"Don't worry, I won't," Oliver lied. "Besides, aren't you always telling me people don't fall in love in a few weeks? However, despite all this great advice, I gotta go." He'd just spotted Luca coming down the stairs, and the last thing he wanted was for him to overhear this particular conversation.

They were already skirting around the inevitable, not talking about it because there was absolutely zero point in subjecting themselves to a conversation that could only end one way—they both knew that. It would be so much worse if Luca overheard his mom lecturing Oliver about a future that wasn't going to happen.

"Hey," Luca said as he approached, smiling in that soft way Oliver hadn't seen on him with anyone else.

Joy shot him a knowing look, and there went the idea that she hadn't noticed it, too.

He loved his mother, but she noticed *everything*. It was the worst.

"Hey," Oliver said. "Ready to go?"

Luca lifted the backpack he was carrying. "Picnic all packed."

"Great."

"Mrs. Billings," Luca said to his mother, nodding in acknowledgment. "Nice to see you. Breakfast this morning was delicious, as always."

Joy sighed and if it was even possible, her next glance in Oliver's direction was even more obvious.

Yeah, he definitely did not need her to tell him they were both getting in deep, and that no matter how deep they went, it could only end one way: with Luca getting on a plane and heading back to California.

It didn't matter if fate was being an asshole about it; fate was still fate.

"You're welcome," she said dryly. "You two be careful. It can be a tough climb."

Oliver said goodbye and practically dragged Luca outside.

Luca was quiet, settling the backpack on his broad shoulders, as they walked toward the edge of town, toward the ocean.

Finally, after five long minutes, he spoke up. "What was that about?"

"Uh, it was nothing," Oliver said. He was a terrible liar—but what was he supposed to do, tell Luca the truth?

It was too humiliating to even consider.

"She was warning you about me, wasn't she?" Luca's voice was heavy.

Oliver stopped in the middle of the sidewalk, the fresh salt tang of the ocean beginning to hit his nose.

This wasn't what he'd wanted at all.

He'd told Luca he had big plans, and he hadn't been exaggerating.

They didn't have much time left, and he wanted everything, and to get that, they needed to make the most of every moment.

He knew that, and he'd planned for it.

"Do we have to do this?" Oliver asked, as Luca turned to face him. His dark eyes were so serious. Earnest, almost.

Oliver didn't think he'd ever seen this look on his face before. It scared him. It exhilarated him.

"We don't have to talk about it," Luca said slowly, "but I don't want to leave the elephant in the room unacknowledged. That's not fair to either of us."

"It's not?"

Luca reached for him, cupped his cheek with one of his big calloused hands. Oliver's eyes fluttered closed and he tried to imprint the memory of Luca's soft, but firm touch in his head forever. So he could pull it out later and remember just how it felt.

"Oliver, you know I can't stay."

"I know." God, did he know.

"But I don't want to just keep doing this like it's nothing, either," he continued. "I don't want to keep doing it without telling you that I wish things could be different."

"Seriously?" Oliver couldn't do anything but laugh. A little bitterly. "Is that supposed to help? Because it doesn't."

"No, but it's the truth and I promised myself I'd tell you the truth. So that's the truth. I wish I could stay. But I can't."

"I just wanted . . ." Oliver tried to ignore the surge of happiness, followed by the equally strong surge of disappointment currently rocking him. "I just wanted to enjoy the time we had together. That's all. That's what I want. To live in the moment."

"We can do that. I just . . ." Luca took a deep breath. "I didn't want you to think I didn't care. I do care." *Too much.* He didn't say the words, but they echoed between them anyway, and Oliver could hear them as loudly as if he'd screamed them.

"I understand." He did, even if it was killing him.

"I thought you might, but . . ." Luca's voice was wry. "I wanted to be sure, as well."

Luca *would* want to be sure, even if it killed both of them to say it out loud.

"Do we have to think about it anymore?"

Luca smiled, his hand sliding back, behind Oliver's neck, tugging him closer. "No," he murmured as he kissed him briefly. "No, we don't."

Oliver leaned into the kiss. Feeling it down to his toes. Then he pulled back.

"Okay."

"So how hard is this climb, really?" Luca asked when they started moving toward the ocean again.

Oliver eyed him. "Definitely not that hard, not for you. We'll probably work up a decent sweat though."

"And Eliza climbed this? Every day?"

"Every day."

Oliver had never really considered how his ancestor must have felt, what must have driven her to do it, every single day, to push her muscles past the aching point, but he thought he might have an inkling now.

"She was something else, wasn't she?"

"I wish I could've met her," Oliver said.

"Oh, I think you've got plenty of her in you," Luca said, his tone amused. "And your mother, too."

He couldn't help but smile at that. "It's not that she doesn't like you," he said.

"I don't think I've ever honestly worried about a parent liking me." Luca paused, like he was considering this. "Though, now that I think about it, I don't think I've ever *met* a parent, before."

Oliver supposed he shouldn't be surprised, but he was. "You really didn't date before this?" How could someone like Luca not be inundated with offers? And surely he said yes to some of them. Oliver thought of his confident and sure touch and knew he definitely wasn't living the life of a monk.

"Oh, I dated," Luca said wryly. "Handful of dates here or there. Lots of guys just like me. Driven. Ambitious. Arrogant. Focused on what they believed was really important."

"I can't imagine why none of those worked out." Oliver couldn't quite keep the sarcasm from his tone.

"It's not like your business isn't important to you, but it's not the *only* important thing. You care about this town. About Marjorie. About Aaron. About your mother. I bet a couple dozen people in this town could need you and you'd come running."

Oliver wasn't sure about that.

"Maybe," he allowed, "but they'd only do it to get the first scoop."

"Or maybe not," Luca said.

They'd made it to the edge of town now, and Oliver guided them to the path that led to a steep-ish slope, the ground rising toward the top of the cliff. The day was warm, just the faintest hint of the beginnings of spring. He tipped his head back, let the warm breeze wash over him. It felt good to be outside, to be drinking in the fresh air. He didn't do this nearly enough.

Maybe after Luca left town, he'd make it a habit, just like Eliza had.

Maybe she hadn't climbed all the way up this hill because she'd wanted to look for Nathaniel. Maybe she'd done it because sitting at home and staring at the walls with only her own thoughts for company made her want to crawl up them.

"So you really meant it, didn't you, when you said you didn't go on second dates," Oliver said after a few minutes of silence passed between them.

Luca shrugged. "You caught me."

"What does your family think about that?"

His gaze swung toward Oliver. He'd taken off his windbreaker, shoving it into his backpack, and his skin was flushed and dotted with sweat. It was a really good look on him.

"My cousin Ren asked me if I'd finally found someone to 'unbend me' or . . .uh . . .what was it? 'Remove the stick from my ass'? So yeah, they don't like it very much."

Oliver felt a rush of shock. "You told your family about me?"

"I'll let you in on a little secret." Luca set his hands on his hips, pausing on the trail. "If you think this town is nosy, it's got nothing on the Morettis. I mentioned you, and they were like a dog with a bone."

"That's cute, though," Oliver said. Not charmed at all. No way. Or pleased that Luca *had* mentioned him, in whatever capacity it had been.

"You only say that because they don't harass you. Though . . ." Luca pursed his lips. "If a random fruit basket shows up on your doorstep, enjoy the fruit and ignore whatever message comes with it."

"A fruit basket?"

"My cousin Ren again. Always a huge pain in my ass. But sort of better now that he's my brother's huge pain in the ass."

"Oh, he's the one who works with Gabe, right?" Oliver knew he shouldn't be memorizing every aspect of Luca's family. It wasn't that kind of relationship. He'd never fly out to California and have to identify a whole slew of Morettis.

Though he knew if he ever wanted to, Luca would welcome him.

But then he'd have to leave again, and history would just repeat itself.

"Yes, they own the food truck together."

"Come on," Oliver said, reaching out a hand. "We're only about twenty minutes from the top. And the view has to be seen to be believed."

Luca took it, and maybe his hand was a little damp, but then Oliver's wasn't exactly dry either. As they climbed, Oliver discovered that really didn't matter.

⁕⁕⁕

Oliver hadn't been kidding about them working up a sweat, but it was different in a gym, somehow.

Less urgent. Less his own power driving him up the hill.

He found himself enjoying this more than he'd expected, the burn in his muscles beginning to fade as they emerged through the tree line and reached flat ground, the ocean spread out around them.

"Wow," he breathed out, unsteady, as he walked closer, taking in the incredible view.

"Wasn't lying, was I?" Oliver sounded smug, and maybe it shouldn't have been adorable, but it was.

"I still kinda can't believe she made that climb every day."

"Maybe it's one of those things that got embroidered after the fact. Makes the story more dramatic," Oliver theorized as he sat on a big flat rock positioned just near the cliff with a perfect view off the edge.

"Or maybe she really did it. Love . . ." Luca hesitated. "Love makes you do crazy things, sometimes."

"I wouldn't know," Oliver said wryly. "Never been in love before."

He wasn't looking at Luca. He was just looking out at the ocean—like it held the answers to every question.

The problem with that was Luca wanted to discover every single question Oliver wanted to ask. Not just discover though . . .be *told* them, from Oliver himself.

"Neither would I." Though he'd certainly seen his share of love. His parents, absolutely. Marcella and her husband. Marco and his ever-revolving door of boyfriends and girlfriends, none of whom stuck around, but all of whom he loved, even if it was only for a little while. Gabe and his boyfriend, Sean. Ren and Seth, and, seriously, who had pegged *that* happening? Luca had been sure Ren would stay single as long as he did, and it had come as a bit of a shock to discover the truth.

If Lorenzo Moretti could fall in love, then *anyone* could.

Even he could.

"I guess we're both just a little fucked up." Oliver sighed, reluctantly.

"I don't think so," Luca said. "Just busy."

Oliver tucked his knees under his chin, wrapping his arms around his legs. He still hadn't looked at Luca.

Maybe this was really why he didn't go on second dates much—if ever. Because he didn't know what to say when things got serious.

Because he didn't know what to say to Oliver now. *You're wonderful and amazing and you deserve to fall in love with someone who loves you and who will always put you first.*

He thought about saying it, but Oliver's words from earlier were still echoing in his head: *I just want to live in the moment.*

If all they were going to get was the moment, Luca wanted that too.

"I'm thinking about getting busier," Oliver said out of the blue. Now he glanced over at Luca. And if there'd ever been a burning regret in his eyes that love wasn't in the cards for them, it was gone now. Or hidden.

God knew Luca had hidden his own deep inside, so deep he didn't have to put a name to it.

"You are?"

"Mrs. Casey, who owns the antiques shop next door, cornered me at the last festival meeting and told me she's thinking of finally retiring. Sometime in the next year. I always told her if she did, I'd buy her out. Expand."

"What would you do with the extra space?"

"More commercial baking," Oliver said with conviction, like he'd been thinking about this for a while. "And expanding the menu. Maybe even trying out a dinner a few days a week."

It shouldn't have hit Luca like a freight train.

He'd *known* Oliver's roots were deep here, that they wove into the ground. He'd come back, after all, hadn't he, from Charleston, after pastry school, and working there for a few years. He *wanted* to be in Indigo Bay. His family had practically founded the town, and he was as much part of it as the red and pink color scheme. So it shouldn't have come as a shock that he wasn't only not willing to leave, he was digging those roots in even deeper, expanding his business.

But it did, anyway.

That thing Luca had buried deep down, the thing he didn't want to name, throbbed.

"What do you think about that?" Oliver asked, less certain now, after Luca lapsed into silence.

He cleared his throat. "I think you could do anything you set your mind to," he said. "Whether that's put together a big commercial bakery or expand into a restaurant. I think you could do it all."

Oliver's voice was quiet. "That means something, coming from you."

"You'd need more help."

"Yeah. Aaron has a friend in pastry school who I've thought about hiring. If we expand, I'll need to hire *someone*. Plus, Aaron's ready for some additional responsibility, I think."

"They grow up too fast," Luca said. "One day Gabe was a gawky teenager, and the next he wanted to manage the deli, and I told him he was crazy, and well . . .I won't lie. That was the beginning of the end for us."

"Not the end. You told me you talked," Oliver reminded him gently.

Something he'd never have done if he hadn't come here and met Oliver and seen a different way to approach things, a different way to approach *people*. If Oliver hadn't told him to stop regretting the past and do something about it.

"We did. It's . . .better. We're better. Probably not fixed."

"Oh, it'll take more than a few phone calls for that to happen," Oliver teased. "You gotta put in the work." He nudged his shoulder. "At least we know that's one thing you're not afraid of."

"Come on." Luca heard the gruffness in his own voice. "Let's eat."

"Sure."

He'd stowed away a bottle of wine in his bag, and when he pulled it out, along with the plastic cups he'd stolen from the kitchen at the Inn, Oliver burst out laughing.

"Listen," Luca said sternly, the corner of his mouth twitching up into a smile he couldn't quite help, "you can take the Italian boy out of Napa, but you can't take Napa out of the Italian boy."

"I can see that," Oliver said.

He'd prepped and wrapped two paninis, and pressed between Oliver's focaccia was salami, capicola, ham, and provolone cheese, as well as some marinated tomatoes and artichoke hearts he'd started storing in jars in the walk-in, with the hopes Giana could be convinced to add this to the menu.

"This is really good," Oliver said, after taking a big bite, chewing and swallowing. "I love the artichokes."

"I'll give you my recipe," Luca said and realized as soon as the words were out of his mouth that it wasn't *his* recipe. It was something he'd adapted from one of Nonna's. She'd used it on olives, but he actually didn't particularly care for olives, so he'd tried it on artichokes instead, and preferred it that way.

Oliver raised an eyebrow, like he'd realized the reason for the frozen expression on Luca's face. He reached up, patting him on the cheek.

"You can," he said. "Or you can *not*. It's alright. I'll figure something out."

Luca shook his head, trying to clear it. "It's just . . ." He couldn't explain it. How Nonna had taken him into her confidence, trusted him, taught him everything she'd known, everything he'd ever need to know. How precious that had felt, how fiercely he'd fought to protect it. How intensely he'd loved her for her complete faith in him.

"I get it," Oliver said, and he actually sounded like he did. "You think I'd give you my mom's scone recipe? Even if you begged really nicely?"

Luca took a drink of wine. This pinot noir was good, probably too good to be drinking out of plastic cups, but he decided he didn't care. "What if I seduced you with sexual favors?"

Oliver grinned, a wild look settling into his eyes that Luca didn't think he'd ever tire of seeing. "I'd love to see you try."

"Seems worth exploring," Luca said nonchalantly, trying to ignore the fact that his cock was already half-hard, just from the idea.

Or the *other* idea he kept having, about Oliver pinning him to the bed and just making him *take it*.

Not listening at all to any of his begging and pleading, just pinning him down, *tying* him down, and making him give up all the control it felt like he'd spent his whole life hoarding close.

He swallowed hard. These were crazy thoughts. Thoughts he had during too many late nights, late nights *alone*. Though he'd certainly never had them before, not with anyone else.

Because you've never trusted anyone to take care of you, not like you do Oliver.

"Maybe later," Oliver replied, equally nonchalant. "Or anything else you happen to come up with."

Luca's fingers tightened on his cup. What would it be like, to give up that part of himself? To give it up to Oliver?

Maybe he wouldn't even like it.

Or maybe he'd love it a little too much, and it would make everything harder.

"I wasn't sure if you had other things to do today, besides me," Luca teased.

"No." Oliver leaned closer. "Just you." Kissed him then, and he tasted like the wine and artichokes and everything in the world that was suddenly irresistible and delicious.

"God," Luca groaned when they finally broke apart. "Why did we climb up this freaking hill again?"

"Because you wanted to see the ocean. The *other* ocean." Oliver stood then and walked over to the edge of the cliff, dusting the crumbs off his lap.

"It's beautiful."

Oliver didn't turn around, but Luca had a feeling he *knew* he wasn't looking at the ocean at all, but at his own back.

Luca wrapped his arms around Oliver's middle and tugged him against him. Oliver leaned in, the warmth of him heating him right through.

By the time they made it back to Oliver's house, Luca's blood had heated from a simmer to a boil.

Part of it was just being with Oliver. Watching him smile, hearing him laugh, touching him as much as he could get away with, even as they hiked down the hill, the afternoon sun warm on their skin.

The other part of it was the thoughts that kept crowding in.

The thoughts about Oliver sitting on top of him and smiling just like that, the corner of his mouth quirking up, as he made him *take it*.

Take whatever he deigned to give him.

He'd never wanted anything like it before.

You never got close enough to anyone to trust them before.

And that was true. He'd kept every hookup, every date, at an arm's length. But not Oliver. He'd just taken Luca's arm and slunk under it, like he simply belonged closer.

They turned the corner, and Oliver's little house came into view, Luca swallowing hard.

If you don't ask for it now, you'll never know. You'll never get what you really want.

What you really need.

"You've been quiet," Oliver said, unlocking the door with keys he'd pulled from his pocket.

"Just thinking." Luca shrugged, trying to make light of it, but Oliver knew him better by now.

He shot him a look as he let them into the house.

They slipped off their dirty sneakers in the little tiled foyer, and Oliver gestured. "Let's get something to drink," he said.

Like they hadn't come back here just to fuck.

Still, he let Oliver wander into the kitchen, and grab two bottles of water, taking one from his hands.

But instead of opening it, he set it down on the table. Had trouble meeting Oliver's eyes but he did it anyway. How did someone even ask for something like this? What if Oliver didn't want to do it? Would it ruin everything?

It was why he hadn't said anything about it before.

He was too afraid of messing up the short time they had together.

"You gonna tell me what you're agonizing about?" Oliver asked lightly, tilting his face up toward Luca's.

It would be so easy to just kiss him and take him to bed. He knew it wouldn't be bad. In fact, he knew just how good it would be between them.

But he wanted more. Was he wrong to want more?

You'd only be wrong if you weren't honest with Oliver about it.

"Promise me you won't judge," Luca said. Even though he already knew Oliver wouldn't. This was *Oliver*.

Oliver reached up and tucked a hand around his neck, dipping under the collar of his T-shirt. He shivered, not just because of the cold brush of Luca's fingers, but his touch, right where he was vulnerable.

"Like I ever would," Oliver said, rolling his eyes a bit. But his expression was so fond. "Come on, you can tell me anything."

"Remember the first time we met?"

"How you almost had me imprisoned for manslaughter?" Oliver chuckled. "How could I forget?"

"I was more thinking about how you lectured me afterward. About crosswalks."

"*That's* what's on your mind?" Oliver was straight out laughing now.

"Sort of." Luca squirmed internally. Could he admit it? Could he tell Oliver how much he wanted it? "But you looked at me, then, and again, when I almost ran you over at the Inn, and I wanted you to look at me like that again . . .in bed."

Oliver raised an eyebrow. "You just want me to look at you?"

"I want you to pin me down. Uh." Luca told himself not to lose his nerve now. "Put me in my place. Make me take it. Whatever you want to give me."

Oliver's eyebrow hit his hairline now. He didn't say anything.

"If you want to. If it doesn't—" Luca nearly lost it then. Nearly turned away. The only thing that kept him rooted in place was the hot look in Oliver's eyes. Like he was interested. *Intrigued.* "If it isn't something you want too, that's fine, I just—"

"I want it," Oliver interrupted. "What, do you want me to tie you up?"

Luca nearly choked. "I . . .uh . . .I don't think I made it that far. But . . .maybe we could start with something a little . . .less terrifying?"

Oliver smiled. "We can. Come on," he said and was sliding that hand down, tangling his fingers with Luca's, tugging him in the direction of the bedroom.

"Do you think you can do what I say and not stop?" Oliver asked archly as he turned in the middle of the room, suddenly pressing their bodies together. He glanced over at the bed. Specifically at the slats of the wooden headboard. "Like you could hold on to those and not let go?"

He could do that.

And not only that, but suddenly, he wanted nothing more than to do just that.

Luca nodded, his throat suddenly too dry to speak.

Just talking about the idea of it, the hazy amorphous thought of it, had made his dick hard as a rock. And then seeing the headboard? Hearing what Oliver was asking him to do?

He'd never been harder in his whole life.

"You gotta use your words," Oliver murmured to him. "That's important, okay?"

"Yes," Luca managed to get out. "Yes, I can do that."

"You need to remember one more thing for me," Oliver said, and he was pulling his T-shirt off.

Luca almost nodded but then he remembered what Oliver had just said. He needed to use his words.

"Yes," he said. "Anything."

"If it's too much, you can say stop, and I'll stop. No matter what, I'll stop."

"No matter what?"

"No matter what," Oliver promised. "And if you're still good, at any point, you can tell me to keep going and I'll keep going."

Oliver's hands slid down his chest and were hovering right above the button his jeans. Surely he could feel how much Luca wanted him. How much he wanted this.

"Okay," Luca said. Considered if it was okay to *ask* for what he wanted, but then he realized, he already had. He'd asked for Oliver to give him whatever he needed—not whatever he wanted—and there was a kind of empty bliss in the idea he was completely in Oliver's hands.

But when Oliver leaned in and kissed him, he *could* kiss back.

Lost himself in the taste and feel of his mouth against his own, the nimble push-and-pull of his tongue. Didn't even realize Oliver had stripped him down until he felt his palm press against his throbbing dick.

He groaned.

"Get on the bed," Oliver said. His voice was firmer, more certain, but it was sweet too.

The best of both worlds.

Luca didn't hesitate. He scrambled up on the bed, shedding everything around his ankles as he went. Settling in, he reached for the slats of the headboard and felt the satisfactory bite of the edges of them into his palms as he gripped them.

"Good," Oliver said. "Such a good boy."

Luca swallowed hard. He didn't want to like it. But he fucking loved it.

"You still good?" Oliver asked, reached for the hem of his own shirt.

"Yes."

Oliver nodded as he pulled off the rest of his clothes. Then he didn't do anything. Didn't move toward the bed. Didn't touch Luca. Just stood there, naked, and let Luca look.

"You're so gorgeous," Luca said, his voice a deep, dark rasp he barely recognized as his own.

"Yeah, you like what you see?" Oliver reached down and gripped his cock, giving himself a squeeze, bliss flooding his expression, and Luca swore under his breath. He wanted to be those hands. He wanted to be the one touching Oliver. Making him feel good.

But he wasn't going to. Not this time. He tightened his grip on the wooden slats and tried to stop gasping so desperately.

"I love it," he breathed out and meant every single word.

He wanted to see it forever. And not just Oliver's slim body, the perfect peach of his ass, the pale pink of his lips and his nipples, but the intent gaze of his hazel eyes. The way he looked through Luca and saw down to the real him.

How many people had ever done that with him? They'd only ever seen the surface. The polished, arrogant, urbane exterior. Even his own family focused on that.

But not Oliver.

"You gonna stay still for me?" Oliver asked as he finally climbed on the bed, dipping his head down, close to Luca's cock. It twitched helplessly, wanting some kind of friction. But instead, Oliver nuzzled his hip, tongue flicking out and tasting him there.

Luca groaned. He was lost in it: the feel of Oliver's lips against his skin, the brush of Oliver's hair on his stomach, the pressure of his own hands around the wood.

"I think," Oliver mused like he wasn't driving Luca insane with want, "I'm gonna ride you. Slide you right in and make you take it at *my* pace. Nice and slow." He pinned Luca with that look, the same one he'd worn the first time they'd met, and the second, too. The look that had turned him on unbearably then, and still did now. "And you're not going to come. Not til I'm good and ready for you to. Not til I do."

The high-pitched whine that came out of Luca's throat wasn't something he even recognized. But it seemed answer enough for Oliver, because he was leaning over him, grabbing lube and a condom from the drawer, his stomach brushing over Luca's throbbing cock, giving him for one brief, blissful second the kind of pressure he was desperate for.

Then it was gone, and he could only watch, helplessly, as Oliver slicked up his fingers and reached behind him.

He whined again.

He wanted to see. He wanted to witness every explicit moment of Oliver fingering himself.

But all he could do was lie here and watch as the pleasure flickered over Oliver's expressive face.

"How many?" he asked, breathlessly.

"Two," Oliver said, his own voice not quite steady. "One more, and then I'm going to pin you down and fuck you so good you aren't even going to know your own name."

"I don't really know it right now," Luca admitted with a laugh. And Oliver hadn't even really touched him yet.

But then Oliver did, unexpectedly dropping down and slipping his flushed cock into his mouth, giving him a hard suck and then another, until Luca was forced to focus on not thrashing, fucking up into the warm wetness.

"Shit," Luca groaned.

Oliver pulled off, and he wanted to groan again, even louder. "You still good?" he asked, and this time his voice had an unmistakable tremor in it. God, what if he'd fucked himself with the third finger while he'd been sucking Luca off?

His brain whited out at the thought, and only the constant pressure of his hands around the wood kept him in place.

"Yes. I'm good. So good," he croaked out after a long moment.

Luca watched him tear open the condom. And braced himself for the inevitable pleasure. He was so sensitive now, only his strength of will keeping him from pushing up into Oliver's touch. From wallowing in the feel of him.

But he was taking what Oliver was giving him.

That was all.

"That's it, baby, take it," Oliver crooned to him as he swung a leg over his chest and then there was indescribable pressure, unbearable pleasure, as his cock began to slip into Oliver's body.

He braced his hands on Luca's chest and trembled as he took him all the way down.

By the end, it was Luca who was shaking. It was so good, so overwhelming. He wanted nothing else but to reach out and take Oliver. Touch him. Be the hand that was working his cock as he worked his body down onto Luca's dick.

But he didn't, because he'd said he wouldn't. Because when Oliver had asked, he'd said he could.

Truthfully, more than he wanted to touch, he wanted to be good for Oliver. Keep his promise. Let him do whatever he wanted and *take* it.

"Shit," Oliver breathed out as he began to thrust down. "God, you feel so good."

Luca wanted to agree, because the pleasure was overwhelming, but he couldn't think about the hot, tight clasp of Oliver's body, so warm and so slick, because if he did, he'd come. He was that close. And he couldn't. Not until Oliver told him he could.

Not until after Oliver had gotten everything he wanted out of him.

It was the only thought he could hold on to as Oliver used him. Took everything he needed.

Good, good, good, he chanted to himself as Oliver threw his head back and groaned, fucking him slow and steady.

"Yeah, baby, you're so good. The goddamn best," Oliver panted, and Luca realized he was babbling all of this out loud.

It was one hundred and eighty degrees different from all the dignified, choreographed sex he'd had in the past. Restrained and skillful. This was real and sweaty and desperate.

"I wanna touch you," Luca begged.

"But," Oliver said with a wild grin, "you wanna be good more. I know, baby. It's so hot."

"So hot," Luca croaked as finally Oliver began to ride him harder. He could see himself disappearing, flushed and wet into Oliver's body and it might've been the sexiest thing he'd ever seen.

Tying with the way Oliver threw his head back and groaned as he stroked his cock.

"I'm gonna come," Oliver cried out.

But he hadn't given Luca permission and so he gritted his teeth together and just *watched* as Oliver's face went blank with ecstasy, his body contracting around Luca's cock in one mesmerizing pulse after another. Painting his way up Luca's chest. Each stripe of come landing on him felt like a brand. Like he'd feel them forever, every time he closed his eyes.

Then Oliver blinked and nodded. "You wanna come?"

Luca couldn't quite comprehend it, for a second. Then . . . *"Yes, God, yes please. Let me, please."*

"Then come, baby," Oliver said, leaning forward, and Luca couldn't help himself. He thrust up once and then twice and nearly screamed as his orgasm overtook him. It felt like it went on forever, his hips moving over and over like they couldn't possibly stop. No doubt Oliver was overstimulated and maybe it was even hurting a little as Luca's orgasm roared through him, but he didn't flinch. Didn't make him stop. Just talked him through it, telling him how beautiful he was, how hot he was, how much Oliver cared about him.

Finally, it ended. Luca felt flushed and distant. Felt the brush of Oliver's hands as he loosened his grip on the wood slats one finger at a time. As he slipped Luca's cock out of himself.

Felt the damp washcloth as Oliver cleaned up his chest.

Then he was cuddling up next to him, the heat of his body slowly bringing him back one breath at a time.

"You good?" Oliver asked.

Luca's eyes opened, looked into his intent gaze.

"Yeah, yeah," he croaked. "Never been better."

"You enjoyed that," Oliver stated rather than asked.

"So did you," Luca retorted. But his voice was so sweet. Had he ever sounded like this? He wasn't sure.

But whatever change Oliver had wrought inside him, it felt like a miracle. His own personal miracle.

Changing him from a cold, remote, distant statue into a real, flesh-and-blood man.

A man who felt things he'd never imagined he would until now.

Until Oliver.

Chapter Fourteen

OLIVER HAD WONDERED IF things would shift between him and Luca after their life-changing sex of the other day.

He'd thought maybe Luca would regret being laid so bare, made so vulnerable. That he'd pull away, because it was so much more than he'd experienced with anyone else. That he'd be smart about it, even a little cold, and start to put distance between them, because in less than a week, that was all they'd have.

Distance.

Oliver couldn't say that he hadn't considered the possibility himself.

Should he cut Luca out? Or at least freeze him out a little? His mom's words echoed through him, a reminder that the only thing he was going to feel when Luca flew away was pain.

But he'd have the memories too, and the belief that he *could* do this with someone.

That in only a few weeks, he could fall for someone.

Because even though he'd rather die than admit it, he loved Luca.

Wanted him in his life, even if it was impossible.

But he couldn't bear the thought of pulling away.

You only have a little more time left, he thought as he glanced up from his laptop. Luca had invited himself over tonight—sort of unspoken, in that he'd showed up just as Oliver was finishing up at the bakery, and they'd walked back to Oliver's house together.

"I'm cooking you dinner again," Luca had announced, even when Oliver had reminded him he had festival business he *needed* to take of tonight.

"It's alright," Luca said, "I've got work to tackle after dinner, too." And who was Oliver to say no when Luca was that determined?

"What are you making me?" Oliver asked, because it was hard to keep his eyes on his screen, on the work he *knew* he needed to get done, when Luca was in his kitchen, and the smells were already amazing. Roasted garlic and something nutty, like parmesan or nuts, toasting in a pan on the stove.

"Something simple. Cacio e pepe, with a roasted garlic and pine nut gremolata," Luca said. "My favorite quick go-to, when I'm home and need some carbs for a long night of work."

"You do that?" Oliver asked, standing up, stretching and then wandering into the kitchen. "If we're having pasta, you should grab that extra sourdough I brought home and toast it up."

"Already found it," Luca said, clearly making himself comfortable in Oliver's kitchen, which wasn't attractive at all. Or the way he'd rolled up his shirtsleeves and already had pasta boiling away in the pot and a pan with garlic and parsley simmering in olive oil.

Nope. Not at all.

"And," he added, shooting Oliver a rueful smile, "yes, way too often, honestly."

"Really?" Oliver couldn't believe it. He worked long hours at the bakery, yes, but he'd spent the time when he'd first opened to automate his billing and ordering systems and hired the best accountant in town to take care of his books, so when he came home, he *came home*. He didn't just spend a few more hours working just because he had to.

Those steps had made his margin razor thin at the beginning, but it had been worth it, because he hadn't burned out, like so many other restaurant owners he'd known in Charleston.

Was Luca like that? But he'd told Oliver he didn't work the line, not normally. So what was he spending all his time doing that he needed to work when he came *home* from work?

Luca glanced up from the cheese he was shredding into a neat pile on Oliver's butcher block.

"Really," Luca said. "And yes, I'm a workaholic normally. This is . . ." He hesitated. "A break of sorts, for me. That's what my mom told me, when I came here. That I should take the time."

"That why everyone's running interference for you at home?" Oliver wondered.

"Sort of, yes, I think so," Luca admitted.

"But still, how are you working so much? How much are you overseeing, day-to-day?" Oliver was curious, because at some point in the very near future, all he'd have of Luca were these little glimpses into his regular life. He'd be able to glance at his watch and think, *right now, Luca's at the restaurant, shaking hands and asking people how their dinner was. Right now, he's eating a family meal with the staff. Right now, he's in his office at home, running through the daily take and reconciling it.*

He already knew they wouldn't be keeping in contact when he left, because it was going to be too hard as it was. They didn't need to prolong the agony, even though Luca had become a good friend, too, in the last few weeks, not just a lover Oliver was desperate to keep.

"I spend some time at the deli mid-morning to early afternoon, working with the manager there, to avoid any issues, then I move over to the main Nonna's location. Sometimes I'll stop over and check in with Marco at the steakhouse, but he likes it when I keep my hands out of his business." Luca rolled his eyes. "But I'll see Marcella, my sister, who is in charge of the front of the house, have a quick meeting with Dario, who's our accountant, and sometimes I'll get to see my parents, too, if they're coming around. Then I work the floor, usually for most of dinner service, but I can usually sneak into the kitchen for a quick meal, before settling in with paperwork and email for the evening."

Oliver didn't ask if he could work less.

He knew that wasn't how Luca functioned. It wasn't even how *he* functioned. He knew Aaron was a competent and capable assistant. He could handle the bake more than one day a week, which was what he was currently doing, but Oliver had resisted changing the schedule. Why? He *liked* having his hands in the dough, having his fingers in every pie, feeling the pulse of his bakery around him.

Luca was the same.

He wanted to be involved. *This* involved.

"It's a good life," Luca said quietly. Like he knew what Oliver was thinking. "Lonely, maybe, but good. I love my family."

Oliver knew it.

But it didn't stop him from sneaking up behind Luca and putting his arms around him, holding him close for a single moment, resting his cheek on the broad planes of his back.

It didn't stop him from wishing for things he couldn't have.

"Same," he echoed in a low voice.

For a long moment, neither of them moved. Then Luca cleared his throat and Oliver let go.

It was killer, the letting go, but necessary. He knew it was.

He returned to his laptop and Luca cleared his throat again, glancing over. The look in his dark eyes burned. And Oliver knew it wasn't only killing him. "Dinner ready in a few," he said. "Once the pasta's cooked, it goes quick."

Sure enough, a few minutes later, Luca set down two plates on his little kitchen table, full of delicious-smelling pasta.

"This looks amazing." Oliver picked up a fork, twirling it in the beautiful mound of pasta. Groaned after he shoved it in mouth, chewing through the bliss. "*Tastes* amazing, too."

Luca's smug expression might've been a turnoff, but he was just as good as he thought he was, and that made it kind of hard to blame him for it.

"Thanks," he said.

"No, really, *thank you*," Oliver said. "Without you, I'd probably have scrounged in my freezer for frozen pizza or something."

"Or something?"

"You have something against frozen pizza?" Oliver had a feeling he totally did. This was Luca Moretti after all.

Oh, well, not everything about him could be perfect.

"There's a reason I haven't invited my mother to my place in ages," Luca said, dropping his voice down, like his mother might spring out from behind the ficus in the corner. "She'd go through every cupboard, every drawer in my fridge, and *definitely* through the freezer."

"What would she find there?" Oliver asked innocently.

"Not just frozen pizza, but *mozzarella sticks*, too." Luca sighed. "Listen, we all need our vices."

"Let me guess, you pair your shitty frozen mozzarella sticks with really good wine."

Luca chuckled. "Guilty as charged."

"See, I knew I didn't run you over for a reason," Oliver teased, waving his fork in the air in Luca's direction. "Knew I'd like you."

Knew I'd love you.

Luca met his gaze directly and was laughing too. And then, suddenly, he wasn't, that burning look in his dark eyes back from earlier.

The feeling pressed, hard and insistent and undeniable, against Oliver's breastbone.

This was the most exquisite pleasure and the worst pain he'd ever felt, all tangled together.

It would be easier if they *could* separate themselves, if he had the nerve to back away now, while things were easier. Not *easy*, but easier.

But he couldn't do it. He just didn't have the courage.

Instead, he was greedy and wanted to grab everything he was allowed, right up til he wasn't anymore.

Luca coughed and returned his gaze to his plate.

Maybe it should've made Oliver feel better that he wasn't alone in feeling this way. But it didn't; in fact, it made it feel *worse*, if that was even possible.

"So," Luca said, "what do you have to do tonight, still?"

"Finalize the placement of the vendors," Oliver said. "And review someone's application that came in *quite* late."

The corner of Luca's mouth quirked up. "Oh, who's that?" he asked innocently, like hadn't sent it over himself just this afternoon.

"Someone trying to get the attention of the town," Oliver said. "If the food's anything like this, I think they'll succeed."

"Inside's spruced up too."

"You convince Enzo to do the mural?" Oliver had both been surprised at the idea—and not very surprised at all. Surprised, because he hadn't once thought of it, even though it was a damn good thought, and not surprised, because of course Luca would be brilliant like that.

There was that feeling again.

Suddenly, the food tasted like ash in his mouth.

He looked up to find Luca staring at him intently.

"No," Luca said conversationally, but with purpose. *Intent.* "No, you didn't want to talk about it, and we're not going to."

Oliver swallowed his food. "But—"

Luca's eyes pleaded with his uncooperative heart. "I thought we weren't trying to make this any harder," he said quietly.

Yeah, that ship fucking sailed. The moment you trusted me the way you did, the way you opened up to me, the way I was there for you, when you came back down.

"We're not," Oliver promised.

He was not going to cry. He was absolutely not going to cry.

"Okay, good." Luca took a deep breath. "Cause I think you might've had the right idea."

"Should I record that? Play it back for you when you become particularly insufferable, especially when you find out where I've put Nonna's table?"

"What, you put us *where*?" Luca demanded playfully.

Had he ever imagined that Luca *could* be playful? Not at the beginning, no. He'd been so serious, so buttoned-up. So worried about doing the right thing all the time. But he was breathing again, Oliver could *feel* it. Instead of hanging on to that, he was going to go right back to holding all the burdens, Oliver knew it.

Couldn't even blame him, because he knew this was how Luca was.

Maybe it was something, a feeling Luca would remember forever, that Oliver had given him a bit of a respite, even if it was only for a few weeks.

That, Oliver decided, would have to be enough.

"Trust me, you should be lucky I put you in at all," Oliver retorted, keeping the same even, playful tone.

"Lucky, huh?" Luca raised an eyebrow. And before Oliver knew it, he was being picked up and carried to the bedroom, their meal and their work at least temporarily forgotten. And he was okay with that.

They wouldn't get many more chances.

The next morning, Oliver couldn't get the taste of the pasta, the remainder of which he'd scarfed down cold and delicious, when they'd finally returned to the table, mussed and satisfied an hour later, out of his mouth.

It lingered on his tongue and in his brain.

In his heart.

"I'm gonna try something," he told Aaron, who had a good handle on the last real bake of the morning. "You need me for anything?"

Aaron shook his head. "I'm gonna finish these pastries and get some dough proofing for the afternoon commercial bakes."

"Alright," Oliver said and tucked himself into the back corner of the kitchen, pulling out parmesan from the big walk-in fridge and black pepper from the pantry, and put together his dough, twisting it and turning it with layers of butter he'd mixed with the rich cheese and the sharp spice of the pepper.

"What's this?"

He looked up and Marjorie was standing there.

Either she and his mother were now sharing the same expression or they'd been talking.

Or, his mind supplied, *they're both on the same page because they love you, and they're worried about you.*

"Just trying out something new," Oliver said.

She glanced down at the counter, at the empty plastic container of parmesan he hadn't thrown away yet, and at the pepper next to it. "Trying some Italian recipes?" she asked.

"Sort of," Oliver said. He really didn't want to talk about this. It was just something he wanted to *do* because it was easier to keep his hands and mind busy than to dwell.

"Ah." It was only one syllable but it was telling anyway.

Damn it, he *did* enjoy living in a small town. Except right now, apparently.

"If you need to talk about . . .well, about anything, you know I'm here," Marjorie said. "Anything at all."

Oliver rolled his eyes. "I'm fine."

"It's okay to *not* be fine," Marge reminded him gently. Patted him on the shoulder. "Bring one of those to me when they're done. They smell delicious."

They tasted amazing too, Oliver nearly burning his fingers on the first off the tray when they came out of the oven twenty minutes later.

But the scorched roof of his mouth was worth it, because as he chewed, he fell right into that moment they'd shared last night. Luca had tasted just like this.

That, he decided, would also be enough.

Five minutes later, he brought one to Marge in the front, wrapped up in a napkin.

"I don't want to talk about it now, and probably not in a few days, either," Oliver said honestly as he handed her the pastry. "That's going to have to be okay with you."

"Anything's okay with me," she said, taking it from him. Took a bite. "Especially if you keep making stuff like this."

Oliver smiled. "Good, isn't it?"

"You going to tell . . ."

But she didn't get the rest of the sentence out, because the front door swung open and there was Luca in the flesh.

Before Oliver *had* decided if he was going to tell him about his new creation.

"Something smells amazing," Luca said, sniffing the air. "What is that . . .it almost smells like . . ."

Like you. Like the food you made us with your own two hands.

Oliver shrugged. Maybe it was better he knew—not everything, but some things. "I tried a new recipe," he said. "Inspired by that pasta you made last night. Cacio e pepe pastry."

He stole a flaky corner from Marjorie's twist and handed it across the counter, ignoring her screech of protest. Luca popped it in his mouth, tasting it deliberately, giving it a long moment against his tongue before he swallowed.

"That's really fucking amazing," Luca said. "You're so . . ."

They stared at each other for a moment, and for a moment, everything disappeared. Marjorie and her outrage, the bakery around them, Aaron in the back, the festival happening in two days, Giana and Enzo and all their problems.

Just for a second, it was just the two of them.

Oliver knew then that Luca loved him too.

Better, he thought, *and also worse.*

"Thanks," Oliver said. "You guys ready for the festival?"

"I think so," Luca said. "I swung by to give you something. You got a minute?"

"For you, yes," Oliver said. "You want coffee?"

"Yeah."

Oliver poured two coffees and at first he thought Luca wanted to sit in the cafe area—after all, it was nearly close, and they were empty, for the first time all day—but then Luca led him outside.

Behind his corner, where he leaned against the brick wall. Shot Oliver a look as he handed him his coffee.

"Thanks," he said shortly.

"You gonna tell me what this is about?" Oliver asked gently.

Please don't tell me you love me. For the love of God, don't do it.

"I should have done this ages ago," was all Luca said as he dug something out of his pocket and passed it over.

It was a piece of stationery from the Inn and scribbled on it was a recipe.

For focaccia.

"What's this?" Oliver asked, frowning.

"Something I should've given you before," Luca said ruefully. "I was stupid. Forgive me."

But Oliver wasn't getting it.

"Is there . . .something wrong with the focaccia I'm baking you?" he asked.

"No, not at all. It's delicious. It's just not—" Luca took a breath. Let it out. "This is my Nonna's focaccia recipe."

Suddenly, realization was beginning to dawn.

"You didn't want to give this to me before," Oliver said slowly.

"You don't understand, they're . . ." Luca hesitated. "When she taught me the recipes, the family recipes, she swore me to secrecy. I think she might've even been tempted to perform a blood oath, she was that serious. I was never to share them with anyone that wasn't family.

But . . ." There was that burning look again. The look that made Oliver catch his breath. "But I don't care. You're . . .well, you should have it. That's all."

"Because I'm making focaccia for your aunt's deli?" But Oliver asked it, knowing deep down, that wasn't why. He just wanted to hear Luca say it.

"If that's what you need to believe," Luca said, "then yes."

Oliver folded the recipe carefully and put it in his pocket.

They were quiet for a moment, sipping their coffee.

"You gonna put that on the menu?" Luca wondered.

Oliver didn't need to ask what he meant. He knew. The cacio e pepe twist he'd created today.

"Seems like a good way to keep you around," he said lightly, even though it was killing him.

Luca set his coffee down. Slowly. Deliberately. "Come here," he said quietly and tugged Oliver into his arms.

Kissing him like he never wanted to let him go.

And Oliver? Well, he knew what that felt like.

Because he felt it too.

⁂

Luca walked into the deli the next morning, the day before the festival, and found his aunt staring at his cousin, who'd begun to prep the wall for the mural he was going to paint.

He'd wanted to get a head start, Enzo had said the day before after Luca had approved his sketches, because he knew with the festival happening tomorrow, they'd hopefully be busier and he'd have less time to work on it.

"What's this?" Giana asked, directing the question not toward her son, but to Luca instead.

"I told you Enzo was going to do a mural. You saw the sketches, I'm assuming. I emailed them."

"I didn't," she said stiffly.

Luca was watching Enzo's back and couldn't miss the way it tensed, under his T-shirt, at his mother's words.

This had gone on long enough.

"Can I have a minute of your time?" he asked Giana.

"You've certainly taken a lot more without asking," she grumbled.

He took her arm and nudged her toward the kitchen door. "*Privately*," he said.

The door swung shut behind him. He hoped Enzo wouldn't be listening in, but he knew better.

"What's this about?" she asked.

He couldn't deny his temper was a little closer to the surface right now. It was probably how angry he was at fate, who'd set Oliver right in his path, the *perfect* person for him, even though he couldn't hope to keep him in his life. So he was generally pretty pissed off, and on top of that, he was *sad*, which wasn't an emotion he normally indulged in.

But getting annoyed with Giana, even if she deserves it, doesn't fix anything.

"Enzo's mural? You don't agree he did an incredible job on the sign?"

"That's not it," she said carefully. "That was just a sign. With chalk. No . . .no big deal if it didn't work out."

"But it did," Luca reminded her gently. "He's got skill, but more than that he's got talent." He hesitated, not sure how far he should go, but he saw her making the same mistakes he'd made with Gabriel. With Chiara and Ilaria. Mistakes he'd told himself he'd work hard to right. Didn't he have a responsibility to say something? "Talent he's wasting, working here with you."

She frowned. "Having a business to support him? A legacy he can pass onto his own children? That couldn't possibly be a waste."

"It is, if it's not what he wants," Luca said.

He'd been blunt, maybe, but Luca told himself as she slumped against the back kitchen counter that she'd needed to hear it.

"He's got so much talent, Giana," he said softly. "You saw the sketches?"

She nodded, finally admitting it. "I just . . .I just wanted more for him than an artist's life, you know? Never enough money, struggling to get by. I thought . . .why shouldn't he have what the rest of the Morettis have?"

"We don't *all* have it," Luca said dryly. "My brother Gabe left, started his own business, and when Ilaria graduated, she not only refused to come back home, she convinced Chiara to join her. They're managing a coffee shop now, and I think they're trying to turn it into a part-time art gallery. Just because we're Morettis doesn't mean we all want the same things."

Wasn't he learning that, the more time he spent in Indigo Bay?

He'd wanted more things, more *different* things, than he'd ever wanted back home in Napa. Even though that life was pulling him back in, he wouldn't forget the way he'd felt here.

"In fact," Luca continued, "maybe you should let him go."

Giana looked at him like he was crazy.

And maybe he was, a little bit. Maybe the thought of losing Oliver was unhinging him.

"Send him off to the west coast, maybe even to my sisters. There's lots of art schools in San Francisco."

She shook her head. "No, no, that's not what he's meant for. I did all this for him."

"I know, but that doesn't mean it's right," Luca said. Trying to be gentle, but feeling like he was talking to a brick wall. Maybe she couldn't see what he could so clearly. But it still felt like he should try. "Don't you want him to have what he wants? Don't you want him to be happy?"

"I wouldn't think you'd give a shit about that," Giana said, equaling his own bluntness. And that was fair. Before he'd come here, he hadn't, not really.

He'd been putting one foot in front of the other, doing the same things every day, because they were "right," not because he genuinely wanted to do them.

Some of them he did. He felt the weight and obligation of Nonna's legacy, yes, but he loved it, too.

But fixing every problem his family had? He was more than that. He *wanted* to be more than that.

Maybe he'd go back to California, but at least he could do it on his own terms going forward.

"I do," Luca said. "More than ever."

She pursed her lips. "You really want to send him off to California, too?"

"It's just a thought. He'd have family there, though. A support system. Just something to think about."

She didn't say anything. Was hopefully actually thinking about it, but Luca wasn't going to hold his breath.

"And now," Luca added, gesturing toward the front, "go back in there and tell him you're excited to see what he's going to create."

"What if—"

But Luca didn't let her finish. He could still be an arrogant asshole, sure of what was right, because he *knew* this was right. "Do it," he said. "I don't care if it turns out looking like a garbage fire. He wants to know you give a shit about him, about what *he* gives a shit about."

She sighed. "Alright." She paused, like this next part hurt. "And you're probably right."

"I usually am," Luca said with a grin.

She smacked him on the arm, but she was smiling now too. It was a little bittersweet, but Luca got it. Sometimes it was hard to let go of a dream, even if it wasn't *your* dream. "Be nice," she reminded him.

"Not my forte," Luca admitted.

"You'd be surprised," Giana said. "You didn't have to come here and help me. I know I wasn't very . . .easy about it."

"No kidding," Luca said. She smacked him again, and he laughed.

"But it was what I needed," she finished.

"Yeah," Luca agreed.

"What I'm trying to say is thank you," Giana said. "Don't make it any harder."

"Wouldn't dream of it."

"You know," she said, right before she walked out the kitchen door, "you should take some of your own advice."

"I'm trying," Luca said ruefully. "It's not that easy."

"Easy isn't worth doing," she said, before disappearing out the door, and Luca froze.

She'd been Nonna's youngest child, so of course she must've heard Nonna say that—it had been one of her favorite phrases, after all—but it hit him harder than normal to hear it repeated now.

Easy isn't worth doing.

It wasn't a question of what was easy, because it didn't feel like any of the available choices were exactly *easy*, but maybe that was the whole point. If getting everything he'd ever wanted was easy, it wouldn't be worth a damn.

Chapter Fifteen

The morning of Indigo Bay's Sweethearts Festival dawned bright and sunny, a perfect day to celebrate love.

Was Luca in the mood to celebrate love? Not really. He'd finally, after too long putting it off, booked his flight, mostly because his father had actually texted him back *finally*, asking when he was coming home.

The guilt, which he'd already felt staying this long when Giana was set on the right course, had overwhelmed him, and he'd set up his return flight without thinking about it too closely.

He'd leave tomorrow, and so today was his last day in Indigo Bay.

Oliver hadn't really said anything when he'd told him, just nodded, and Luca had believed—had *wanted* to believe—that he understood.

Still, it wasn't easy.

Nonna, nothing's easy. How do I choose when every choice is the hard way through?

But she didn't answer, and neither did the covered hotel pans full of sauce and meatballs and rolls set up in front of him.

Luca sighed.

He'd seen Oliver a few times in passing, as he and Giana had gotten their booth set up, but every single time, he'd looked busy and at points even frantic as he had directed traffic and vendors to where they were supposed to be.

"You want to talk about it?" Giana asked as he followed Oliver, crossing the square again, with just his eyes.

"There's nothing to talk about," Luca said.

That wasn't exactly true, but he didn't *want* to talk about it.

Thinking about it was hard enough.

"I know Enzo was really into him for a while, but I've never seen him date someone in town," Giana said. "He doesn't do that. I have a feeling you don't either. If both of you are willing to date, and *each other* . . .doesn't that mean something?"

Luca shot his aunt a look. "Okay, there might be something to talk about, but I'm not interested in talking about it."

"You should. Before you leave and regret it."

"No matter what happens, I'm going to regret it," Luca said wryly.

"You know my mother wouldn't have wanted you to do this to yourself," Giana said.

"Bringing out the big guns now, huh?" Luca said.

But he supposed he shouldn't be surprised. Still, Giana rarely talked about Nonna, even though she'd been her mother.

"Family is a lot," she continued, like he hadn't even said anything, "but it's not everything, Luca. Deep down, I think you know that."

"Except I'm the one who promised her I'd take care of the family."

"And you think the family didn't promise to take care of *you*?" Giana asked archly.

Luca opened his mouth and then clamped it shut again. Had she really? He'd question it more, but that sounded like a very Nonna thing to do.

"I just think you should take your own advice, that's all," she finished. "Think about it."

Like he'd been doing anything else.

He'd been doing so much thinking, he was sick to fucking death of his own brain.

Luca glanced down at his watch. It was eleven now, and more and more people were now filtering into Indigo Bay's central square. They'd be getting hungry soon, and hopefully they'd be busy enough he wouldn't have time to think at all.

An hour and a half later, Luca leaned back and stretched, the red apron he'd borrowed from Enzo pulling tight against his chest.

"Well, that's about it," Giana said, grinning over at him. "I can't believe we sold out."

"I can," Luca said.

She rolled her eyes. "I guess I should thank you again."

"No thanks necessary. We do this for one another because we're family. Because we're Morettis."

He didn't want to feel the weight of that right now, but the fact was, it was truth.

He had certain obligations.

Just the same as Oliver had his own here, and nothing had made that more apparent than today and how in demand he'd been, arranging things and running around with barely a moment to check in with Luca. When he had, Luca had sat him down behind their table and made him eat something.

He was one of this town's favorite sons. Owned one of the town's most beloved businesses.

No, if it had *ever* been a thought in Luca's mind that maybe he could take Oliver out of Indigo Bay, even if he'd wanted to go, Luca knew now he couldn't do it.

He was meant to stay here. Applaud on the sideline as his mother stood on the little stage and told the story in the same beautiful, stark detail as Oliver had of Nathaniel and Eliza.

He and Giana had just been about to finish cleaning up when Oliver arrived, out of breath and with a surprising look of panic on his face. No matter how busy he'd been today, there'd been absolutely no alarm to be seen before now.

"What's wrong?" Luca asked as he stacked empty pans.

"One of the couples dropped out of the dating game," Oliver said.

"Why?"

"Ironically, they broke up," Oliver said, a wry edge to his voice. "So yeah, not much help to us, now."

It seemed the easiest, most natural thing in the world to do, to ask him, "What can I do?"

"You're not going to like it," Oliver said.

Luca untied the apron and folded it up. He had a feeling he knew what was coming, and he also knew why Oliver didn't want to ask him. Also knew why Oliver had come to him. "Let me be the judge of that."

"I wouldn't ask . . .not if . . ."

"You need me to do it with you?" Luca interrupted him gently.

Oliver's hazel eyes widened further. "You would? Even though . . ."

Even though you're leaving tomorrow.

"Yes," Luca said. He couldn't do much for Oliver. But he could do this.

Oliver hadn't wanted to ask. It was bad enough Luca was leaving tomorrow. Bad enough and not at all a surprise, either, but he hadn't wanted to grind in the inevitable pain of his departure any more.

And participating together in the Dating Game, in front of the whole town and all the tourists who'd come in for the day, who might believe they were really together, that they were in love, that they might actually believe they had a future together?

That sounded like a little slice of heaven—and hell.

"You sure you're okay doing this?" Oliver checked in again, as they stood at the side of the stage, waiting to be introduced.

Marjorie was the emcee for the game, and she'd shot him a worried look when he'd arrived with Luca in tow.

It was not a perfect solution, for sure, but Luca would be good at this. Maybe they'd even gotten to know each other well enough they'd have a chance of getting a few questions right.

"I'm fine doing it," Luca said, flashing him one of his most devastating smiles. "You ashamed of me now, Oliver?"

"Never," Oliver said and reached out and took his hand, squeezed it. "I—" But he couldn't quite get the words out. Hadn't he promised himself he wouldn't make a fool of himself over their goodbye?

Telling Luca that he wasn't only *not* ashamed of him, but he'd never been prouder to introduce someone as *his*, even if it was only for a little while, was defeating the whole purpose.

"I know," Luca said and squeezed his hand back.

Not for the first time, Oliver believed he *did* know.

"Come on, let's get this shindig started," Marjorie said and led them onto the stage.

There were three sets of couples: Clare, the town's realtor, and her wife, Becca. Ned, who managed the grocery store, and his wife of nearly thirty years, Colleen, who'd worked with him every day for practically their entire lives. And Oliver and Luca.

"We don't have to win," Oliver murmured under his breath.

Luca raised an eyebrow. "Why are we here if we're not going to try to win?"

First, Marjorie asked them to introduce their partner, or as she put it, *their better half.*

Oliver listened to Clare tell everyone how amazing Becca was, how insightful and supportive, and how she created a perfect place for them to be together at home. Then Colleen talked about how hard Ned worked, how he'd fought against her working with him before he'd realized how strong a partnership they could have together.

He told himself he wasn't worried about what Luca would say about him—*I was just here for a few weeks and Oliver was a good way to pass the time, when I wasn't convincing my aunt to see sense*—but he was, a little.

He shouldn't have been.

Luca took the microphone from Marjorie with a charming smile that Oliver *knew* took in the crowd, because it had never once failed to take *him* in.

"I haven't known Oliver very long," he said, "but I *do* know just how incredible he is. He's giving and kind and sweet as hell, but he's not one of those people who's too sweet. Just when you think he might kill you with all that sugar, he gets snarky and honest. That's what I love most about him. How he never fails to give me the most real part of him, the most honest part."

Oliver's fingers, already trembling, straight up shook when he took the microphone from Luca. That was what Luca thought about him? He saw past the sweet, pleasant exterior he didn't necessarily put on for the world, but that he knew protected him anyway.

Luca saw *him*.

The Oliver underneath it all.

"You know," Oliver said, glancing in Luca's direction, "I didn't like you much at first."

Luca threw his head back, laughing hard. If the audience hadn't been won over by that moment, they were now.

"Seriously!" Oliver said with a chuckle. "You were kinda arrogant. Way too certain of how gorgeous and smart and perfect you were. Then I got to know you, and you *are* those things. But you're more too. You're loyal and the people you care about? You love them so fiercely."

Luca's gaze softened.

Maybe it made his love too obvious, like he was wearing it on his sleeve for everyone to see. But perhaps that was okay.

He hadn't ever wanted Luca to feel guilty about leaving, because Oliver *understood*, even though he hated it. But maybe it would be a good thing for Luca to know someone out there cared this much about him.

"You guys are absolutely adorable," Marjorie cooed.

But she still shot Oliver a quick look before she turned back to Clare and Becca to ask them the first question.

"Let's kick this off with the best question *I* could come up with," Marjorie continued, "Becca, what is your wife's favorite junk food? Their *deepest, secret* guilty pleasure?"

Becca laughed. "Oh, this is easy. Hands down, Taco Bell."

"Especially the Mexican Pizza," Clare cried out.

Everyone laughed.

"What about you, Colleen? What's Ned's favorite junk food?"

"Jellybeans. *All kinds*," she said, "but especially the licorice ones."

"Yep, she's got it," Ned said, a slow, fond smile breaking across his wrinkled face. "They're the best."

"What about you guys?" Marjorie said, turning toward where Luca and Oliver were sitting.

Now, Oliver had suspicions what Luca's guilty pleasure might be, at least when it came to junk food, but he *knew* Oliver's—at least if he remembered it.

"Oh, that's easy." Luca winked at Marjorie. "Frozen pizza."

"And you're not mad about that?" she asked archly.

"Hell no," Luca insisted. He shot Oliver a sweet, dopey smile, the kind of smile he'd never have in a million years believed Luca could possess. "How can you be mad at someone who creates such amazing things all day and then just wants a quick dinner?"

"You should be cooking for him," Becca pointed out.

"Trust me, I do."

Oliver watched Luca's face as a shadow crossed over it.

He *had*. But he wouldn't be cooking for him anymore. Not if he flew home tomorrow.

When he flies home tomorrow, Oliver reminded himself. He'd very scrupulously not even suggested to Luca he should stay—because they both knew he wouldn't even consider it—but also because if he asked and Luca said no, he wasn't sure he'd ever get over it.

"Good," Becca said. "You gotta win them over stomach first, right?"

"Right," Luca said weakly.

"Alright," Marjorie said. "First kiss! Who wants to describe theirs first?"

Becca and Clare nailed theirs, even acting it out on stage, to wild cheers.

Then Colleen talked about how Ned had been holding off, wanting to do something very silly, she said, like *respect* her, and she'd finally had to just grab him by the shirt collar and kiss *him*.

Then Marjorie turned to them, and suddenly Oliver didn't know if he had the stomach to do this.

But Luca had smiled at him, kind and sweet, the opposite of everything he'd once believed the man was. Maybe they were really more similar than he'd imagined. Maybe he was a little saltier than he'd realized, and Luca much sweeter.

"I kissed him," Luca said after taking the microphone from Marjorie, "because I couldn't imagine doing anything else. He'd just told me Eliza and Nathaniel's story and it was so romantic and he told it *so* well, can't imagine where he gets that from," he teased, glancing over at the audience, where Joy sat, "but he was just standing in front of me, and I realized if I didn't kiss him then, I'd regret it the rest of my life."

Oliver took a deep breath and then let it out slowly.

There was no way Luca wasn't looking at him with love in his eyes.

The game moved on, Marjorie teasing out answers from the other couples, even from them, but it passed in a haze of bittersweet longing for Oliver.

He'd found the man for him, the man he'd probably love for the rest of his life, but just because fate had placed him right in Oliver's path didn't mean they were actually *meant* to be together.

For the first time, as Oliver hugged Marjorie and then Becca and Clare, and even Ned, he thought hard about the possibility of leaving all this behind.

From the beginning he'd told himself going to California wasn't an option. His life was here. His family was here. His *bakery*. And Luca was right, his family's history and its love was literally woven into the town. How could he leave it? But how could he let love escape him without doing anything to stop it?

Oliver didn't know.

It was too much to think about, so overwhelming, he finally shoved it to the side as he found himself alone with Luca, standing by the edge of the stage. Luca looked apprehensive and a little guilty, like he'd said more than he'd meant.

Maybe they hadn't said the words, but they'd said enough.

"What do you want to do?" Luca finally asked, shifting from one foot to the other. Oliver didn't think he'd ever seen him anxious, but he was now.

That much was clear.

"I think—" Oliver breathed in and breathed out. He couldn't really come to terms with the idea of leaving now, but that didn't mean he couldn't *ever*, he'd have time to think about it after Luca left. "I think I want you to kiss me goodbye."

Luca raised an eyebrow. "That's all?"

"No, that's not all," Oliver said, reaching out a hand and gripping Luca's. "Come on, let's go. They don't need me to clean up, and I'm assuming Giana's taken care of already."

"Yes," Luca said, and he didn't put up any argument, just let Oliver tug him silently in the direction of the Inn.

He didn't say a word until they were through Luca's door, the lock turned behind them, and he looked at Oliver, that intense burning look in his dark eyes making Oliver swallow hard. "Did you mean all of that?" he asked.

"Did you?" Oliver countered. He already knew the answer. Luca knew it, too, but Oliver understood why he'd asked.

It was stepping right up to that line without actually crossing it.

Because Oliver had a feeling if they did cross it, there'd be no going back.

"You know I did," Luca said in a low, desperate voice, and cupping his cheeks with his palms, leaned down and kissed him.

There was a part of Oliver that desperately wanted to overthink.

But another, much stronger part that told him, that *insisted* in fact, that all he should be doing was feeling.

So he *felt*.

The bristle of Luca's scruff against his chin, dragging down in a deliciously rough slide against his neck, the brush of his fingertips along Oliver's spine as Luca pulled his T-shirt up and pulled it over his head.

They tumbled into bed together in one half-naked pile, rolling back and forth until Oliver ended up straddling him, leaning down to nip at Luca's lips again.

"You want it like this again?" Oliver ground down, caught the exhaled gasp from Luca's mouth. He wasn't going to think that in some version of the future, this would be the last time they'd do this. So he didn't say it.

But he saw the thought cross Luca's face.

"No . . ." Luca gasped again as Oliver rolled his hips. Unable to help the smirk that bloomed across his face as he did it. There'd been a time—it seemed impossible to even believe now—when he'd been sure Luca was cold.

But he wasn't cold at all. He was *fire*, underneath his icy, arrogant reserve.

"No," Luca repeated, "not quite. Not like . . .before." He stretched out, his fingers reaching for the drawer in the bedside table. He came back with the bottle of lube, and yeah, they had used half of it. Oliver wasn't going to feel guilty about that at all. They'd had fun and a hell of a lot of great sex. "Me, this time," he said.

Oliver's jaw dropped.

It wasn't like he hadn't thought about it. Of course he had. Personally, he liked both, but he'd expected Luca wouldn't be that way.

Wouldn't want to give up that kind of control.

"I don't . . .I don't trust many people to see me like . . .like that," Luca said, and his eyes were burning again, right into Oliver, making his pulse jump and his cock twitch. "But you, you're different."

You're everything.

Oliver heard the words even though he didn't say them.

"Okay," he said, shuffling backward. He tugged Luca's boxer briefs down his thick thighs, revealing his hard cock, flushed red and already wet at the tip.

He *really* wanted this.

If Oliver let himself think about it, he'd burn up from the inside out, and he'd never be able to give Luca what he wanted. What he *needed*.

"Please," Luca said and even when begging, he sounded semidignified, which shouldn't make Oliver love him more, but it did.

"I've got you," Oliver murmured and dipped his head down low, licking up Luca's cock, as Luca groaned and slowly spread his legs. Oliver slicked up his fingers and then circled his thumb against his exposed hole.

"You done this before?" Oliver asked, between long, tender licks of his cock. Taking his time because Luca deserved that—deserved the whole fucking world, as far as Oliver was concerned.

"Yes," Luca said between gritted teeth. "But not . . .not often. And not for a long time."

"We don't—"

But Oliver didn't get the rest of his sentence out before Luca was pushing up and his kiss was hot like a brand, burning him the rest of the way.

"Yes," Luca said when it finally ended, before he collapsed back on the bed. "Yes, we do."

He nodded. Took a deep breath and leaned down again.

Oliver wanted it to be good, knew what he liked—though *Luca* knew what he liked, too, the bastard, because now he'd miss sex with him almost as much as he'd miss the man himself—and so he took his time. Stretching him carefully, one finger and then two, with plenty of lube to keep him wet.

While Oliver fingered him, he kept up the teasing blowjob he'd begun. Nothing too deep, nothing too strong, just enough to remind Luca who was in charge, who was calling the shots here, enough to let him relax enough to let him in.

Luca moaned, loud and insistent as Oliver added a third finger. He tried a few different angles, and then finally found it, and this time Luca made zero noise at all, just thrashed his head against the pillow when Oliver massaged his prostate.

Oliver's hands weren't exactly steady as he found the condom, rolled it on, and slicked himself up.

Luca already looked fucked out, his cheeks ruddy and flushed, his eyes wide, the pupils blown out, his hands seeking out any part of Oliver he could reach, before he finally braced himself and slid the first inch in.

It had been forever since he'd done this, too, and the pressure was so tight and warm and intense, Oliver needed a moment himself.

"God," he said, hearing just how rough his voice sounded, "you're so good."

Luca reached up, cupping his cheek as Oliver slid home the rest of the way. Neither of them spoke, but maybe words were overrated just then. Maybe they'd both said everything they needed to.

Oliver didn't push it, didn't thrust hard or particularly fast, because almost from the beginning, it felt like just this was enough. He ground, slow and steady, into Luca's ass, and let the incredible feel of tight heat pull him away.

Luca reached for his own cock, and Oliver knocked his hand away, leaning down and giving him just a little bit of friction as his lips found Luca's.

Luca's mouth was so pliant and sweet against his own as they kissed and kissed. One of Oliver's hands gripped Luca's, and he squeezed it tight as Luca finally groaned loud and insistent, body shaking underneath Oliver's.

They'd had a lot of sex, Oliver thought, finally letting go and letting his own orgasm overtake him, but none of it had ever felt this sweet or intimate.

Even after it was over, he didn't move, because Luca had an arm clamped tightly across his back.

Like he didn't want him to go.

That makes two of us.

Finally, Luca's eyes opened and he looked unbearably sad.

He was going to say it now.

I don't want to go.

I love you, and I don't want to leave you.

If he did, Oliver was going to do something crazy or stupid or even worse, *both*, and he knew it was too soon to be making those kinds of decisions.

So instead, he wiggled out of Luca's grasp, feeling his eyes on him as he walked to the bathroom on unsteady legs, depositing the condom and washing up, wetting a second washcloth for Luca.

When he came back, Luca was already sitting up, and he took the washcloth from his hand, like he didn't want Oliver to even dream of using it on him.

Oliver didn't know if he was relieved or not at how closed off Luca's expression was.

Certainly it was easier to deal with than the impassioned longing he'd seen before, the look that had sent him running to the bathroom. But there was a pang of disappointment too.

Had he, deep down, truly wanted to hear what Luca had been about to say?

Even if it was going to hurt like hell tomorrow?

"Stay," Luca said, patting the pillow next to him.

He didn't ask if Oliver could.

Oliver debated. He'd already told Aaron he wouldn't be in tomorrow morning. Had fully expected to spend it curled up on the couch, crying with a tub of Jenni's ice cream, eating all his feelings.

As much as he *wanted* to spend one more night with Luca, the idea of prolonging this goodbye was painful.

You can have both, he reminded himself. He'd just slip out early. Kiss Luca on the forehead and leave before things could get any more fraught between them.

Make it easy. Simple.

Two things they weren't at all, but still, maybe they could make it a clean break in the end.

At least before Oliver could figure out if he was willing to take the wild and slightly insane step of leaving Indigo Bay.

"Okay," he said and settled back in bed.

Luca went to the bathroom. When he returned, he didn't even bother putting his underwear back on. Before Oliver could ask him what he wanted, he was sliding into bed next to him, and tugging him over, until Oliver was lying draped across his chest.

It was easier this way, not being able to see his face.

Not easy.

But *easier*.

"I'm going to miss you," Oliver said, hating the way his voice cracked.

Also, what a fucking understatement.

"Yeah." Luca's voice wasn't quite steady either. And even though he didn't say he'd miss Oliver too, Oliver knew it was true.

Chapter Sixteen

Luca woke in the gray dawn of morning, felt the cold side of the bed next to him, and hated everything.

This was how it had always been. Before he'd come to Indigo Bay, he'd never shared a bed. Never shared his real self with any of the guys he'd dated. Certainly never shared his heart.

But he had, with Oliver.

And now this was how it was going to be, starting with today.

Waking up every morning alone.

Going to bed alone.

Being alone.

It wasn't just the loneliness that unexpectedly swamped him. It was the fact he was going to be alone because *Oliver* wasn't there, next to him.

"What are you doing?" he asked the ceiling, even though he believed he'd already known.

He was going to go home to California, because his family loved him and needed him.

But what kind of Moretti would he be, what kind of son and brother and nephew, if he just ignored the organ beating so hard in his chest, not wanting, for the first time in his thirty-five years, to be ignored?

A Moretti who wouldn't be a Moretti.

His Nonna, she would be disappointed, if she could see him now. He knew it, as well as he knew how to breathe.

It was obvious then—though it had been rather obvious for about a week now—that he could never say goodbye to Oliver.

Not the permanent kind of goodbye.

He had no idea how this could possibly work. He had obligations and the businesses in Napa, and not only was Oliver's home base here, he was so intricately woven into this community—but Luca also knew he was *better* with Oliver. The best part of himself.

He couldn't lose that.

He couldn't lose Oliver.

But he was gone.

Luca checked, sliding out of bed, and going to the bathroom, finding it cold and dark.

He'd left.

He'd told him, *I want you to kiss me goodbye*, and for Oliver, that had been what last night had been, then. A goodbye.

But Luca wasn't going to goddamn accept that. He was Luca fucking Moretti and he loved Oliver, and he knew Oliver loved him, and he wasn't going to say goodbye, not that way, not any way at all.

He threw on a sweatshirt and jeans and shoved his feet into his sneakers and headed downstairs.

The walk to the bakery was cold in the pre-dawn, but he didn't mind.

He banged on the back door for ages before someone opened it.

But it wasn't Oliver. It was his assistant, the one with the shaggy blond hair and the sorta clueless smile.

"What is it?" he asked, the clueless smile even more pronounced than usual.

"Oliver's not here?"

Aaron shook his head. "Took the morning off."

Luca turned abruptly and walked away before Aaron could ask him what he was doing.

Fuck if he knew. He just knew he couldn't say goodbye.

Not now. Not ever.

But Oliver's house was cold and dark too, no lights to be seen.

Luca slumped against the closed and locked door and tried to think where he could've gone.

Maybe to his mother's? But she lived at the Inn, and he wouldn't have stayed there. Not while Luca was still under its roof.

There was only one place he could think of.

It seemed like a shot in the dark, but wasn't that all love was? Life? A shot in the fucking dark.

He barely remembered the path Oliver had taken him on because he hadn't been thinking about where they were going, only who he was going with.

It was more than a little embarrassing how long he'd been head over heels for Oliver and had spent all that time pretending his feelings didn't exist.

Finally, after fifteen minutes of crossing back and forth on the quiet streets by the wharf, he found the entrance to the path that led up to the cliffside park Oliver had brought him to.

The same hill Eliza had climbed every single day, her constancy a proof of her love.

Oliver had never told him he was a romantic, but he hadn't had to. It was in every word of the story he'd told about Eliza and Nathaniel. It was in the way he'd refused to go on a second date with Enzo—and then refused to be resentful at how angry Enzo had been with him afterward. The truth was in his eyes every single goddamn time he'd looked at Luca.

As he climbed, Luca's mind emptied out. If Oliver wasn't there . . .

He's going to be here. He has to be there.

And if he wasn't, Luca wasn't giving up. He'd go to every single fucking house in Indigo Bay if he had to. He'd search everywhere, because if anyone was worth that Herculean effort, it was Oliver.

Finally, he reached the top, and as he lifted his eyes to the horizon, there, just as he'd expected—as he'd *hoped*—there was the man he loved, sitting on the bench they'd shared last week, staring out at the ocean.

"Oliver."

There was shock in Oliver's eyes as Luca crossed the clearing toward him.

"What are you doing here?" Oliver said, wiping his cheeks.

God, he's crying. You're the biggest asshole in the world. You were gonna leave him, and even if it made both of you miserable, you were still gonna do it.

Maybe he *was* an asshole. Maybe he was cocky and arrogant and way too certain of how things should be.

But he also loved Oliver with every fiber of his being.

Surely that should count for something?

"First, I'm an asshole."

Oliver laughed wetly. "What?"

That was not quite what he'd intended to say.

Luca re-grouped. He could do this. He was a Moretti. He was *Italian*. Gabriel had won over his boyfriend. His father and his mother were still disgustingly in love. Marco still believed in love, even when it continued to fuck him over. Surely, all of this meant that inside him, inside the blood that ran through his veins, was proof he could *do* this.

"I mean, *yes*, I am an asshole sometimes," Luca said. "And maybe that's too much, maybe I . . .maybe I should pay for the fact that I was still going to leave you, even though I didn't want to. Even though I really don't want to. But I can't do it. I can't say goodbye, not to you. Not today. Not tomorrow. Not ever."

Oliver reached up, cupped his cheek. His hand was cold—how long had he been up here, recreating Eliza's devotion?

"It's funny," he said.

"It's really not," Luca said. "I love you. And I hoped —"

"No, no." Oliver shook his head and he was smiling now, the brightness of it taking over and transforming his entire face. He was beautiful like this, in the light of the sunrise, eyes still damp but filled with an undeniable happiness now. "No, it's funny because I was up here and I'd just decided that I couldn't say goodbye to you either."

"Really?"

He'd never have asked Oliver to leave Indigo Bay. How could he?

"I love you, too, you ridiculous man," Oliver said and pressed his cool lips to Luca's.

For a long moment, Luca fell into the kiss. Let everything but the fact that they definitely loved each other, that he hadn't fucked things up beyond repair, that he didn't have to say goodbye after all, sweep him away.

But then he broke off.

"You can't leave here."

Oliver raised an eyebrow. "And you can leave Napa?"

"We're gonna figure this out," Luca said. "I don't know what it looks like. I don't know how it works. But we're gonna do it together."

Oliver leaned against Luca's chest, their embrace the most natural thing Luca had ever felt in his whole goddamn life. Why had he fought so hard against this?

Oh, that's right.

"Come home with me, just for a little bit," Luca said, before he could be logical and keep the words to himself.

"What?" Oliver glanced up at him in surprise.

"Come home with me. Just for a few days. I want . . .I want you to meet my family. I need to talk to them about the changes I'm going to be making. And then I'll come back here with you. I can't promise I'll never leave again, but I'm . . .I'm going to do this. Surely Marjorie and what's-his-name can hold down the bakery for a few days."

"I . . ." Oliver wet his lips. "I *want* to. But I think . . .I think maybe you should deal with your family on your own?"

Luca shook his head. "If I'm going to move across the country, they're going to want to meet you."

"So they can hate me forever?" Oliver asked wryly.

"No," Luca said, chuckling, "so they can meet the man who's stolen my heart, completely and utterly. They're going to love you, every bit of you. I promise."

The last thing Oliver had expected when Luca was on his way to Charleston to fly back to California was to be next to him.

But he was.

It had been a frantic few hours. He'd called up Marjorie and also Aaron's friend, the one he'd been tentatively talking about hiring. He'd gathered them for a quick pow-wow at the bakery, and they'd all promised him unequivocally that they could manage things while he was gone. The good news was he *was* normally incredibly organized, and so it wasn't too hard to make sure Marjorie would have everything she'd need to handle the bakery.

Then he'd run home, packed by throwing random shit he still couldn't quite remember into a suitcase, taken the quickest shower in the world, and had been ready when Luca had driven up in his rental car, ready to go to the airport.

He'd taken five minutes out of his frantic rush to call his mother, who'd only said in a very satisfied voice, "Good. Now don't you dare let him go, Oliver."

"I won't," Oliver had promised.

And looking at Luca, sitting in the driver's seat of his rental car, Oliver felt the echo of that sentiment still. *I'm not letting him go.*

"I managed to get you a ticket next to me, thank God," Luca said.

Oliver didn't want to ask what that had cost. Maybe it was better not to know.

Then Luca flashed him the brightest, happiest smile he'd ever seen on his face, and suddenly the price of the very last-minute plane ticket didn't matter.

Of course, that was until they got to the Charleston airport, and Oliver realized the ticket wasn't just for the regular cabin, but a first-class ticket.

"What?" Luca asked, as he checked them in at one of the kiosks. "You ever fly across country in *coach*?"

"Yep," Oliver retorted in a teasing voice. "I flew to *Mexico* once in coach."

Luca flushed. "Well . . . uh . . . that was the seat that was available."

"It's alright. You can still be that guy," Oliver said, tucking a hand into his arm. Squeezing. "I love you anyway."

Still, Oliver couldn't deny it was *really* nice to fly first-class. The seats were big and comfortable and they got a meal and, in Luca's case, a glass of wine.

That Oliver ended up partially stealing.

"You know," Luca said, brimming with affection as he glanced over at Oliver when he returned the glass to his tray table, "you could get your own glass of wine. We are in first class."

"I know. I'm just . . ." *Nervous. What if your family hates me for taking you away?*

"What did I tell you? They're all going to be goddamned grateful to you for taking me off their hands," Luca said gruffly. "They're going to love you, just like I do."

"They're not going to hate me for living on the opposite side of the country?"

Luca sighed. "Honestly, they're probably going to be grateful."

"Really?" Oliver couldn't quite believe this. Luca worked so hard for his family's company.

"They want me to fix things, sure, sometimes, but the rest of the time . . ." Luca sighed again, more resigned this time. "The rest of the time I'm sure I annoy them."

"Well, you don't annoy *me*," Oliver said with a grin.

Luca pressed a kiss to his cheek, and then, only about an hour later, they were descending toward the Oakland airport.

"How long will it take to get to Napa?" Oliver asked as they waited for their baggage. "To your . . .you own a condo, right?" God, this was insane. They barely knew anything about each other.

Except Oliver knew that wasn't true.

Yeah, they'd only known each other for a few weeks, but he knew Luca well enough to understand he'd never regret picking him. Never regret *choosing* him.

"About an hour, if there's not bad traffic. And yes, actually a town-house, but we're not going there." Luca shot him a knowing grin. "We're going to the restaurant. To Nonna's."

"We are?" Oliver had to tamp down his apprehension.

"I texted Nicoletta—my mother—and she said I'd better be bringing you around right away, so that's what I'm doing." Luca looked pleased about this turn of events, but Oliver couldn't deny he was still horribly anxious about it.

Sure, Luca thought it was going to going to go fine, and his family would love him, but what would they say when they realized Oliver meant he wouldn't be around all the time? Sure, Luca believed he annoyed them by being underfoot all the time, but the fact Oliver was here at all was proof of how very attractive that could be.

They weren't going to want to give him up. Oliver sure didn't want to.

When they picked up Luca's car in the long-term parking, Oliver was not surprised to see it was an expensive-looking black Mercedes, all leather interior, sleek and elegant. Just like the man himself.

Oliver shot him a look as he climbed into the passenger seat. He was beginning to get a better picture of the man, now that he was out of Indigo Bay. He still loved him, yes, but it was definitely a much more complete view. "You're rich," he said.

Luca looked sheepish. "No, no, not *rich*, not like millionaire rich. Comfortable? Well-off? That deal I made for the sauces, though, it certainly helped my entire family."

"Which is why you did it."

"The restaurant business is notoriously fickle," Luca pointed out as he pulled onto the freeway. "I wanted something that I knew would give my parents and my siblings a comfortable living forever. And the sales have been good enough, if we have a little slump at one of the restaurants, nobody has to suffer for it."

Oliver was quiet for a moment. Then Luca added wryly, "It's not like your mother doesn't own the biggest building in Indigo Bay. In which she runs a *very* successful bed-and-breakfast. It was never empty. And I heard her telling someone on the phone they usually book up months in advance, especially at the peak times. I guess I got lucky to get my room so last-minute."

He wasn't wrong. He didn't own the inn; his mother did. But maybe it would be his, someday.

"True," Oliver conceded. "But it's not *mine*, not yet."

"But it will be," Luca pointed out. "Also, not like your bakery is doing poorly. You're just as much of an entrepreneur as any of us. More so, if we're counting some of us." His voice grew dry at the end.

"Tell me about them. Your siblings."

"Well, you know about Gabe. He's the middle child, and also the *middle child*, if you get my drift. Ren, our cousin, likes to call him the King of Feelings, and that's sort of saying something, since we're all emotional by nature already. Gabe and Ren own the food truck together, down in LA. But other than that, starting at the top, there's Marco, who runs the higher-end restaurant, the steakhouse. He's the chef and the sort-of manager there."

"Sort of?"

Luca shot him a lopsided smile. "I'm *supposed* to be the manager, but I sort of let him do his own thing. It's how we keep from killing each other. Marcella, his twin, runs the front of the house at all the restaurants. Then it's Gabriel. After him is Dario. He's our accountant."

"Just the accountant?"

"He's kinda quiet, especially when you compare him to the others," Luca said wryly. "But he's brilliant with numbers. Good kid, Dario."

"Surely, he's not a kid anymore."

"Okay, okay, he's not a kid. He's . . .uh . . ." Luca thought about this hard. "Twenty-eight? Twenty-nine?"

"I just realized . . ." Oliver trailed off, more than a little embarrassed. He'd told Luca he was willing to blow his whole life up for him, and he didn't even know how freaking old he was.

"Thirty-five, I'm thirty-five," Luca said. Shooting him a lopsided smile, like he'd followed that entire train of thought.

"Twenty-nine," Oliver said, and he couldn't help laughing. "You'll be back in town for my big thirtieth birthday bash that my mother keeps insisting on throwing for me. And the best part of that is that she won't have to show up with a blind date for me anymore."

"No," Luca said darkly, "she will not."

"Awwww, a little jealous?" Oliver teased.

Luca took Oliver's hand and pressed a hot kiss to his palm. "Not if I'm the only one in your bed and your heart."

"Damn it, I suppose that hot date I have next week is out," Oliver joked.

"It's a good thing you're really cute."

"So, the two sisters who live in San Francisco, those are the youngest, after Dario?"

"Yep," Luca said. "I keep hoping they'll move back, but they're probably better where they are."

Oliver knew how hard that was for him to admit.

"Sometimes, we've got to do our own thing for a while," Oliver said. "My mom was really surprised when I ended up coming back to Indigo Bay. I was *so* ready to get out of town when I was a teenager. It was right to leave, when I did, and I was right to come back, too."

"I guess I'm leaving too, now, so I can hardly judge them for doing the same," Luca admitted.

"You're making a choice for you, putting *you* first," Oliver reminded him gently, "not abandoning your family. I'd never want you to do that."

"See? This is why they're going to love you."

God, Oliver hoped so. He didn't want to be a source of friction between Luca and his family.

Finally, Luca pulled up to a big building, set back from the road. It was painted a bright pristine white, nearly glowing from the well-lit, impeccably maintained grounds. *Nonna's Fine Italian*, it read in elegantly scripted neon letters above the door.

Oliver had seen pictures of their flagship restaurant when he'd looked up the Morettis, but the view when he got out of the car put them totally to shame.

"It's gorgeous," Oliver breathed out. And so much bigger than he'd imagined? This was a huge restaurant. Three of Rudy's could've fit in just the parking lot, nevermind the building itself.

The size of Nonna's shouldn't have intimidated him, and it didn't, not really, because Luca was right, he was just as much of a successful business owner as the Morettis, but that didn't calm the anxiousness currently crawling around in his stomach.

"Thanks." Luca's chest puffed out a little in pride, and it turned out Oliver loved that about him, too. His sense of pride in his own and his family's accomplishments was undeniably attractive. Reaching out, Luca took Oliver's hand. Squeezed it. "You ready to go in?"

He glanced over at the car window and tried to fix his hair. Not that he really could, but he made an effort.

"Don't worry, you look amazing," Luca said. "And I love you. That's all that matters, in the end."

Oliver wanted to believe him, but still couldn't help but worry.

Opening the front door, Luca ushered Oliver inside and for a minute, all Oliver could do was smell and look and *feel*.

First off, it smelled fucking amazing. Like Giana's deli had begun to, in the last week, but so much more. Basil and roasted garlic and tomatoes, with the deep rich scent of meat underneath.

Oliver hadn't expected the restaurant to be so elegant, but it was, with tables and chairs and tall booths all done in a shiny dark wood, the floors just a few shades lighter. There were trailing green plants and ivy in corners, and old wine bottles stoppered with dripping wax scattered through the arrangements. The overhead lights were low and there were candles everywhere, reflecting the shine on every surface.

"Natalie," Luca said, greeting the young woman hovering near the hostess station at the front.

She brightened the moment she saw him. Oliver understood that look. He probably wore it every single time he spotted Luca. "Oh, Mr. Luca, it's so good to see you. I know your mother missed you. And Mrs. Marcella, too, of course."

"Of course," Luca said dryly. "Thank you. Is Nicoletta in the back?"

"They're all in the lounge," she said.

Still hand in hand, Luca took Oliver through the dining room, winding between tables, heading toward the bar, which must be in the back.

When they entered the small lounge area, an enormous wood bar running all the way along the back of the room, a group of dark-haired men and women turned to look at them.

"It's Luca," an older woman, with Luca's eyes and his nose cried out, and approached, and before Oliver could offer a hand or introduce himself or *anything*, he found himself being pulled into a tight, warm embrace that smelled like the best version of all the scents that had seduced him from the moment he'd set foot in the restaurant. Lemons and thyme and rosemary, and that earthy scent of garlic under it all.

"Mama, you're crushing him," Luca warned, but Oliver didn't mind because every single one of his worries was currently being demolished by this greeting.

"Oh, Luca," the woman said, finally pulling back and looking at him with a very satisfied expression, "he's so cute."

"Mrs. Moretti," Oliver said, trying to re-gain his footing and his voice. "It's so nice to meet you." He'd considered adding *finally*, but was that really true? They'd only known each other for three weeks. There wasn't much *finally* about anything.

"Oliver, yes?" she said. "Everyone, come meet Oliver."

He'd never been laboring under any false belief that Luca wasn't deeply, *incredibly* attractive. But seeing him alongside the rest of his family?

It was a lot.

Everyone was beautiful, in a careless, sort of thoughtless way, like they didn't even realize their bone structure and their hair and the impact of their smiles were something special. They just *were*.

Then a man, with shoulders almost as wide as Luca's and with a charming smile that no doubt had left a slew of happy sighs in its wake, broke off from the group and Luca's eyes widened.

And trailing behind him was another man, slightly younger, who looked like his face had been formed by Michelangelo himself.

"Gabriel, I can't believe you're here," Luca exclaimed, wrapping him up in a big hug. Oliver could hear the joy in Luca's voice. "And you even brought Lorenzo."

There was a time Oliver had believed the man was cold; it was impossible to even imagine now. Around his family, his walls came down and he radiated warmth.

"Thought I'd take a break and head up with Ren, make sure the restaurant was still standing without you here, supervising every brick and every table," Gabriel said, making Luca roll his eyes, but fondly.

The incredibly attractive one—and really, that was saying something, considering the rest of the Morettis—turned to Oliver.

"Ren," he said, holding his hand out. "Short for Lorenzo, but nobody but Luca gets away with calling me that. I run the food truck with Gabe. I'm their cousin."

"The black sheep cousin," a beautiful woman in her mid-thirties, dark hair curling to her shoulders and a very sweet smile added with a smirk. "I'm Marcella." She hugged him then, and Oliver needed a second to place her. Oh, she was Marco's twin. The third oldest.

"My reputation precedes me," Ren said with a grin, and holy hell, Oliver was crazy in love with Luca, but Ren was something else.

"Your reputation is a cesspit," Marcella teased. "But not anymore, I hear? Did you really settle down?"

"You know I did," Ren said. "Finally found a guy able to tame me." He winked at Oliver, who didn't know what to say. What to do. *Jesus.* He was almost a little glad he'd gotten to meet Luca's family *after* he'd already decided he was in this for the long haul.

"Oliver," Marcella said, taking his arm, "come and meet my father." *Oh God*, that would be *Luca's* father too.

But he met the older man's gaze with a friendly smile—hoping, at least, that it would hide how nervous he was. "Papa," Marcella said, "this is Oliver. Luca's man."

Oliver extended a hand but found himself being pulled into a tight embrace instead. "It is so good to meet you, Oliver," the man said when he finally let Oliver go. "I'm Matteo, and I'm so happy to welcome you to our family."

"Ah well . . ." Oliver didn't know how to say, *is it that serious, we've only been dating three-ish weeks?* But then he glanced over at Luca, surrounded by his mother and Gabe and Ren, and their eyes met, love brimming in Luca's gaze, and Oliver couldn't help but think, *yes, I think it might be.*

An hour later, Oliver had been given a glass of exceptional red wine—"from Italy," Matteo had told him, "from one of the vineyards we invest in there"—and then fed, a huge platter of chicken parmigiana placed in front of him. He and Luca had shared it.

"The sauce," Luca had told his mother with concern creasing his forehead, "it's a bit salty tonight."

Oliver hadn't agreed; it had been some of the best Italian food he'd ever eaten.

Of course when Marcella had sat down opposite him and shot a very frank look in his direction, asking if it *was* the best, he'd said so. And if he counted the atmosphere and the camaraderie of the family, always teasing and laughing with one another, in this beautifully appointed room, full of love and care, he hadn't lied.

Then a while later, Marcella's brother Marco had arrived.

He was the most serious looking of the bunch. He and Luca had shaken hands, Luca pulling him to the side for a murmured conversation, before he'd turned to Oliver and introduced himself.

Oliver had been expecting things to feel very different from what he was used to, but to his surprise, there was a feeling here, in this room, that echoed Indigo Bay.

He'd worried he'd be taking Luca out of his comfort zone, out of what felt familiar, but Oliver was beginning to realize maybe they were more similar than he'd ever dreamt.

Maybe Oliver's actual family was small, and Luca's was big, but he had an extended circle of people who watched over him and teased him, too, and made sure he had everything he needed to succeed—and vice versa.

Luca had recognized it the night of their first date, but now Oliver saw it too. What he had back in Indigo Bay was not that dissimilar from what the Morettis had built here in Napa.

"So, what do you think?" Luca asked softly as the evening finally began to wind down and he couldn't stop himself from yawning. It had been a *long* day, and he hadn't gotten much sleep on the plane, no matter how comfortable the first-class seat had been.

"I think . . .I think you're a very lucky man."

"That I am," Luca said, the soft, loving glow in his eyes as he stared at Oliver making it clear he included him as part of the luck.

"Your family is amazing. A *lot*, but also amazing."

Luca nodded. "And they'll always be here. I don't need to be here all the time to have this." He sighed. "I thought I did. I thought I had to shepherd it, to protect it, to care for it all the time or it would fade, but maybe not."

"Maybe not," Oliver echoed, agreeing with him.

"Luca!" his mother exclaimed as she looked over at them. "Look at Oliver—he is dead on his feet! Take him home. He needs rest."

Luca's eyebrow quirked up, like he was saying, *don't you see?* And Oliver saw.

He hugged everyone again, even serious Marco, and then they were back in the car. Complete with doggy bag full of food.

"Does your mother think you're . . .I don't know . . .going to starve between now and tomorrow morning?" Oliver asked as Luca pulled back onto the main drive.

Luca laughed. "Maybe. She did tell me I looked too skinny. Asked me what Giana had been feeding me."

"You'd better not have told her *I* was the one feeding you," Oliver said.

"Don't worry, I wouldn't hang you out to dry like that."

The drive to Luca's townhouse was not far, and it only felt like a few minutes before they were pulling up to the modern-looking unit, last in the row.

Oliver took in the painfully neat and organized garage as Luca drove the car in.

"Welcome home," he said wryly. "How about we save the big tour for tomorrow? I'm exhausted, and you look just how I feel."

"Works for me," Oliver said, barely able to hold back another yawn.

"I'm just—" Luca took a deep breath and reached over, taking his hand in his. "Incredibly happy you're here. I didn't think it was going to end up like this; it was too much to even hope for."

"You saying I'm a dream come true, Moretti?" Oliver teased.

But Luca's expression stayed serious. "Yes," he said.

Chapter Seventeen

LUCA WOKE THE NEXT morning and knew before he even opened his eyes this was what he wanted, more than anything else.

The warmth of Oliver next to him, even as he snored quietly away, the peaceful sound of him sleeping, filled his heart with joy.

He'd meant it last night. He hadn't thought a happy ending, specifically with Oliver or generally at all, was in the cards for him. But seeing the way Oliver had met his family and hadn't flinched and hadn't been overwhelmed by their overwhelmingness, made him feel like even though the decision he'd made was the right one.

It wasn't going to be easy not being here.

Even if he came back every few weeks, to check on things, it wouldn't be his home anymore.

That's because home isn't a place. It's a person, and it's Oliver.

He'd sort of expected his mother to panic at the thought he could be this serious about someone after only knowing them for a few weeks, but he'd seen the love and approval in her face, in her gaze, as she'd looked at him and Oliver together, and when someone felt *this* right, it turned out length of time didn't matter.

He and Oliver were both adults. They'd established their own businesses. They'd taken hits and experienced misses and learned what worked for them and what didn't.

It was why Luca knew, deep down, in a place he'd spent all these years ignoring, that Oliver was the right man for him, and he'd love him, no matter how everything turned out, every single day for the rest of his life.

"I can hear you thinking over there," Oliver muttered into his pillow, and Luca realized that he'd woken up.

"Oh . . .uh . . .yeah," Luca stammered. He turned over and was rewarded with the adorable sight of Oliver, pillow creases running along his cheek and hair a complete and total mess. "Good morning."

"Is it good?" Oliver asked quietly. "Or are you over there wishing you hadn't made so many big decisions yesterday?"

Luca was shocked. "Do you really . . .*no. No.* I don't regret a thing. Do you?"

It had never occurred to him Oliver might regret it. Not after he'd fit in so well with his family, just like Luca had known he would.

But maybe he did regret it. Maybe he thought they'd both been too hasty, dragged along by so much excess emotion. Maybe he was worried Luca regretted it, because *Oliver* did.

Oliver burst out laughing. "No, never. Not at all, actually. I don't really know how this is going to work, not at all, because I sort of thought, yesterday, you were going to basically move to Indigo Bay, but now I'm here, and you *belong* here. So I guess I could get a place here and—"

Luca stopped him before he could go any further. Just pressed his fingers against his lips, which was distracting for various other reasons.

"I want to move to Indigo Bay," he said. "I don't know much about how any of this is going to work, but I do know that."

Oliver looked surprised. "But—"

"I love them. But . . .I need a life outside of them. At least *some* life outside of them."

"How are you gonna manage that?" Oliver asked.

Luca couldn't help it; he made a face. "Ask an easier question, okay?"

"That's why you came back, didn't you? To figure it out."

Luca nodded, and Oliver moved closer, draping himself over Luca's chest.

"That makes me happy," he murmured into Luca's pectoral muscle. "Really fucking happy. Maybe it shouldn't . . .but it does."

"Because I want the life that *isn't* my family to be you?" Luca asked absently, sifting his fingers through Oliver's very messy hair.

But Oliver tensed up, and only then did Luca really think about what he was saying.

That wasn't a very casual statement, was it?

It was serious as hell.

Clearly you don't do this often.

Had he freaked Oliver out?

What else could he have possibly meant when he told Oliver he loved him? He'd never felt romantic love before, not like this. It was serious for him. Totally fucking serious, picket-fences-and-exchange-rings-someday kind of serious.

But then Oliver propped his chin up on his arms, gaze staring right into Luca's face, and he didn't look freaked out at all.

He looked pleased. He looked *happy*.

That's the look, Luca realized, *you're going to devote yourself to putting on his face for the rest of your life.*

"How did *anyone* think you were a cold, hard asshole?" Oliver demanded to know. "When you say romantic shit like that, I can barely even breathe."

"I also told you I loved you first," Luca said proudly.

"Exactly," Oliver said, flopping back down onto Luca's chest. "You're a huge sap, and I love it. Love *you*."

For a minute—or ten—they didn't move. Just lying there together, Luca's hand in Oliver's hair, enjoying the peace. Enjoying the true contentment they both felt now that they knew this wasn't going to just end in a few days, or in a week, or in a month.

"But," Luca finally said, clearing his throat, "I *do* need to figure this shit out with my family, while I'm here."

"Yeah, you do." Oliver's voice sounded regretful. "They love you. And you love them. It's not going to be easy."

"My Nonna used to say something: *easy isn't worth doing.*"

"Yeah?"

"I think she's looking down on me now, smirking. Because she's right, but it still sucks."

Oliver's expression was wistful. "You think she'd have liked me?"

"You gonna make me happy every day for the rest of my life?" It was a big ask, Luca knew it. But he was *all-in* on this. Oliver had to know that by now.

"Yeah," Oliver said, reaching up and cupping his cheek. "I absolutely am."

"Then, I think it's safe to say she'd have absolutely adored you."

"Good."

Luca's hand slipped down Oliver's neck, to the smooth line of his spine, his fingertips hesitating right over the waistband of his briefs, considering going even lower.

They weren't going to have much time to be alone, and maybe they should take advantage of the quiet morning.

But right when Oliver's breath caught in his throat as his fingers slipped under the elastic, his phone dinged. Then dinged again. And then it went off a *third* time.

"Shit," Luca muttered.

"That's your family, isn't it?"

"This is why I'm looking forward to being in Indigo Bay. Way less distractions," Luca said.

But Oliver was grinning so brightly, like he didn't even mind. "You think," he asked, as he flopped back on the other side of the bed, giving Luca room to retrieve his phone from the bedside table, "they're actually going to leave you alone once you're across the country?"

Luca glanced at the screen. Two messages from Gabe. One from Marco. Two from his mother.

At least half of these must have come in before he woke up, which meant that he had limited time before one of them—undoubtedly his mother—panicked and showed up at the front door.

"No," he admitted. "But I can turn a phone off."

Oliver chuckled. "What do they want?"

"Gabriel says he and Marco are going to the restaurant, meeting up with Marcella and my parents. He says Ren refuses to deal with 'family drama' and is going to head out to breakfast and then to a few wineries. He asked if you wanted to go with him."

"What's Ren's deal?" Oliver asked.

"Oh, *God*, that's a kettle of worms. He's just . . .well, *Ren*. Didn't want a relationship, so basically made it a habit of hooking up with anyone and everyone, and you can see from the way he looks that wasn't particularly difficult."

"What's wrong with that? What's wrong with not wanting a relationship?" Oliver asked, curiously.

What *was* wrong with that? At least Ren had always been unapologetic about how he conducted his business. Luca had been pretending for years, saying he wanted to find someone but never trying very hard.

"Nothing," Luca admitted. "We're just very different and he—"

"Likes to annoy you?" Oliver finished with a laugh. "Yeah, I can see that."

"If it's not too much trouble . . .please keep him occupied."

"For you?" Oliver asked archly. "Cause going to breakfast and a few wineries doesn't exactly sound too strenuous."

"It won't be. But Ren is *still* Ren, even though he's settled down now."

"I like him," Oliver offered. And it was true. After he'd gotten used to seeing that face, he'd discovered Ren was hilarious—snarky and absolutely outrageous, without an ounce of shame about it. "I don't mind hanging out with him today. I know you've got stuff to do. Family to deal with. I don't want to be in the way of any of that."

Luca dropped the phone into the covers and wrapped his whole body around Oliver's. "You could never be in the way," Luca murmured into his ear. "It's just—"

"I get it. I really, *really* get it," Oliver promised. "And I have a feeling I'd have more fun with Ren anyway."

"What does it say about how much I'm dreading this conversation that *I* think I'd have more fun with Ren?" Luca asked.

"Nothing easy is worth doing, right?" he said, chuckling.

Luca sighed. "It's annoying when you're right."

"Me *and* Nonna," Oliver said with a wiggle of his body that made Luca want nothing more to pin him to the bed and forget real life for the next few hours.

But he needed to face his family.

Plus, in two days Oliver had to fly back to Indigo Bay, and while he hadn't made any promises to him about how soon he'd be able to join him, Luca wanted to be on the same flight, right next to him. *Going home.*

Luca pressed a kiss to Oliver's bare shoulder and reluctantly slid out of bed.

It was time to face the day.

Time to face the music.

Luca dropped Oliver off with a kiss at the local diner his whole family liked for breakfast.

Bracing himself, he drove over to the steakhouse where they were all meeting. He didn't know what he'd be walking into, but he knew it wouldn't be easy, whatever they all wanted to say to him.

What he didn't expect was to walk into the back kitchen and see Marco—and just Marco—working the espresso machine.

Marco glanced over his shoulder. "Oh, good," his brother said, "it's you. I've got your cappuccino here. Double shot. Or do you want a triple?"

"I don't know," Luca said, leaning against the back counter. Wondering also where the rest of the family was lying in wait for him. "Do I *need* a triple shot?"

"Depends." Marco flashed him a knowing grin. "You stay up half the night with your new boy?"

Luca thought back to last night, when they'd both been so tired they could barely see straight, Oliver leaning against him at the bathroom counter as they'd brushed their teeth together, side by side.

"No," Luca said.

"Double it is," Marco said, heating up the milk.

"So, you gonna tell me anything about how it went while I was gone?"

"I know this is very hard for you to understand, but we managed alright without you," Marco said. He sprinkled the top of the cup with cinnamon, just the way Luca liked it, then passed it over.

"*Alright* is not what we do here," Luca reminded him.

"And yet you're the one who's planning to fuck off semipermanently," Marco retorted mildly, turning around from the machine, his own coffee in his hands.

His brother looked as serious as he usually did, but more tired than normal.

He couldn't argue with it, he couldn't deny it, he couldn't avoid it.

It didn't feel good to be forced to just accept the unpleasant guilt sweeping through him without even trying to fight against it.

"I get it. I do," Marco said. He reached out, touched Luca on the shoulder. "Why shouldn't you do something for *you* after everything you've done for us? And Oliver's great, really. The kind of guy I always thought you might end up with, if you got out of your own way for long enough."

"Really?" Luca hadn't ever imagined Marco might be wondering about his love life—or the complete desert that had been his love life before he'd met Oliver.

"Yeah. Nice. But not so nice he wouldn't call you on your bullshit," Marco said. "And he won't complain about you working too much. Cause he'll probably be doing the same."

Luca wasn't sure what he'd imagined, but it wasn't this. He'd been sure there'd be more pushback. More frustration. More deeply buried betrayal rising to the surface when it became clear what his plans were.

"Don't look so surprised," Marco said. "I always knew you'd fly the coop someday."

"I'm not *flying the coop*," Luca retorted from between clenched teeth.

"Sure you are." Marco flashed him an unexpected grin. "And it's okay, you know?"

"You ever going to tell me what happened while I was gone?" Luca asked, changing the subject.

"The normal bullshit, of course. Dad had to jump in on the line a few times. Gabriel's here, which . . .hell must've frozen over, because I could hardly believe it when he showed up here with Ren. Saying he was taking a break from the truck, or that it wasn't busy."

"They hired people," Luca said, because he did know at least that much. "Must be working out well, if they think they could both be here."

"Huh." Marco took a sip of coffee. "But really, it was fine. I mean it. Even Dario . . .well . . ." Marco flashed him an apologetic smile. "It turns out he's more like you than anyone realized?"

"What? *Dario*?"

"Come on, I'm sure they're all talking about you anyway," Marco said, gesturing toward the dining room. "They might as well do it in front of you."

"Thanks," Luca said dryly.

Just like Marco had promised, they were all there. Well, mostly. Chiara and Ilaria were still in San Francisco, obviously, but the rest of the family was there.

His parents, sitting in one of the booths, coffee in front of them. Marco, standing next to him. Gabriel and Marcella, at one of the tables. And Dario, rising to greet him.

There was something different about Dario. Had he always had this direct look in his eye? The confident tilt of his jaw? Or was Luca just noticing because he'd been gone for long enough to see the changes?

But then, when his gaze swept over the rest of his family, they all seemed the same.

Gabe had that stupid grin on his face. His mother still looked peaceful, his father alert. Marco, as serious as always, and Marcella, as frantic as ever, despite being twins, ultimately the two opposites of the spectrum.

But Dario reminded him of *him*. Nicoletta had always told him Dario resembled him the most physically, and Luca had been able to see the seeds of it in his face before he'd left, but now it was like looking into a mirror.

"Hey, welcome back," Dario said, pulling him into a firm hug.

"I told you," Marcella said, before he could open his mouth. "I told you he'd see it. He looks like someone just blew his mind with a nuclear bomb."

"Marcella," his mother chided quietly.

"Told you we were fine," Marco said from next to him.

Luca looked back at Dario, who just shrugged. "You were gone, and things needed done," he said.

"But you're the—"

"The accountant?" Dario finished for him. Then shrugged again. Like it was no big deal for him to take on more work. "Our systems are mostly automated at this point. I had the time. So I dealt with some stuff."

"It was more than just *some* stuff." It was the first time Matteo had spoken up, but when he did, all his children looked over at him. "He walked through the restaurant, with me, and we greeted the customers together every night. Just like you do, Luca. He's learning."

His mother rose from her chair and took his hand in hers, squeezing it. "What we're trying to say, darling, is that we're *okay*. You can go. You can do whatever you want, whatever you need."

There was a whole group of murmured agreement at her words. "I don't understand," he said uncertainly.

"There's nothing to understand." Finally Gabriel spoke up. There was something more honest in his gaze than Luca saw in the others. "We got your back. The way you had ours, for so long."

Luca's fingers tightened on the cup in his hands. "I'm going to come back, often. Maybe once a month . . .maybe more, if you need me. Whatever you need."

It felt pathetic to say it now, when they'd all decided they had their new savior in Dario. And where had *he* come from?

Luca felt a pulse of undeniable guilt—joining the rest of it, swirling around, unsettled, in his stomach—at the memory of describing him to Oliver as just "the accountant," and then, "the kid."

Oliver had been right; Dario was not a kid anymore.

"That often?" His mother sounded disappointed. "What does Oliver think of this?"

Like suddenly, her number one priority was Oliver. And honestly, that tracked.

He slumped down into one of the booths behind him. Marco shot him a sympathetic look. Which didn't exactly go a huge distance to making him feel better.

His family didn't need him. He was *replaceable*.

"Here, I thought you'd be happy," Dario said, sounding disappointed.

Well, kid, that makes two of us.

"I'm not . . .unhappy," Luca said, testing out the feeling. He didn't know what it was. He just knew it tasted bitter on his tongue and swirled unpleasantly around in his stomach, making even Marco's exceptional coffee nauseating. "I'm glad you were there for the family. That was . . ." He didn't know how to even finish that sentence. "It was really good of you."

".Thanks," Dario said shortly. He didn't look pleased that Luca's praise hadn't been more effusive. But what was he supposed to do? He was still reeling from the fact that his younger brother, who he'd thought had been perfectly happy locked away in his office, had been greeting customers and doing *his* regular walk-throughs of the dining rooms; from the fact his family was totally okay waving goodbye to his departing figure.

He'd expected *some* questioning of his decisions, *some* gnashing of teeth, *some* fucking wailing about how he was abandoning them for a guy he'd known for less a month. Instead they were all . . .*happy* for him?

"I think you expected we'd all be lost without you," Marcella said.

Well . . .*yes.*

"Marcella, be nice. He's dealing with a lot of shit right now," Marco warned his twin.

Marcella rolled her eyes. "He has emotions—he should at least be familiar with them, even if he spent years pretending they didn't exist."

He wasn't happy about Marcella talking about him like he wasn't even here. Normally, he'd have cut her down with a few well-chosen words, but he just ignored her today.

Why?

Because she was so fucking right.

He should be familiar with what he was feeling right now.

Oliver kept telling him he wasn't cold, not all the way through, and he *wasn't*.

He fucking felt things. Lots of things.

He was feeling right now like all those never-ending years of dedication and sacrifice and hard work were evaporating in a snap of fingers. Why had he worked so goddamn hard if it didn't matter? If they could just wave goodbye to him like he didn't matter?

"I didn't pretend they didn't exist," Luca finally said, slowly, glancing at each of his family in turn. Serious Marco. The bedrock of his parents. Snide Marcella. Smiling Gabe. Confused Dario. "I just . . .felt like something was more important than the way I felt."

"And that is my fault." Matteo spoke up again, and this time he stood and walked over to where Luca was sitting. He put both hands on his shoulders. His expression was as serious as Luca had ever seen it. "I let you handle things, because after Nonna died, I couldn't. It hurt to even walk in here, so I let you take care of everything."

"It hurt me too," Luca croaked. He could remember, like they'd been yesterday, those weeks, feeling like a part of him he'd never considered living without had been forcibly carved out of him.

But he'd put one foot in front of the other, because his father and his family and the whole business *needed* him.

"I know," Matteo acknowledged. "I let you do it anyway because I was too broken to care. But then a few months later, the fog lifted, I looked up, and you were taking care of everything. I told myself it was easier not to demote you, so I just let you keep going. Even though I should've said something. Told you that it wasn't necessary to shoulder every burden of this business. Of this family."

"Oh. *Oh.*" Luca was beginning to understand. Those confusing emotions were beginning to sort themselves into recognizable forms.

He was understandably sad that this chapter was closing.

He felt regret that he'd ignored everything he wanted for so long.

He was relieved and happy and completely, utterly grateful that everyone in this room wanted the best for him—that they recognized the best for him was to start something new, something of his own, with Oliver.

"We love you, Luca," his dad said seriously. "We want you to be happy. And I don't think you've been that happy, doing this with us. If you moving to Indigo Bay means you're happy, and you work less, and we see you a little less often, it's not going to be easy, *because* we love you. But we still want you to do it."

"Okay." Luca swallowed hard.

"I'm sorry, too, that I let you shoulder it all for so long," Matteo said. "You were just so good at it." His mouth twisted into a wry smile. "And I think you're going to be amazing at whatever you choose to do after this."

"I don't know," Marco teased from next to him. "He might be total shit at relationships. We better hope Oliver's a patient guy."

"Oliver's practically been sainted already," Marcella offered. "But I think he'll keep Luca on his toes."

"He'd better," Gabe said.

"If you didn't think he could face off with me, should you really have sent him off with our cousin?" Luca questioned, raising an eyebrow.

Gabe, that betrayer, just *laughed*. "Oh, I think he and Ren are gonna do just fine together. Ren's excited to indoctrinate him into all the Moretti bullshit."

"What Moretti bullshit?" Marco asked.

Luca rolled his eyes. He loved his brother, but he was real slow sometimes.

"You really think dealing with all of this is easy?" Luca asked, waving his hands around.

"I thought we were being pretty easy," Nicoletta retorted tartly.

Luca laughed. "It's part of your charm, honestly, Mama. The whole thing. Even your King of Emotions bullshit, Gabe."

Nicoletta leaned over to where Marcella was sitting. "Change is hard," she said, "and it's clearly broken your brother. Oh well, it was nice while it lasted."

"You going to sell your place?" Marco asked.

"No, I think I'll keep it," Luca said. It had made good logical sense to buy it a few years ago, and it wasn't like real estate had stopped being a solid investment.

"What the hell are you going to do in that small town?" Gabe asked.

"Yeah, Giana's already *got* a Nonna's there," Marco pointed out.

"I don't know," Luca said slowly. Though he did have an inkling—a few inklings, honestly—but he didn't want to tell his family before it was a sure thing. "But I'm sure I'm going to figure it out."

"The one thing I'm sure of," Matteo said, patting him on the shoulder. "Is that you won't ever be bored. And if you *do* ever get bored, come back here for a bit."

"I won't need to, cause like I said, I'll be back regularly." Luca hesitated. "More than you probably want me to be," he added wryly.

"I think probably just enough," Marco said, and that, Luca realized, was all he'd ever wanted.

To be appreciated. To be missed a little. And lastly to be told that it was okay for him to go find his own way.

· · ·

"So," Oliver said, leaning back in their private booth. "It's all figured out, huh?"

Marco had insisted on them coming to dinner at the steakhouse tonight to have a "real dinner" during their last night in Napa, before they both flew out tomorrow.

As promised, Marco had prepared them an amazing meal—filet with marsala and mushroom sauce, cauliflower gnocchi and braised radicchio, following it up with a decadent and light tiramisu that they were supposed to be sharing. Luca glanced at the three-quarters demolished dessert and realized he'd eaten most of it.

Whoops.

Well, it was hardly his fault, if it was right here, delicious and nearly irresistible, but Oliver kept eyeing Luca across the table, like he was the truly irresistible one.

And now, just as Luca had expected, was the question they'd been dancing around.

They'd talked about it of course. After Ren had dropped him off yesterday, it wasn't like Luca had kept his conversation with his family a secret. He hadn't.

But today, he'd spent much of the day closeted in the main office with Dario, going over details, and finally, with his father's assistance, and Gabe's surprising gift for enforcing cooperation and collaboration, they'd put together a rudimentary schedule, splitting up Luca's duties.

"It's a work in progress," Luca admitted, toying with his dessert spoon. "But yeah, I think . . .I think it'll work out. Dario surprised me."

Oliver had spent much of that time with Marco in the steakhouse kitchen, which had surprised everyone but Oliver. "What," Oliver had asked in surprise when the offer had come in, "you didn't realize how alike we are?"

Luca hadn't. But then he also hadn't realized that Dario had turned into a younger version of himself, either. "I guess," he'd retorted, "I should be grateful you aren't spending more time with Lorenzo."

"Ren went back to LA. Some food truck emergency. Left Gabe here, with the hope he could stop you from killing your brothers or your father."

Not that it had ever come close to that. And to Luca's shock, Gabe had actually offered to help out, if needed.

They'd all agreed it would have to be on an emergency basis, but it had meant a lot to Luca that Gabe had volunteered.

Could tell it had meant a lot to Gabriel that he'd been appreciative of the gesture.

They weren't fixed, not by any stretch. There were too many years of bad blood for everything to be fine, now, but they were better than they'd been in ages. Luca believed their renewed relationship was half Oliver's doing, for encouraging him to reach out in the first place, and also half the fact he was going to be three thousand miles away and understandably less interested in micromanaging every Moretti family member.

"Told you Dario wasn't a kid anymore," Oliver said with a smile.

Luca barely refrained from rolling his eyes. "You hadn't even met him when you said that. You can't possibly be right about everything."

"Oh, but I can," Oliver teased. "And I will."

"Is this how it's going to be?" Luca wondered out loud. Taking another bite of tiramisu because it was right there and it was delicious and also, he was trying this new thing where he actually *enjoyed* life.

Enjoyed the fact he was happy—wallowed in it, in fact. Didn't hesitate to take Oliver's hand. Didn't try to put a respectful distance between them. Ate what he craved. Drank good wine. Made love like every day could be his last.

It was so different from how he'd lived before Indigo Bay, and change wasn't easy, but it felt like each day was better than the one before it, and that was a blessing Luca wasn't ever going to take for granted again.

"I sure hope so," Oliver said. He was smiling again. Content this time. Like he knew, too, that Luca felt the same.

"I keep thinking we're being smug about this," Luca said, "but if you can't be smug about your awesome, glorious love life, then what *can* you be smug about?"

"Oh, I'm sure you'll find something," Oliver teased, eyes sparkling. "But this is good, for now. Perfect, actually." He paused. "You ready to go back home?"

Luca reached across the table, took his hand in his and squeezed. "Yes," he said.

Epilogue

"Luca!" Oliver yelled, "do you have the shrimp appetizer?"

Luca ran a hand through his hair, frustrated, overwhelmed, and happier than he'd ever been in his whole goddamn life.

"*What* shrimp appetizer? We don't *have* a shrimp appetizer!" he called back through the pass-through.

It was their third night of dinner service in the expanded cafe, and things were . . .well, Luca could say they were a work in progress.

Oliver would probably say they were a garbage fire.

But still, it was *their* garbage fire.

"I added it last night, after service," Oliver said, his face appearing now in the window gap between the heat lamps and the stainless steel countertop where the rest of the table's appetizers sat.

"You just *added an appetizer*," Luca ground out. Swore under his breath. Fumbled for the copy of the menu he kept by the pass-through. Glanced at it, and sure enough, there was the shrimp appetizer, listed right there in black and white on the page.

"Shit," Luca muttered. The good news was from the description, it looked like the dish was already basically prepped, cold poached shrimp salad with preserved lemon and diced chilies.

It was a dish he remembered well, because they'd shared it during their last vacation to Italy, on the coast, sitting high above the ocean, at this little family owned restaurant that had reminded him so much of Nonna's.

Then later that night, they'd made love with the windows wide open, the sea breeze cooling them down just as the heat became too much to bear.

Of course, Oliver had to add it to the menu, and *last-minute too.*

The fucking sentimentalist.

He leaned down and poked around in the fridge they'd had installed under the pass-through for the salads and the cold dishes they could prep ahead of time—one of the ways they'd figured out how to juggle this new venture, along with their others.

Six months ago, he'd officially bought Nonna's Deli from Giana. She still worked part-time for him, and even part-time for Oliver sometimes. Right now, she was probably somewhere behind him, tossing pasta into sauce, getting the rest of this table's meals ready for service.

She said it was good for her, kept her busy while Enzo was out on the west coast, going to art school and living with Chiara and Ilaria.

"I got it," Luca called out, pulling out the dish he recognized from the fridge.

He set it on the counter, added the wedge of lemon he thought it needed, even though Oliver's expression made it clear he thought it was overkill.

Was everything easy? No, it was not. Owning, now, a bakery, a cafe adding more services to their schedule, and also a deli, was a challenge.

Add to that their personal rule that they went to bed and got up at the same time, and nothing was easy.

But what had Nonna always told him?

Easy isn't worth doing.

Everything about their new life together in Indigo Bay suited Luca down to the ground.

He'd really started to grow and thrive, without the constant need to supervise a whole passel of Morettis. And the Morettis, too, had grown. Dario was coming into his own. Gabe was closer to them than he'd been in ages—even closer to Luca, which was the most shocking part. Even Marco had stopped trying to be such an island.

Change was never simple, but, Luca thought, as he slid the rest of the appetizers over to Oliver, it was an integral part of life.

"Did you get the clam sauce?" Giana asked, from someplace behind him, and he realized he'd forgotten to grab it from the walk-in.

"No," Luca grumbled and went to fetch the pre-prepped sauce he'd made this afternoon from fresh clams brought in by the fisherman down at the wharf.

He was just finding the pan on the shelf when the door popped open again.

Glancing up, he saw Oliver haloed in the light from above the doorway.

He shut it closed behind him.

"Is everything okay?" Luca asked.

Their wait staff was new—well, *everything* was new, wasn't it? They'd only been open for dinner for two and a half days now—and Oliver was supposed to be supervising them.

"Yes," Oliver said and leaned in and kissed him, his lips surprisingly warm against his own and surprisingly much more determined.

For half a second, Luca forgot about the clam sauce, forgot about the ten tickets currently printing out in the kitchen, forgot about the Nonna's supplier who'd just emailed him about a price increase, forgot about everything. Wrapped his arms around his boyfriend and kissed him like he was the happiest guy in the world, a guy with no worries, no cares, and certainly not a shit ton of work waiting for him.

It turned out that *both* of those things could be true, at the very same time.

Oliver's tongue flicked out and tasted his bottom lip as he pulled away. "That," he said in a low, rough voice, "was for the way you looked at me when you saw the shrimp appetizer."

Luca raised an eyebrow. "We gonna go make out in the walk-in every time someone orders it? Because I can't say I hate that idea."

Oliver laughed. "Can you imagine?"

The thing was, Luca could now.

Oliver had raised the curtain, giving him the briefest glimpse of a kind of life he'd never dreamed of having for himself, but now, every day, worked his ass off to *own*.

To be worthy of having.

"Yes," Luca said. "Fuck them all. They can wait." And he pulled Oliver back and kissed him again.

"Tonight," Luca said, when they finally broke apart, and Oliver's eyes were glazed, nearly dazed with arousal, "we have something we need to do."

"Sex?"

Luca had never laughed as much as he did now. Like the joy simply couldn't be contained anymore, it just exploded out of him, without any hope of control whatsoever. At first he'd been surprised, then confused, then he'd learned to embrace it. Maybe *he* was the new King of Feelings. "That, definitely that, but also . . .we need to talk about the menu."

"The shrimp appetizer?" Oliver looked momentarily disappointed, like it hadn't been the best kind of surprise. And yeah, it had *definitely* been a surprise.

"That, and a few other things." Luca tried to sound stern, and no big surprise, mostly failed at the attempt.

Oliver pecked him on the cheek. "Don't worry," he said, "I promise not to add anything else without checking with you first."

"You swear?"

Oliver laughed, skirting away from Luca's attempts to reel him back into his arms. "Come on, we have dinner to serve," he teased.

Like Oliver hadn't come in here with the express purpose of kissing him.

Luca would be totally pissed off if he wasn't so fucking charmed.

At the last moment, right before ducking out of the walk-in, he spotted the clam sauce and grabbed it.

At least Giana would think he hadn't totally lost his train of thought.

She eyed him when he returned to the big stove.

"You get lost?" she questioned as he handed over the pan of clam sauce.

"Yeah," Luca said. Meeting Oliver's gaze as he peered through the pass-through—no doubt, about to launch some complaint about why the clam pasta was behind, even though he knew *perfectly well* why that was the case—and exchanging a hot look, tempered with love.

He'd known, of course, that when he committed, it would be for life. There would be no half-measures for Luca Moretti, but it was something else to experience what forever really meant, every single day.

Easy isn't worth doing, Nonna whispered in his ear, and this time he sent her a message back.

Love isn't either, and it's worth even more.

Three years after the end of *Sweet as Pie*, Luca's family has one question on their minds: why hasn't Luca popped the question yet? To read the bonus scene, click here.

Interested in reading more Morettis?
Enzo's book is now available! You can read *Cherry on Top*, a fake boyfriend standalone, to discover just how he redeems himself and finds his own HEA.

-

Make sure to check out Gabe's book, *On a Roll*, and Ren's book, *Ride or Die*—both are part of my Food Truck Warriors series, but you can read them as standalones!

INTERESTED IN READING MORE OF
BETH'S BOOKS?

CHECK OUT A FULL LIST OF TILES
BY SCANNING THE QR CODE
OR VISITING HER WEBSITE

WWW.BETHBOLDEN.COM/BOOKLIST

WANT TO FOLLOW BETH?

MAKE SURE YOU NEVER
MISS A RELEASE?

SCAN THE QR CODE BELOW
OR VISIT HER WEBSITE
FOR A SOCIAL MEDIA LIST,
NEWSLETTER SIGNUP,
AND SO MUCH MORE!

WWW.BETHBOLDEN.COM/ABOUT